GODFREY JOSEPH PEREIRA was born in Pali Village, Bandra, Bombay. He was the assistant editor of *Society* magazine, and a correspondent at *Sunday* and *India Today*. He also covered the first Gulf War from Israel. In the United States, he worked as a reporter/writer in *News India*, *India Abroad* and *India Monitor* in New York City. Godfrey currently works as events director at the Monroe Center for the Arts in Hoboken, New Jersey. He is also writing his next novel, *Letters to Esther*.

BLOODLINE BANDRA

GODFREY JOSEPH PEREIRA

HarperCollins *Publishers* India

First published in India in 2014 by
HarperCollins *Publishers* India

Copyright © Godfrey Joseph Pereira 2014

P-ISBN: 978-93-5136-442-9
E-ISBN: 978-93-5136-443-6

2 4 6 8 10 9 7 5 3 1

Godfrey Joseph Pereira asserts the moral right to be
identified as the author of this work.

This is a work of fiction and all characters and incidents
described in this book are the product of the author's
imagination. Any resemblance to actual persons,
living or dead, is entirely coincidental.

All rights reserved. No part of this publication may be reproduced,
stored in a retrieval system, or transmitted, in any form or by any
means, electronic, mechanical, photocopying, recording or otherwise,
without the prior permission of the publishers.

HarperCollins *Publishers*
A-75, Sector 57, Noida, Uttar Pradesh 201301, India
77-85 Fulham Palace Road, London W6 8JB, United Kingdom
Hazelton Lanes, 55 Avenue Road, Suite 2900, Toronto, Ontario M5R 3L2
and 1995 Markham Road, Scarborough, Ontario M1B 5M8, Canada
25 Ryde Road, Pymble, Sydney, NSW 2073, Australia
10 East 53rd Street, New York NY 10022, USA

Typeset in 10.5/14 Casablanca Regular at
SÜRYA, New Delhi

Printed and bound at
Thomson Press (India) Ltd.

To
Hartman de Souza,
For giving me courage to re-enter the darkness,
and
Raymond Fernandes,
Who never got that second chance

Prologue

'HUT, MEN, SHADAP your mouth. Shee baba, bleddy stoopid bugger, saying same, same thing, every day, men.'

There is something quaint, even poetic in the bastardization of the English language in Pali Village in Bandra, Bombay. The rest of India knows them as 'Mack-Ah-Paos', a tag originally meant for the Indian Goans, and was then extended to all 'Cat-licks' (Catholics) in Bombay. To a non-Christian in India, a Goan or East Indian Catholic is a 'Mack', or 'Pao-wallah', which literally translates into 'bread seller', but the crust of this word is singed with a complex litany of negative connotations. Stereotype says that to be a 'Mack' is to be a genetically damned drunk, with no personal or professional ambition; a lazy-marrowed individual to whom procrastination is a way of life. 'Bleddy, bekar bugger, only playing gee-ta all day and chasing girls, don't want to do no bleddy work, men.'

Pali Village was my village. I was born David Francis Cabral, named after Saint David, the patron saint of Wales, and Saint Francis of Assisi. Catholics from Pali believed that these saints would be my guardian angels and protectors. I spent twenty-five years of my life in this village and then travelled to the vortex that is New York City. I wanted to prove that I could make it 'abroad' for a better life like my friends working in Dubai and Oman. My flight was 7,802 miles long; but the journey covered more ground.

BOOK I

1

DAVID HAD KNOWN his Gulf-returned friends for twenty-odd years, but they were different now, somehow foreign. They now spoke proper English too, these village boys. He felt inferior, somehow small, jealous, confused and angry, like an unkempt goatherd around these sophisticates. The men were back in Pali Village on vacation, visiting their families and some friends. They had gathered in David's living room. One of the men, Roy Gonzales, flashing his gold Seiko watch as he picked up his drink of rum and coke, announced: 'I prefer drinking Scotch, single malt.' Victor Pereira, David's childhood friend, piped in: 'Bombay is getting worse, men, what's happening to this bleddy place?' And Michael DeSouza, who went to elementary school with David said: 'I can't travel by local train anymore, these people smell.' David sat silently listening to his three friends trash talk his Pali Village and talk about Dubai like it was the Promised Land, while sucking down their Triple X rum and coke.

They had come to visit him as old friends, to share a drink and talk about their brave new world. He resented his status, was ashamed of his toilet, his living room, his furniture, his existence. Victor turned to David and stage-whispered jokingly: 'You know . . . wish the house was air-conditioned. In Dubai . . . everything is air-conditioned, men, you know.' From the street outside, a vegetable vendor was yelling: 'Bheeeeeee-deeeeeeee-yaaaaaaa-ayyyyyy'. His Gulf-returned friends thought it was hilarious. They had heard these cries a million times, now suddenly they were contemptuous of the high-pitched wailing. They jeered at the shrillness of the street vendor. David took it personally – this was his world, his people.

David thought: 'Dey look like bleddy outsiders, men. My gosh!' They sauntered around. Confident and cocky. People in this East Indian village of Bombay City do not saunter. Here, people shuffle, like they've been accused of some shameful act. They drag their feet guiltily. Their arms are loose; their heads are tilted, ever so slightly to the right or left. They seem to be constantly looking over their shoulder, shifty-eyed, at another person who is in turn looking over his or her shoulder. Everybody is always 'only bleddy looking, men'.

Petty accusations were common, nobody took them seriously. 'Ah-ray, wot men, you bleddy laughing at me again? Why for, huh?'

Outsiders called it 'Mack-Ah-Pao English'. Pali villagers would say: 'We are East Indian buggers; we speak like dis only, but you must hear those bleddy Goans, dey are much worse, men! We speak bleddy okay English, men.' And so they spoke ... a tableau of the absurd, birthed by a deep humiliation of existing in the rubbish heap. If you don't have it, shit on it; or at least fart around it. Now it does not look so good, does it? Does it, bleddy baster?

Yes, Pali Village was a whopper of a Big Mack.

The villagers were argumentative and touchy about their rough edges. Hell help an outsider who muddled that line in the muck. A stranger discovered what that meant, the Pali Village way. It started as a flawed inquiry, flamed into a vociferous argument and meandered into a fistfight that culminated in a history lesson. A group of villagers were 'standing on the junction', a little after sunset, watching Bandra go by, making inane conversation and passing rude personal comments at random, 'just for bleddy fun'. A stranger approached them; he wanted to purchase a suckling. His daughter was getting married, they needed to slaughter and roast it for the wedding dinner.

'I heard this whole East Indian village is full of pigs. I need to buy one,' he said.

Perhaps the sentence did not come out right. Bosco Big Stomach growled: 'Ah-ray baster, wot you mean, men? You saying we are all pigs or wot?' The stranger tried to clarify.

Salt Peter added a pinch. 'Whom you heard from, men? Who bleddy told you dat; your stoo-pid fadder told you dat?'

The stranger, now riled, spat at Salt Peter: 'Don't bring my father into this, okay!'

And back and forth it went. Freddy Fakir said, 'Ah-ray, we are sons of da bleddy soil. We are da original pee-pils of Bombay. Why for you be calling us pigs?'

Bosco Big Stomach violently shoved the stranger. Salt Peter was in the process of delivering another idiotic original composition when the stranger swatted his face. A cut opened up on Salt Peter's right eyebrow as he fell to the ground. Simultaneously, Bosco Big Stomach and Tommy-Eat-Shit-A-Lot moved in and viciously pummelled the stranger until he faltered and dropped. Salt Peter kicked the prostate body. Someone got a rope and they hog-tied him to the concrete cross at the junction. A crowd had gathered. Freddy Fakir lit a candle, then a Charminar cigarette and blew smoke on the stranger's bleeding head wound.

'Go get da Professor,' he ordered.

A young girl scampered into the village and returned

with the 'Professor' who was a history teacher at the local Pali school. Freddy Fakir explained the cause of the quarrel.

'Tell, him,' he said, 'Professor, tell him who we are, men. Den he will know da difference between a damn pig and a bleddy East Indian.'

The Professor, delighted to oblige his captive audience, did not waste a moment. 'Our ancestors were Koli fishermen and farmers,' he told the trembling stranger. 'We have been here, in Mumbai, on da coast since da Stone Age. Apostle Bartholomew, one of da twelve, later came to Bombay in da first century AD 55, you know dat? He came to da city of Kalyan which was den a bleddy big sea port, it is just fifty-one kilometres from our Pali Village, did you know dat? How he talked to da people there, who were all Hin-doos, I don't bleddy know. The bugger spoke Aramic and da people spoke Hindi and Marathi. But dat is not important. Are you bleddy listening, men?' The stranger nodded. 'When he went away, he left behind a Gospel of Saint Matthew written in Hebrew and many brand-new Christian buggers. Sometime after dat, don't know when, da Christian farmers from Kalyan and other Koli fisher people started coming to live in Pali Village which was only rice paddy and toddy tapping tree fields den. It was nice even for da Koli fisher people, because from here, you just cross Pali Hill and go down, and you come to da Arabian sea, lot of fish there, men. At dat time, Bombay was ruled by Sultan Bahadur Shah, he wanted protection against da powerful Mughal emperor Humayun, so he signed da Treaty of Bassein with da Portuguese, who were already ruling Goa. Dey wanted another base for all their spice trade and so dey took charge of Bombay on 23 December 1534.

'Da bleddy Portuguese were fully surprised dat there were so many Bartholomew Christian buggers running here and there around in Bombay and da Portuguese turned dem into Roman Cat-licks and began converting many Brahmin buggers by offering dem cheap land and giving dem special privileges, and da other low-caste Hin-doo buggers also converted because dey wanted to get out of da social gutter. Da converts had to take da surnames of da Portuguese padre, military person or common man who stood as godfather at their baptism ceremony. Dat is why we have bleddy Portuguese last names and dey made us Western, and our first names are Western too, because we are Cat-licks, named after our bleddy saints. We started to play gee-tas and all da cooking changed, and we began eating da cow and da pig, and drinking good port wine and our ways changed and we began dressing like dem Europeans. You understanding all dis or wot? After about a hundred years, in 1661, da Portuguese gave Bombay away to da British as a dowry gift to Charles II of England who had married Catherine de Braganza, da sister of King John IV of Portugal. But Bandra was not included in dis treaty, no-no, Bandra remained with da Portuguese Jesuit priests who owned Bandra till 1739. After dat year, da Maratha buggers came in, with full force, men, and took over Bandra. The Maratha buggers' power went away by 1775, and da bleddy British with their East India Company took over Bandra. Den later, dat Gandhi fellow came and threw salt on da British and asked da buggers to leave da whole of India and go back to their home.

'Many people confuse us and da Goan Christians. But we are different. Now, when da British were in Bombay, those dam bleddy Goans were still ruled by da Portuguese at dat time, remember dat? Da Goans and Mangalorean Cat-licks were coming to Bombay like bleddy flies, looking for work and dey were saying dey are "Portuguese Christians". The British did not like da Portuguese Christian people, because dey were Portuguese subjects and we were British subjects. You understanding all dis I am telling or wot, my tongue is getting tired saying all dis! And den da English on da day of Queen Victoria's Golden Jubliee sorted out da whole bleddy dam mess once and for all, men. On 20 June in 1887, dey named da Bombay Cat-licks "East Indians" after da East India Company, so dey could tell da difference between us who were born here, and outsiders like dem bleddy Goans and those dut-eee Mangy buggers. You want to know something very, very funny, men, we live in da Western part of India but we are called East Indians, it's comic, no? We were given preference, given all da good gour-mint jobs because we were da sons of da Bombay soil, loyal British subjects, and da Jesuit priests had taught us good solid bleddy English and we could read and write da Roman numbers and all, you listening or wot, men?' The stranger nodded again. 'And dat is how we buggers are coming to be named bleddy East Indians. Now do you have any questions?'

The stranger was silent. He didn't get his pig, he got a lesson. Finally, Tommy-Eat-Shit-A-Lot untied the man, patted him on the shoulder, politely asked him not to return and walked away. The villagers dispersed, the evening's entertainment was over. The junction gang walked to 'Auntie's' to drink and laugh about the incident.

Pali Village is a sunken, low-down one-street circle. A cracked, soiled saucer at the end of opulent Pali Hill. Still, the village was homey in a twisted sort of way. Quaint cottages on either side of the street. Scores of white-washed crosses. Little gardens with mango and banana trees. Well-fed pigs strolling the street, sows with scampering sucklings, their snouts browned by faeces, mangy dogs, skinny cats, waddling ducks, ever-hungry chickens, mysterious turds, and of course, the villagers. A cacophonic symphony. Complicated lower-middle-class folk with rustic values and non-existent morals. The 'aunties' and 'uncles' made no apologies for their bankruptcies and revelled in their crude mannerisms. It was a shield that they used to defend their rural nature. It was abnormal not to abuse normality. 'Bleddy, thinks he is a big bugger, men, saying "thank you" and "please" all da bleddy time, and dressed in a suit and tie; bugger wants to act like gora Englishman. Ha! Look at his face, black as bleddy coal. I heard da bugger has no money. Just showing off. All greenery men, no bleddy scenery!'

When David heard about the fight, he felt sorry for the stranger. He knew it was impossible to reason with them. To tell them that their actions were barbaric would elicit scorn and vitriol. They were a fearful enigma to outsiders with their 'Bleddy, my fadder wot going?' attitude. In normal English that meant, what will my family or I lose if I do this? This was convoluted logic to a non-villager. The basis of street credibility in the village was a dare-devil attitude that was desired in 'a man'. Such a man was considered 'A Big Bugger'. But this tag had nuances. Men who showed off, were also spat on with the accompanying 'bleddy, become big bugger, men'.

And that is exactly what David was thinking of his friends. 'Dey have become big buggers, bleddy baa-ster, men.' His friends' clothes did not have that second-class, marinated, railway traveller appearance; that eroded dhobi look. They appeared terylene drip-dried and pressed. Crisp – or 'crips' as they say in the village. The triumvirate had joined the Gulf Stream five years ago and was back, looking at home through a periscope manufactured in Dubai.

Richer, fatter, smoother, cleaner, a foreign-returned cologne bubble surrounded them. They did not possess that distinctive Bombay whiff of raw sewage, body odour and dust; they even talked different. David watched them move about his Pali Village, Bandra home, these now-refined Gulf-returned friends of his. His fingers were tightly interlocked over his groin as he sat rigidly in embarrassment and rage brought on by jealousy. 'Bleddy, dam dem all.' They made him feel like a villager. A gutter that David was trying to claw out of.

It was an ironic secret that he wisely kept to himself. David felt the difference between the villagers and himself often. He was from them, but not of them. He liked them for their rustic wisdom sometimes, and disliked their abrasiveness for anything outside the circle of Pali Village. He had a secret fondness for Western classical music. He liked to look at fashion magazines, read about good wines and exotic places. David considered himself a well-read individual. He liked Tolstoy and Hemingway, Steinbeck and Márquez, and understood the subconscious labyrinth that was Joyce. But this was his forbidden chamber. Nobody entered here, not even David's closest confidante Brian. David indulged in these pleasures within the confines of his room. The villagers would have roared with laughter and called him a sissy if he was heard listening to anything but English pop and East Indian music.

Godfrey Joseph Pereira

Sometimes he wandered through the maze of his roots and wondered why they viewed selfishness as a virtue and were genuinely not bothered by the fallout of their contemptuous laughter. They sucked their reasoning from the nipple of ignorance and concocted divine justifications for their actions. 'Bleddy gave her two tight slaps, men. Now she is walking straight, no more bleddy flapping her mouth for nothing, men! My gosh! She is asking, why I am drinking? Ah-ray, one or two pegs, men, dat is all I am having, and she is making bleddy big noise, men. Every night she is saying same, same thing. All da neighbours are listening. Had to teach her who is da bleddy man of da house. So I gave her a good hiding. One, two slaps; now she be fine. She made bleddy long face for two, three days. So wot? Ah-ray, all bleddy twelve apostles drank at da Last Supper, so you tell me now, wot is wrong with me having one or two pegs, men? It's dat bleddy mother of hers, men, da old ugly swine. My gosh! Keeps poking her big, fat, bleddy nose into everything, for nothing, men.' The exclamation 'My Gosh!' was the prologue of many a defence to suggest extreme disbelief.

The boys went to a Catholic boys' school and the girls to a Convent School, a short walk outside Pali Village, if their parents could afford the meagre school fees. The rest went to Pali School at the end of the village. It was a sub-standard shack with a rusted tin roof, but here the children were taught the 'Cat-lick way', which meant teaching them the Ten Commandments and other dos and don'ts that Rome had prescribed. The temptation of sexuality 'Thou Shalt Not Covet Thy Neighbour's Wife' confused the three-year-olds, but this meant nothing to the teacher or the villagers. Students' questions at Pali School were usually met with:

'Shet up. Don't disturb da class. Will tell you tomorrow.' The important fact was that they were being 'Christian schooled' and that was enough for everybody. They were 'Cat-licks'. The rest of humanity fell into one colossal ignoble category – non-Cat-licks.

When little Richie Walk Funny got into trouble at Pali School, the teacher summoned his father, Langda Jeffery.

After listening to the teacher, Langda Jeffery sighed deeply and told the teacher: 'Ah-ray, baba, cum on, men. I don't have no time for dis bleddy nonsense. If he do same ting again, just bleddy kill him, men. No tension.'

This was harsh even for Pali Village standards and the English teacher gasped: 'Hut, men, wot you saying? My gosh, you gone mad, or wot? Shee baba. Go home, go, go, men. Useless, bleddy bugger. No wonder dis bleddy child is become like dis!'

That is the way they were here, in this village called Pali. When Dominic the Pig was accused of showing his genitals to young girls in the village, someone in the village told him: 'Ah-ray Dominic, wot men baas-ter, wife not giving you enough? Baster, show your cock to your daughter. Go to bleddy church tomorrow, men. Say ow fadder, ail Mary, you stoopid, dut-tee, bleddy man.'

Where village children were concerned, parental care and supervision ran from absolute indifference to minimal care-giving. Nobody in Pali Village, especially the fathers, ever looked at their children and said: 'I love you, darling.' That kind of tender softness would be an affront to the tough fishmonger tradition; talk like that was quickly filed under the 'girly' category. And a sissy was automatically hot-iron branded 'a homo', and nobody, *nobody*, wanted to be a homo, not in Pali Village, no baba.

Kids were treated like semi-trained farm animals. They had their specific uses. 'Hey, Allan Baba, go to "Auntie's", men. Dada wants a half-bottle of liquor. Tell her to give bleddy good stuff, men, which she keeps under da bed.' Kids were used for errands; from procuring illicit liquor to 'Go to Maxi aunty, men, tell her I want bleddy half coconut and dat masala she keeps in da bedroom. Go now, men. And tell her, I will give back her bleddy dried fish tomorrow dat I took last month. And bleddy ask her if she is coming to seven o'clock mass today? Hope dat baster husband of hers is not drunk again. Why she married dat swine, don't know. Go, men, idiot, wot you bleddy just standing there looking?' That children had to be fed, cared for and minimally educated was often viewed as a matter of cruel divine retribution. 'God only knows, men, why da bugger was born, just trouble every day for bleddy everyone.' If bones were not broken and the child was not dying, life villaged on. Low fevers and rashes were generally ignored; if the fever persisted for a couple of days, the child was dragged to the local doctor, who after examining the child had his 'compounder', Jo-Sef, concoct a 'mixture'. The doctor's advice was grudgingly sought only in dire circumstances; otherwise village remedies often solved an ailment. Treatments included a paste of turmeric for swellings and a warm rum rub for stomach-aches, or the stern admonishment: 'Bleddy, why you stomach paining, men? Told you, bugger, not to eat dat dam pig meat, it was bleddy three weeks old. Bleddy child never listens, men. Go to bathroom, try making kaka. I am fully fed up with you, men.'

The children grew up tough and wild and free, with no rules and few regulations. But when the street lights came on, all activity stopped and they scampered home. That was the unwritten rule. To ignore it would mean a vicious stinging slap on the ear that rang in the brain for two days. Still, the village children were relatively happy with the little things that life afforded them. Smacking the tin rim of a used bicycle tire with a stick, they galloped around their Roman arena in Ben-Hur fashion, whooping and hollering, making a hurried, half-sign of the cross in mid-race so that they would not fall and break a leg.

For a community so steeped in the convolutions of Catholic dogma it was interesting to see that the village's outlook to life goose-stepped to the Cârvâka philosophy, an Indian hedonist school of thought that arose approximately in 600 BC and died out in the fifteenth century AD. But in Pali Village, shreds of its philosophy thrived. The Cârvâka philosophy believed that the Hindu scriptures were absolutely fictitious, that all priests and gurus were liars, and that the afterlife and its eternal chakra were deceptive, devious spinning wheels of theological cow crap. The villagers believed pleasure should be the aim of living and 'everything else can go to bleddy hell, men'. Unlike other Indian schools of philosophy, the Cârvâkas argued that there is nothing wrong with sensual indulgence. And, unlike the tenets of Catholicism, the villagers believed that too: 'Stoopid people make a big, bleddy deal out of these bleddy sex things men. Bleddy skin to skin is no sin men. God made sex; so dat we can bleddy enjoy, men. And sometimes you get bleddy children after too much enjoyment. But wot to do about dat, men?'

And so when Harry Homo, who incidentally was happily married and had five children, began surreptitiously beckoning village teenage boys and taking them to abandoned buildings, the villagers chuckled. They knew about his 'dirty pictures'. Harry Homo did not live in the village, but he was a big part of its growing-up process. They knew what he was doing; they laughed and tacitly agreed that he was harmless. Harry Homo was Bandra's unofficial sex educator and titillator-in-chief. He was fiercely heterosexual. He knew what people called him; it did not seem to bother him. Harry Homo sincerely believed that he was a sex educator of sorts. 'You buggers should know all dis stuff, men. Your Fadder and Mudder will bleddy never tell you about all dis, but bugger it is OK, men, wot do you want to know, ask me. Dis little thing here in her . . . And dat is called a bleddy . . .' He dealt exclusively with young boys. Harry Homo usually met teenage boys coming back from school: 'Hey, bugger, want to see bleddy dirty pictures, or wot?' he would say with a leer, his hand in his satchel. For a teenager from Pali Village to view florid photographs of lusty European fornication and fellatio in four colour was an exquisite journey into the forbidden walled city. It was a crotch-tingling epicurean education crafted at the Playboy Mansion by Marquis de Sade. Harry Homo was not a predatory paedophile. He never 'touched' the boys as he explained in staccato short sentences who was doing what and how in the pictures. It seems he got his thrills from the teenager's trembling excitement as he noticed the sweat on their foreheads and the little hard bulge in their short pants. Everybody knew Harry Homo. He was the kind, wise, understanding Bandra medicine man of troubled teenage sexual exploration.

2

FOR SOME 'OUTLYING East Indians', Pali Village was the New York of India. It was the gateway to 'The Queen of The Suburbs – Bandra'. A few fortunate 'East Indian Cat-lick immigrants' sometimes meandered in surreptitiously from the fishing villages on the outskirts of Bombay to join their families. It was not easy to come and live in Pali Village. You had to be connected by thick, congealed, bottle-masala blood and sautéed in vindaloo paste to apply for a post of permanent residency. And there were always 'Family Problems', mostly involving bitter property disputes that landmined a relative's entry and gradual acceptance or slow banishment.

You could not 'buy' a house in the village, 'even if you were bleddy, almighty Lord Falkland', so they said; there were none for sale anyway, and land to build on was non-existent. An East Indian's home was his only major lower-middle-class possession. And finance was always a problem. 'I have bleddy balls in da bank, men', was a common chorus heard from the East Indian choir. Most men in the village worked as clerks for the 'Gour-mint', Western Railway, Central Railway or the B.E.S.T.; the lucky ones were bank tellers, and the women clacked away as secretaries at firms in Bombay city. Homes were handed down, generation to generation, father to son, and 'outsiders', which meant Hindus and Muslims, were not entertained. Colour of skin was important when it came to marriage. To be 'Blake' was to be put at the bottom of the fish basket. Little chance of being sold in the Big Bazaar if you were born 'Bleddy Blake'.

Sometimes relatives came for the Bandra Feast and never

left. People who were allowed to stay in Pali Village came with dreams, with hopes of making it in the brave New World. Maybe a good job in Bombay city. Salt Peter was one of them. He had arrived at his sister Fighting Elsie's place one Christmas morning 'drunk and jolting' and said he wanted to stay; said that he was going to kill himself by drinking kerosene if he was turned away, and then the whole village would curse them, said he was a proud man but he was ready to beg ... Fighting Elsie, her husband and five children discussed it, argued the pros and cons of Salt Peter, dissected his woebegone history, and finally decided that 'it would not look nice' to turn him away, and 'dat bleddy aunty Hilda would keep on saying da same bleddy thing again and again and again, how we kicked him in da stomach. So better let da bugger live here, even though da swine took dat bleddy aunty Hilda's side with da U-Tan property. Remember how he put da knife in our back? Bleddy dutty bugger he can be sometimes.' But the Fates, it seemed, were on Salt Peter's grimy side, and he was allowed to stay with a solitary menacing warning from Fighting Elsie: 'Bleddy you give trouble, and I will bleddy remove all thirty-two teeth from your bleddy face, okay?' Salt Peter nodded, affixing his solemn acceptance to the draconian agreement.

Salt Peter was the court jester and general layabout from U-Tan, a fishing village on Bombay's coast, who arrived at Pali Village to take on the role of village idiot. For Salt Peter this was a steep professional upgrade. He did the filthy work. If someone wanted their pig sty cleaned out, or the rotting carcass of a dead dog buried, Salt Peter was the man they called. If somebody needed to steal electricity from a government electrical line, Peter was the idiot who risked life, possible paralysis and prison to do the job. 'A First-Rate Master with Fifth-Grade Tools' was his advertising line. Salt Peter was the idiot who said he could do anything. From plumbing to roof repair, painting and electrical work to the slaughtering of pigs, Salt Peter did it all. The job was never done 'fully right', as Salt Peter explained, but 'it bleddy worked, men'. And he always had something entertaining, idiotic or sarcastic to say. Salt Peter had been eyeing a pile of bricks lying in Trembling Teresa's garden. He wanted to steal them and sell the bricks to the milk shop owner who was building a wall, but, against his better judgement, Salt Peter decided to ask her. Trembling Teresa, like everybody else in the village, had one ear to the ground.

'I know you want to sell da bricks to dat dam milk man,' she said. 'Don't think I bleddy don't know.' She said she had no time for Salt Peter as she had a lot of volunteer work to do at the local church and she had to attend mass too.

And Salt Peter said to her: 'You are not going to change just because you go to bleddy church; charity starts in da home, so give me da bricks now and maybe you will stop bleddy shaking so much.'

Trembling Teresa did not like that; she cursed him and turned to go, her hands trembling from Parkinson's disease. Salt Peter laughed, rubbed the crack in his arse, called her 'Bleddy Trembling Teresa' behind her unsteady back and walked away.

Salt Peter was paid in used clothes, liquor, food, old utensils, old shoes and sometimes money. He had a thin, five-foot, bag-of-bones structure, with a curved spine, a small pointy ferret-like face and long, very long, artistic fingers. He dressed his hunched body in a loose, brown pair of khaki shorts, a short bush shirt and rubber sandals. His shorts hung low, tied by a jute rope around his slender waist, the crack in his arse permanently exposed. Somebody once asked him why people called him Salt Peter. And Peter said: 'Ah-ray . . . bugger, without Peter, life would be bleddy tasteless. Peter is da main ingredient here, okay . . .' And he constantly offered wisdom or what he thought was an intellectual understanding of any given situation. A Salt Peter quotation stolen from someone: 'Light travels faster dan bleddy sound, men. Dat is why some buggers appear very bright until you hear dem bleddy speak.'

Legend had it that Salt Peter had actually gone to college for one year and then dropped out stating that he had had enough of 'the bleddy big books'. He said they had transformed him into an absolute idiot. The villagers agreed. Nobody contradicted his rustic ramblings. There is an old adage: 'Never argue with an idiot. He will drag you down to his level and beat you with his vast experience.' That is the way the villagers viewed Salt Peter.

And now, here he was, listening to David and his friend Brian Lullooh, injecting his idiocy when there was a break in the conversation. Below Brian's balcony a middle-aged woman was begging for money. The villagers knew her. She knew one song. She arrived once a year, screamed her song, collected some money or old clothes and disappeared. Salt Peter yelled at her to sing her song, poured a drink and settled back in an easy chair. And Cotton Mary sang:

I went to see my Dah-ling;
last Saturday hoo, last Saturday hoo,
I seen my dah-ling waa-kin,
last Sat-day hoo, last Saturday hoo . . .

naa-een-naa-mee nee-naa . . .
last Sat-day hoo, last Sat-day hoo . . .
Seen my dah-ling waa-kin . . .
eee-ya, eee-ya-yo.

Cotton Mary rapped out a rhythm with two bits of roof tile, and on and on she ginned, singing the same lines over and over until Salt Peter asked her to shut up. Cotton Mary's face went dark with rage.

'Hey bleddy idiot, baster bugger . . . pass money, men, stop pissing from your bleddy mouth,' she shouted. 'Come down, bugger, I will show you how I shet up your bleddy, fat mouth. Come down, I will shet up your bleddy, full face, men.'

Brian, sensing a war, threw down a one-rupee bill. Salt Peter said something obscene to Cotton Mary. Fondling the one-rupee note, she smiled at him, said that was the sweetest thing she had heard since yesterday. Salt Peter waved at her magnanimously; said he had more insults but they had to wait as he had important things to do. Cotton Mary smiled, said she would 'keep him in mind', swished her sagging behind at Salt Peter and walked away to another part of the village.

This was how the people of Pali Village were entertained. Sometimes a man would bring in a dancing bear, or a turbaned 'snake charmer' would arrive with a cobra in a wicker basket. He would place the basket on the dirty ground, uncover the basket, poke the cobra and, in a flash, there would be the cobra's hood. In splendorous fury, its forked tongue appearing, flicking ominously and disappearing. He then produced a flute and played it, swaying to the tune. The defanged cobra, venom sacs removed, followed the flute, moving from side to side in a hypnotic trance. The village children loved this show and were told by the elders that the snake charmer possessed special powers over death; that was the reason he was still alive after the cobra had repeatedly bitten him. Even the wise men of the village were unaware of the fact that cobras, as all snakes, are deaf. The villagers enjoyed the spectacle, and that was all that mattered. When an outsider tried to explain the facts, Bosco Big Stomach growled: 'Ah-ray, shet up, baster. You just want to bleddy spoil da fun, men.'

The superstition that grabbed the prize was of course the 'Goo-Goo-Bile'. A turbaned man, leading a bullock whose back he had decorated with a shining shawl embroidered with tiny inlaid mirrors, would saunter through the village, randomly stopping at homes. The bullock's horns were festooned with multicoloured scarves and bells. The housewife would give him a rupee and whisper a set of questions to ask the bullock. The man would nod solemnly and commence rubbing a small drum with a crudely fashioned bow.

The drum emitted an eerie 'goo-goo-goo' sound and the man would shoot a question at the bullock. Would Little David Duffer pass his fourth grade? If the bullock nodded up and down that would be a 'Yes', if the bullock moved his head from side to side, Little David Duffer was going to fail. The crowd gathered around and watched with bated breath. Nobody seemed to notice the man gently tugging on the rope tied to the bullock's neck. The drum went goo-goo-goo. Finally, the bullock nodded up and down. Little David Duffer was going to pass. They howled with good cheer. Another question. Will Jambool Joe stop drinking? The bullock's head went from left to right and everybody groaned. It was pure bull-theatre.

And when 'Devil Power' came to the village, even the elders looked on in awe at the awesome satanic power trapped in his lithe body. The 'Devil Power' was a muscular man dressed in a multicoloured skirt, his torso naked, gleaming with coconut oil and sweat, his waist-long, black hair flailing with his movements. His thickly mascaraed eyes gleamed coal black, and a heavy silver earring in his right ear reflected his black glow. His accomplice in hell was a woman who caressed the skin of a drum, her body swaying sensuously to its beat, breasts bobbing, and sari, draped over her sweat-drenched body, trailing in the dirt. Devil Power whipped himself with a thick hemp rope, two-stepping to the drumbeat and exorcising the demons caged in his body. The whip, cracking against his naked skin, fractured the air like gunshots. He appeared to be in a trance as he danced in a self-mutilating, demonic frenzy, whipping away Satan. Suddenly the drumbeat ceases. Not a sound is heard. Even the children fall silent. His eyes turn upward, white in his skull; he falls to the dirt, exorcised. Streaks of blood trickle from his arms and chest, his body is in an epileptic state, spasmodically jerking to the silent echo of the drumbeat. A full, long minute passes. Softly, the drum starts up again, then the gyrating woman snarls and begins pounding the skin. Devil Power, in excruciating slow motion, resurrects his body from the dirt. Holding the whip in his extended left hand, he goes around the circle of gathered villagers, two-stepping to the beat, his right hand extended for money. This was the kind of entertainment the villagers loved, it was the only entertainment they were offered. Perhaps a film at the New

Talkies Theatre on Hill Road once in a while, but nothing could top the dark, drum, evil, roped, bleeding Devil Power. Nothing. It made the villagers want to go to church the next day and grovel for redemption on bended knees.

3

THE COMMON JEST about Pali Village was that if you threw a stone in the village you would hit a Pereira or a pig. There was a third P: the amateur palmistry practitioners. Superstition was a fearsome metaphysical entity that no one wanted to cross. If a crow cawed incessantly on a window, a guest would be dropping by with bad news. If a snake slithered into a house, death would be calling and if you broke a mirror, only Saint Anthony could save your miserable, pathetic soul from seven years of bad luck. The fears were myriad; the answers to all the fears were palmistry and prayer. A Hail Mary, an Our Father, perhaps the whole rosary and a novena all helped soothe the fear of impending disaster, and if you knew what was coming, well that helped, sometimes.

Everybody knew that Carla Four Eyes was 'da bleddy best hand-reader'. People swore she had prophesied to One Eye Mary that the stars were clashing above her husband's soul. 'Something bad was going to happen to da bugger, and, my gosh, bugger died da next month. Just like dat, men. Bleddy nothing wrong with him. Strong as a bleddy buffalo. He just died, men. Don't know'ow? Went to work morning, came home in da evening, had a small drink, had good supper, duck moile and bleddy just died. He used to drink, but so wot . . . nice man, men! He never beat her, not even once. Po Mary, now who will marry her? Thank God dat she has no bleddy children. Just imagine wot would happen den? And she is quite dark, if she was fair, den bleddy maybe some boy would come forward, you know, but . . . but she carries on, men, po thing. Must be hard to be a widow, so young, shee baba, her whole life just bleddy gone to da dogs, men.'

Carla Four Eyes was the Palm Princess, but every second house had its very own amateur chirologist. They knew that the left hand was the 'Birth Hand', that's all that was required for a doctorate in palmistry in Pali Village. They told you the length of your life, major events in your life, career, health, love life, marriage and children. And the all-important question that had to be answered was: 'Will I go abroad?' The answer was never 'no'. Everyone in Pali Village was told that they would have a chance to go abroad at some time, everybody but Salt Peter. The stars had hog-tied Salt Peter to Pali until the peter ran out of his salt; even Carla Four Eyes said so. When Salt Peter called her 'a bleddy idiot for believing in dis bleddy nonsense,' Carla Four Eyes spewed wisdom. Aristotle, she lectured Salt Peter, had said: 'Lines are not written into the human hand without reason. They emanate from heavenly influences and man's own individuality.' To try and translate verbatim what Salt Peter called Aristotle would be a terrible insult to the original composition of his dialogue. Salt Peter called the Greek philosopher a 'Bleddy Big Homo' and then described unrepeatable violent actions to Aristotle's behind by the thick hoary horn of a rabid rhinoceros. The argument continued until Salt Peter finally said: 'Hey, bleddy Four Eyes, just bleddy let it go, men.'

Brian's hand stated that he would get his turn to fly to a foreign land; but Brian shocked Carla Four Eyes by telling her that he intended to live and die in Pali.

'I am happy here,' he said, with as much humility as he could muster. 'I don't need to be rich to be happy. I don't want to see the world and I don't want to live in Saudi Arabia or Bahrain or New York.'

'Why?' people wanted to know.

'Because . . . bleddy dat's why,' Brian explained.

'Po bugger has read too many books, men,' Salt Peter proclaimed, closing the case of Brian Vs Abroad once and for all.

The truth was that Brian did not like people. The only human being he could talk to was David. The villagers irritated his sensibilities with their small talk, tall stories and general ignorance. He did not talk much but was known to have a quiet sense of humour, sometimes. Once, when asked to go on a blind date, Brian grudgingly agreed. He and David were supposed to pick up two 'chicks' from a neighbouring town to go to the Christmas dance at the Bandra Gymkhana. He warned David: 'Look, men, if da girls are good looking, and dey look like dey might give sex, we will take dem to da dance by taxi, okay? If dey look, so-so, den we will take dem to da dance by bus. Okay?' When they knocked on the door of the house and saw the ugly girls, Brian nudged David in the ribs and said in mock disgust: 'We are going to bleddy walk, okay!'

Brian was the only one to sneer when the story of the 'Grave' swept the village. At one of the many dances held in Bandra on Christmas Eve, a teenager named Lancy Lamba from the village went 'stag', hoping to find a girl at the dance. He did find a young woman and danced with her all night. Her name was Janice. She told him that she lived with her mother in Mahim, which was adjacent to Bandra. She said she had come to the dance with friends who had left early, because someone had died, but she was glad that she now had a partner. When the dance was over, Lancy Lamba dropped her home in a taxi. On the way, she asked for his coat as she felt the wintry chill. She asked the taxi driver for a paper and a pen and wrote down her address for Lancy Lamba and swore that she would love to meet him again. When Lancy Lamba got back home, he realized that Janice still had his coat. The next week, he journeyed to Janice's home. He knocked on the door. An elderly lady answered it, and asked him what he wanted. Lancy Lamba told her.

The old lady smiled sadly. 'I am her mother. You must have my Janice mixed up with someone else, my dear,' she said. 'My Janice died last year.'

She invited Lancy Lamba in, and there in the living room was a picture of Janice, the girl he had danced with. He pointed to the photograph. He showed her the address, told her about the dance, the lady looked at him in disbelief: 'This does look like Janice's writing,' she said, 'but I am sure it is just a coincidence. I wish that you would leave now, please leave, my dear.'

Lancy Lamba had one final request though. The old lady smiled that sad, lonely smile again. She told him the place where Janice was buried. Lancy Lamba rushed to the Sewree Cemetery and walked to the gravesite.

The engraved name on the white marble read: Janice Fernandes. And there, on the cold white gravestone, neatly folded, was his black coat. Lancy Lamba's knees buckled, and he wished he had a strong drink. He wished that he could touch his coat, to see if it was real; he wished that the wetness on his thighs was sweat, not urine. He looked around for some human comfort, but he was alone in the cemetery. He thought he heard something, he whipped around in panic, thought for a moment that he had seen her, thought someone had touched him and whispered his name.

Lancy Lamba fled from the cemetery; he left without his coat.

The next day, Pali Village was on fire with the news.

Many months later, he discovered that Janice had committed suicide over a love affair gone bad. Brian laughed. Said he was sure that Lancy Lamba was drunk. 'Bleddy, ignorant village pigs,' he said, 'will believe anything . . . dancing dead people, ha ha.'

Lancy Lamba emigrated to Canada. He never returned to Pali Village.

Outsiders, trying to decipher Pali Village jargon, found themselves flummoxed by the linguistic brain scramblers. The 'lingo' was coded and the codes were encrypted. The double entendres were an absolute ambiguity. Expressing obscenity or talking about sex without sounding dirty was classic village doublespeak.

Here's Tommy-Eat-Shit-A-Lot speaking with Thelma Two Teeth.

Tommy-Eat-Shit-A-Lot: 'Ah-ray, Thelma!'

Thelma Two Teeth: 'Wot, men, wot you want bugger. I can see your leg is shaking.'

Tommy-Eat-Shit-A-Lot: 'My hands are scratching, men. If your hands are scratching like mine are scratching, we can scratch together, no . . .? Maybe we can bleddy, you know . . .'

Thelma Two Teeth: 'You know wot, men, I feel same.'

Tommy-Eat-Shit-A-Lot: 'Let us go to the Bandstand, sit behind da rocks and bleddy make Happy Divali, men.'

To an outsider this conversation was as confusing as the communication of the Choctaw Code Talkers of World War

One. When The Choctaws said 'little gun shoot fast', they were talking about a machine gun. When a Pali villager referenced 'little gun shoot fast', he was talking about a very short man with a small penis who possessed great sexual prowess.

The village whore, Lorna Leg Spread, was tolerated and accommodated as a black sheep who tainted a family's good name. Her family had lived in the village for generations, she was entitled to stay. Her transgressions were accepted with indifference and Christian forgiveness. The whole village turned the other cheek when Lorna Leg Spread turned her tricks. She was known to let her punters run a tab. 'Hut, men, why you bleddy not said before you climbed on me like a sweating dog you have no money? Okay baba, pay tomorrow.' The punter promised that he would come by 'tomorrow at six-thirty sharp'. Tomorrow slid into 'next Sunday, after I come back from Church', and then slipped into next month. 'Cannot pay now, Robert has first communion. Bleddy why you not understanding, men, I have to give money to my wife for communion party, we have to have party, you know how people will talk if there is no big party, huh!' And eventually, the tab was washed away by the first monsoon shower, 'Wot? My gosh! Dat was so long ago. Shee baba, I cannot believe you are still asking about dat same, same thing every day. I am going now, men. Bleddy rain is coming fast.'

Lorna Leg Spread was a necessary pastime, socially important as 'standing on the junction'. Every evening, groups of villagers stood at the junction that bifurcated the village from Pali Hill. They stood there, swapped stories and watched the world go by. One day a film star stopped to chat. That

Bloodline Bandra

was a big moment. 'Just like dat, men. That Dilip Kumar bugger stopped. Asked us how we are. Wot? How are we? My gosh, wot to say, men. We are fine, bleddy same as yesterday. Ha! Ha! Wot to tell him, men? But he was very nice. You would think someone like him, big car and house and all dat money, would walk with his bleddy nose in da air. But no, men, he seemed like a nice bugger, even though he is a bleddy Muslim bugger.'

Then there were mysteries that fed their gossip. Terrance Bertrand De Souza, who 'walked like a bleddy girl', was mercilessly hounded for his femininity. The villagers thought it was entertaining to point and yell, 'Hey T.B., why your bleddy bum shakes side to side when you walk, men? Bugger, why for you can't walk straight, huh?' The villagers called him T.B. because Terrance was anorexically thin and they often compounded the insult with: 'You a bleddy homo, or wot, men?' One evening, alone at home with his solitude, when the water was on the boil and Catholic condemnation was hissing like Satan in heat, T.B. coiled his sixteen bitter years around his neck and severed his cervical vertebrae. His mother found her only son, at peace, hanging like a feather frozen in mid-air. And the village talked. 'I heard T.B. was ashamed of himself, men. Dat's why da bugger quietly put rope to his neck. Somebody told me dat he liked to do things with men, you know, from behind, in da bum. Shee baba, bleddy terrible sin, men. Bleddy homo. Disgusting. His mudder and fadder ... po things, men ... at least now dey don't have to hear talking behind their backs. Po bugger, T.B., I really don't know how he became like dat, men. God bless his soul.'

They revelled in this mindless cruelty that served as

daily gossip and entertainment. 'You hear wot dat bugger said, just cannot believe it, men. And his wife, fat ugly thing, bleddy has hair on her lip, is saying same bleddy thing. Cannot believe it, men. They are giving us a bad bleddy name, da stupid swines.' They stood there, on the junction, talking, joking and arguing until the sun went down, then it was a stop at 'Auntie's' for numerous pegs of illicit liquor and finally home to a hot East Indian bottle-masala meal. Ball curry and boiled rice, a little spicy mango pickle on the side, and maybe another drink.'

Sometimes the liquor led to disaster. The argument started at 'Auntie's'. Nobody remembers what really happened. But, the next morning, Spunkless Joe was found in the village with a meat cleaver protruding from his stomach. Kenny Card Sharp was fast asleep with the blood of Spunkless Joe splattered all over his clothes, when the police, directed by Auntie, arrived at his cottage. He said he had blacked out and did not remember stabbing anyone. Yes, he remembered drinking with Spunkless Joe. Yes, he remembered an argument, did not know what it was all about. No, he did not stab him. Why would he kill his best friend? he asked himself and anybody who would listen. No, he did not know whose dried blood was on his hands. The police said they could not answer his questions, and arrested him. Later, a forensic laboratory test proved that the prints on the meat cleaver matched the lines on Kenny Card Sharp's nimble fingers. A week after the murder, they dragged him back to the spot where the body had been discovered. He was 'bound and manacled like a bleddy frothing mad dog' and paraded before the villagers who watched in shocked silence. The police nudged him along with a metal spike, slapped his head and kicked him in the stomach as they spat questions and demanded a confession. Kenny Card Sharp said he did not remember killing his friend. Said he really liked Spunkless Joe. Said he was sorry, but he did not care anymore anyway, his friend was dead. Said if he did do it, he deserved what was coming. He wanted death. They gave him life; sent him to prison. The villagers sighed. There was never an easy answer these days, they lamented. It was that 'dam bleddy liquor, men'. Kenny Card Sharp was a good man; gambled a little, cheated sometimes, drank a little, used to steal . . . just a little, but he went to church every Sunday. He was a very good man.

4

DAVID'S MOTHER AND father walked into the small living room to say hello to his Gulf-returned friends. He felt ashamed of Olive, his slipper-less mother, in her cheap, red-and-white-flowered A-line cotton dress with yellow prawn-curry stains down the front. David's father, Bertrand, smelling of illicit liquor, in his short pants, faded brown and frayed, looked pitiful. His soiled white cotton undershirt, called a 'gun-gee', freckled with mysterious stains, smelled, and his considerable paunch jutted through like a smooth, round drum. His blue-and-white Bata rubber slippers were worn paper thin where the heels and toes met the rubber. David burnt with embarrassment.

David's mother said, 'Ah-ray baba, good to see you all.' Ow you, men? My gosh, you all look bleddy very fine.' David's head drooped in shame. But, he told himself, these foreign-returned friends of his had heard his mother before. Why was he ashamed now? David's mother continued, 'Ah-ray, Roy, your ol' girlfriend Betty Bigmouth, her brother, you know Danny boy, no? Betty got married, men, but den she lost da baby. My gosh, terrible. Den all dat drinking and all started with her husband, and dey got a bleddy divorce, men. Now he stands on da junction day and night, men, just like dat . . . bekar.' David said he had to go to the bathroom. His friends had brought expensive gifts. Foreign things which smelt nice. He began to hate their Gulf-returned success. He liked these people, they had gone to school together, shared hashish at college, got drunk on rot gut and went to Grant Road to satisfy nocturnal urges with diseased Nepali

suddenly, a chasm of distinction gaped, ous. David ground his teeth, his jaw taut

re visitors, and he, a miserable, caged animal, hrough the bars at the opulence of a foreign, free He sat there, listening to them talk of a fishing trip. id had never been on a boat where drinks and food had en served. His poverty hurt. He lived in a village, would die in a village.

Will I ever go abroad? he thought, looking at his friends. He sat there, with a smile of fake interest cloaking his embarrassment as he thought: 'Yes, I have a decent job, but God, look at them. I am a reporter for a paper ... who cares? Who knows; who bleddy cares? My parents wish I was like them. They would have a better life if I went to the Gulf. Look at my mother looking at me. I hate her. Look at my father, pouring another drink ... I hate him ... yes, drink, drink it's for free ... single malt ... don't know when it will come again. Whiskey and ice ... really nice.'

'You should go to the Gulf,' Roy was saying. 'India has no future. Go to the West. Go anywhere. That is where the money is. You are nothing without money. And David baba, you are an experienced journalist; your BA in English Literature will help.'

David's education meant that he could double speak. He used 'Proper English' at work, but when he came home to the village, his vocabulary reverted to rustic. The reversal came naturally. Right now, his village gear was in overdrive. He looked at his friends and thought, 'Saala ... bleddy halcuts!' It was the ultimate bitter insult; he was accusing them of hypocrisy, of selling out, of just being terrible human beings.

Godfrey Joseph Pereira

'Ah-ray, baba, why don't you try, David boy?' his mother urged gently. 'Your friends will help, no? Dey are like your brothers. Cum, anyone want prawn curry? David boy, you go Gulf one day. Ah-ray, Victor, my gosh, stop lagao-ing dat whisky, you will get tight, men.'

David heard himself say: 'Yes, yes, I will try . . . you know . . . not too many jobs in the Gulf for a journalist, you know.'

But he was thinking: 'Yes, yes, I have heard how the Indians are treated in Gulf countries, don't tell me. I know. They are worse than servants there. They have no women. They lick TV screens as they watch porn movies in their homes, leave saliva running down the TV glass screen, rushing to the bathroom to masturbate. They cannot fool me. Ahaa . . . I wish I could leave . . . wish I could go to the Gulf. Come back smelling like them, telling people I work in the Gulf, have to go back in one month, company cannot do without me. Talk about catching a plane instead of the nine o'clock fast train to Churchgate. People will point and say, "Ah-ray, baba, he works in the Gulf. Doing very well for himself. Lucky bugger, men. Smokes 555 cigarettes. Drinks Scotch single malt and wears clothes made in England. Goes for vacations abroad. Who knows, might marry a bleddy American? Why would he settle for a bleddy Indian? Works for a good firm in the Gulf, you know. Lucky bugger. Wish I was like him."'

Suddenly it was time for his friends to leave.

'See you on the next trip,' said Roy. 'If you get to Dubai, call us. Maybe we all will take a trip to the West, London or New York . . . We'll go to Fifth Avenue, meet American women. I heard the bleddy Yankee girls are fast, man. Ha!'

'Keep in touch, okay? We have to catch the Qantas flight

at six in the morning. I can't stand these planes, but what to do, have to fly, you know . . . anyway it's better than the first-class railway compartment, you know what I am saying . . . haa. Bandra to Da-der, Da-der to Marine Lines and then to Churchgate. God, I can't even think of that anymore. The smell of Mahim Creek, the crowds, the pickpockets. David boy, I don't know how you do this anymore. Get out, man. Go somewhere; I will talk to the agent who sent me, okay? Bye, now. Keep in touch.'

'Okay, okay,' said David, smiling. 'Let me know when you talk to that agent. Write me a letter. I will go and see him, okay? And one more bleddy thing, baster, stop calling me David boy, okay?'

He shut the door and lay on his couch. David heard his mother start saying the rosary. 'Ail Mary, full of da grace, da Lord is wit' dee, blessed art t'ou women . . . David baba, come say prayers, men, see if fish curry is boiling in kitchen . . . and blessed is da fruit of tie womb, Jesus . . . olly Mary, Mudder God, pray for us sinners . . . David, you checking curry or wot, men? And until da hour of our death . . . Amen.'

David smiled; he wondered if God understood the East Indians and forgave them in his infinite kindness. The East Indians were a religious people but sometimes they strayed.

There was an East Indian obscenity that surfaced, though rarely, during the Mount Mary Church Feast.

'Hey, Dennis boy, where you bleddy going, men, all dressed up with starched shirt, shining shoes and all?'

And, Dennis Boy would answer: 'I am going to *MOUNT* Mary!'

Unfortunately for Dennis Boy, this time, Uncle Tommy Big Mouth heard the sexual innuendo as Dennis Boy playfully shouted it. He slapped Dennis Boy in the middle of the street, dragged him home and belt-whipped him before delivering the trembling boy to his parents. When his parents heard what Dennis Boy had said, they made him kneel on bricks for one hour outside the house, so everyone could see that they were good parents. This kind of blasphemy had to be made public. Later, they dragged him inside. His mother said the rosary and sprinkled him with special Easter holy water that she kept in an old rum bottle for special occasions. 'Glory be to fadder, son and holy ghost . . . Bleddy, dutty boy saying stoopid things against God, you will bleddy suffer for dis . . . Ail Mary . . . Shee Baba, I cannot hardly believe dis is my own son, stoopid bugger . . . 'Ow can I now show my bleddy face anywhere now, men? 'Ow,'ow? Holy Mary, don't know wot will become of dis boy! Mudder God. He is going to hell. Pray for us sinners now. I feel like I am going to bleddy die. And at da hour of our death. Amen.'

This was not the first time that Dennis Boy had stepped on a religious landmine. Once he was talking to Chutney Mary in the churchyard. She could be as rambunctious as Dennis Boy when she was in the 'mood'.

'What's the word, Chutney?' Dennis Boy asked with a leer.

'Oh!' replied Mary, 'the word is "Legs".'

And Dennis Boy said: 'Bleddy spread da word, Mary, spread da word.'

Madcap Aunty Hilda overheard them; lodged complaints with their families and when they got back to their respective homes, they were both thrashed with fine bamboo canes and made to recite the whole rosary kneeling on sand.

The beating for his Mount Mary joke had been more

severe, though. Dennis Boy, who was thirteen years old, wept in agony and swore on the Bible, all the saints and the holy Pope that he would never ever think of mounting Mary again. His defence that everybody said it earned him a thunderous slap to the head, which put him in a five-second coma. Of course, he was dragged to church by his parents the next day. They lit a dozen candles and prayed that Mount Mary would forgive their sexually deviant, heathen spawn.

David smiled. His mother continued with her rosary.

Across the street, he could hear Auntie 'Ugly May' Martha haggling with a meat seller; she was telling him that his pork smelt like her pig's arse. That was the reason he would never get the ridiculous price he was quoting for a kilo of pork. Like all the villagers, she pronounced pork as 'poke'. The vendor shot back his response, telling her what she could do with her pig. She said she had done that already, last night after supper. And the pig had had the courtesy to thank her, but this bleddy 'poke' meat . . . He said, take the damn kilo of pork, and hoped that both she and her pig would rot in shit. She said thank you.

The villagers called this 'bargaining'.

David decided to walk to the junction to get some cigarettes. Near Jude Cold Storage he heard his name being called. 'Hey, David boy.'

David gritted his teeth. It was Stella Gurl.

'Hello,' said David.

Stella Gurl squealed: 'Ah-ray David, heard dat your friends are down, men. Did dey bring you anything?'

'Yes, yes,' replied David. He tried but failed and his eyes darted to her chest. Stella Gurl was called 'Small Tree Big Fruit'. She was five feet two inches tall, with a round cherub face, pert little nose, straight black hair that fell to her waist and she had humongous breasts.

'You know,' she was saying, 'my bleddy sister is coming down, and now da fight for da dam house will start again.' Stella Gurl was the archetypical East Indian when it came to land acquisition. The lust for property was hardwired into her DNA. She had forsaken a chance to be a secretary at an export house in Bahrain. Yes, she had stayed behind to fight 'da bleddy swines'. The 'swines' were her two sisters who were laying claim to their ancestral home in the village. They wanted the house sold and the money divided. Small Tree Big Fruit had reasoned with them. Told them that she still lived there. Now the case was in court and the sisters, who were all married and living 'abroad', occasionally arrived at the house to raise Cain and torment Small Tree Big Fruit. The fight had been going on for twelve years.

Now Small Tree Big Fruit said: 'Ah-ray, David boy, you know my sister, da swine who is living in Switzerland, Sandra, she is bleddy coming down, men. Hope she gets smallpox. My gosh, and dat other one in Canada, Marie. Bleddy has no children, getting fat as a sow . . . See, God is punishing her. She has kept two dogs instead, so I have heard. And dat husband of hers, like a bleddy mouse, men. She keeps him in his place. Gets tight slap if he dares say anything. Ah-ray, wot dey want with dis bleddy house, men? I don't know. They have enough. Still they are stretching their hands for more, like beggars. Bleddy, greedy swines.'

David said he agreed with her and tried to walk away.

Small Tree Big Fruit said: 'Ah-ray, David . . . where you going, men? So now dat Sandra is coming, and I am tired but I will fight dem till I am bleddy six-feet deep and rotting.

Bloodline Bandra

Sometimes I think, I will just pour kerosene on me and set fire to da bleddy full house. Den it will all be over, men.'

David told her that would be a good idea.

She laughed. 'Hut, men! Come on, bugger, stop poking fun at me. And I heard she beats him.'

David was going to ask which of the sisters was the one with the whip, but Big Tree Small Fruit clarified: 'Both my sisters, men, I heard dey slap their husbands from time to time. Buggers cannot say a word, men, bleddy my sisters raise their hands on da buggers all da time. My gosh, David boy, just imagine, men, just imagine . . . I wonder wot people must be talking. See, my name gets dragged in da mud too, since I am their sister. Shee Baba! Our fadder and mudder must be turning in their graves, men. But wot to do, David?'

David said she should marry a rich man and go abroad.

'No, no, men,' said Small Tree Big Fruit, 'I am happy to be a bleddy spinster. I am queen in my own hut, Cleo-Patra, men. Eat wot I want to eat, when I want to eat. Dat day, I took small piece ginger, garlic, little onion, put in bottle masala . . . Ah-ray, cannot get servants to grind good masala these days, men . . . anyway I threw some chicken in, and da curry came out good, men. But, my sisters . . . you know, I am spending all dis money on lawyers, wot a bleddy waste of time, dey are like vultures, I will go to my bleddy grave before I give dem anything just you wait and bleddy see!'

David took one last look at her breasts and said he had to go.

'Okay,' said Small Tree Big Fruit, 'if you want chicken curry just come home, men, but not in da afternoon, I have to go to bleddy Hill Road, men. It is so crowded these days . . . and you know, my friend from New Jersey in America sent me a letter, you know da one who works for da post office there. Her husband is very nice. Sometimes he gambles ... She is quite happy in America, only real friend I have, men ... so, are you bleddy coming or wot, men, da chicken curry needs little more salt, I think?'

David darted across the street. He tolerated her rambling and found her wearyingly repetitive, but her breasts were 'a sight for sore eyes', and so, like most young men in the village, he talked to her, stealing glances at her bosom.

5

LATER, WHEN HE was home, he thought of his job, his life and the grinding wheels of the monotony of his existence.

'Tomorrow to Churchgate, like every day . . . smell sewage, train passes over Mahim Creek, see slum people defecating by the side of the tracks,' he thought. 'Women, open torn, black umbrellas, covering grimy private parts, the shame of poverty, the necessity of defecating by the railway tracks . . . the sheer futility of it all . . . every day . . . this putrid river of shit. Some latent homosexual presses his crotch against my buttocks, trying to spread them in the crowded train. Is my wallet still there? What happened to my life? Ticket collector wants to see the railway pass. Beggar wants money. Unwashed man wants to get off at the next station, he snarls, pushes, abuses. Gets off at Grant Road, the cart vendors, the fast-walking crowds, the street people, the walk to Colaba, Regal Theatre, black-market movie ticket sellers, fake watches, doctored hashish, fake Gucci handbags, fake everything. American tourist saying: "Isn't the Far East cool?"

'Wish I could walk out of the Gateway of India, walk right through the portals and never come back. Leopold Restaurant, abode of pimps, fast-talking drug dealers, cheap foreigners, get into Esperanza building by Colaba police station, masturbate furiously at typewriter. Eat fried cow in curry at the Olympia in the afternoon. Proofread, page-setting, photographs. Press function: get drunk, free liquor, Press Club near Victoria Terminus, more drinks, cab to Churchgate, back over river of faeces, home in the village. Tuesday. A whore. Wednesday. A bar. Thursday. A Hindi movie press conference. Have to get out. Masturbating on the keys of that jaded Remington getting bloody boring. Need to find a real woman. A real life, a job abroad . . . yes, a job abroad. That will solve all the problems. Beggars on the streets, lepers, this village, crowds, trains, Hindu–Muslim riots, corruption, bribes. What a cesspool, this country, this India. Have got to go abroad, anywhere, somehow, anywhere.'

The letter from his friends that David was waiting for never arrived.

6

THERE WERE TWO big blue bottle flies standing at ease on the spotted table top. David lifted the chipped glass and slurped his rum and Thumbs Up. He looked at the flies. David had read somewhere that a female blue bottle fly lays her eggs where she feeds, usually in decaying meat, garbage, or faeces. The flies did not bother him. The restaurant was grimy and noisy; its patrons dirty and drunk. Cigarette smoke and body odour mingled with the thick sour smell of stale alcohol, hot spices and nostril-stinging cheap perfume. David and Brian were sitting in a bar on a Colaba side street, in Bombay City. The bar was jammed with the usual backstreet men, foreign drug addicts and Bombay prostitutes. This was a local haunt, a workingman's cheap night stop beyond the slimy hustlers, yuppies and regular tourists that trolled the Colaba causeway. David looked out through the pock-marked window and remembered the now defunct discotheque, Slip Disc. Aha ... those were the days. Led Zeppelin played there, once upon a time. Yeah, when he was in college.

His friend, Brian, was pushing the *Times of India* towards him. 'Some Indian paper in New York has advertised for a journalist,' he said, 'maybe you should see this.' David shrugged. Old Monk rum was coursing through his veins. He lit a Four Square, squinting at the minuscule advertisement in the classified section.

A busty, ugly prostitute walked in, taking a break from the night. Men gaped at her, stripping her, openly displaying their lust. She sat down, close to David's table, ordered a whisky and scratched her left breast. David heard her painted nails biting into the fabric of her gaudy blouse. Her crimson mouth opened in slow motion, displaying satisfaction as the itch disappeared. He turned and smiled at her. She scowled. This was her break time. Brian looked at her and made theatrical sucking noises. She heard him and laughed as one would at the sight of an imbecile trying to explain the Pythagorean theorem to the village idiot. David smiled. It felt good to be here. It had been a long day at the office. He was assistant editor for a respected political magazine and had just returned from Israel after covering the first Gulf war. His friend Brian was an accountant. They discussed whether they should take the whore upstairs to a no-questions-asked room. After a brief discussion, it was mutually agreed that their money was better spent on another bottle of Old Monk. The whore gulped down her drink and stood up to go. She had heard them.

She brushed Brian's shoulder with her hand. 'You sister-fuckers cannot afford me,' she said haughtily. 'I only sleep with tourists. With Americans. They are real men, not like you two. They have real money. Doll-ahs.'

David smiled. Brian too.

'You should apply for dat job in America,' Brian said in mock seriousness. 'Den, when you return, you will be a real big bugger who can afford Angelina Jolie who just walked out on you.' They both laughed. The men at the next table made obscene hand and finger gestures, exhorting them to go after the huffy whore.

It was all good. David nodded, tore off the advertisement from the classified section and slipped it into his pocket. Tomorrow, he told himself, he would read what was wanted. Tonight, America would have to wait. It was 2 a.m. when

David and Brian hailed a taxi. On the ride home to their village in Bandra, Brian slept, his head back on the seat, arms folded across his stomach, spittle dribbling from his open mouth as they drove past the huts lining the railway tracks. He smelt human faeces. A woman defecating by the rail tracks. A homeless child walking in the darkness. A man, hunchbacked, stumbling to his hut after the night shift, his empty tiffin-box dangling in a plastic shopping bag in his right hand. A leper singing a Hindi movie hit tune about life being sweet. A young homeless couple, fingers intertwined, bodies close together, sleeping on gunnysacks on a pavement. A man in a three-piece suit, hair slicked back with coconut oil. His wife decked in gold bangles and a diamond studded necklace, returning from some celebration. Images flashed by as the rickety taxi jolted and moaned in the blackness.

Poverty is a crime, someone once said. He had heard that New York City had homeless people too. He wondered what the legendary New York skyline really looked like. Like everybody else, David had seen pictures, but to see it in real life – now wouldn't that be something? They got off at Bandra station. The urchin beggars and homeless were fast asleep at the side of the station. They jumped into a rickshaw and in fifteen minutes were at Pali Village. Someone had lit candles at the bottom of the white stone cross that stood sentinel to the right of Pali junction. The streets were quiet, the shops closed. The village barber was sitting at the junction where the village sloped down, stroking his flowing beard and smoking his hash pipe, all alone.

The Barber of Seville and my idyllic village in repose, thought David sarcastically. Someone should write about this bloody place. An elegy, maybe.

Brian's home was the third house down the lane. David's was the first. 'See you tomorrow,' said David. Brian mumbled and shuffled on. David unlocked the door, taking care not to awaken his parents, stripped and lay naked on his bed. He lit one last cigarette, and as the match flared, he remembered the advertisement stuffed into the pocket of his Levi's. Sleep, aided by Old Monk, was coming on though. He crushed the butt into the ashtray, sighed and rolled over. America he thought . . . wonder if the Red Indians are still around. Night finally came to David at 4 a.m. David's sleep was interrupted by his mother pounding on his bedroom door. 'David baba, get up, men, time to go to bleddy work.'

His dry mouth belched ethanol. 'I am awake,' he yelled back. That would shut her up for the time being. David stretched, thought of the day ahead and decided to call in sick.

He walked unsteadily to where his jeans were lying crumpled on the tiled floor and checked the pocket. Yes, the advertisement was still there, that New York dream. Now came the hard part. He walked out of his bedroom, pyjamas now on, shirtless, rubbing his navel.

'I am not going to work today,' he announced to all who would listen.

His father had left for Matunga where the Central Railway office was located. He was chief clerk and had recently refused 'an officer's position' because it demanded relocation. Living in Pali Village was important to him. His mother launched into a familiar tirade about the dangers of alcohol. She knew instinctively that her only son was suffering from a hangover.

'Yes, yes bugger, drink more. It helps. I am like a barking

Bloodline Bandra

dog, nobody listens. Don't know why I bleddy talk at all. Shee baba, I am fully fed up, men.'

It was 10.30 a.m. She was already cooking lunch and talking to the coal fire. She yelled at David without looking at him. He hated that.

'Drink. Uncle Wally died like dat. In da gutter, like a dutty bleddy dog. Yes, drink is good. Helps you get a good wife, have a good life. My gosh, you think da people don't know about your drinks, you think da neighbours don't know, eh? Dey all know. Shame. Shame. And I have to bleddy answer ... I have to hear all da talk ... Like a bleddy, barking dog I am. Best thing to do is to keep quiet. Go drink some more. Ah-ray, David, when was da last time you bleddy went to Church, men, said some prayers?'

David's wisdom cautioned silence. He walked into the bathroom, stuck his finger in his mouth and vomited into the lavatory. Of course, his mother heard the retching. She continued what David usually termed 'the Sermon on the Mount'. They had been through this scene many, many times. Her brother, Wally, had refused to get married and had turned to the bottle in which he eventually drowned. His father's brother, Shaking Steven, was still living. David's mother was often heard saying: 'I wonder why da bleddy bugger bothers to bleddy live? Bleddy man looks dead already, men.' Shaking Steven usually had his first drink at 5 a.m. 'Dat is where you will land, in da bleddy gutter,' David heard her scream.

His father, Bertrand Badak Chor, often compared his wife to a 'bleddy upset stomach that never stops grumbling'. Although his father often scoffed at his son's profession, he was proud that his son was a journalist. One day, he had asked David, 'Ah-ray, David baba, why did those Americans not bleddy kill dat bugger Saddam Hussein? I would have made mincemeat out of da bugger, men.' David said he did not know. 'Bleddy, I thought it was your job to know these things, men,' his father scoffed, shaking his head.

David poured himself a cup of tea in the kitchen. His mother, stirring a pot of goat curry, was silent. She had said what she had to say, for the moment. David went back to his room, read the advertisement and smiled. This was a job made for him. Maybe, *maybe*, his luck would change with this advertisement on this shrivelled piece of paper. His head was throbbing, his hands unsteady. He looked at his bed, a seductress today. He made a move towards the bed, then stopped and headed for his portable Remington. David began typing his bio-data. Despite the hangover, he managed to stay focused. In an hour's time he had proofread his professional life, sealed it in an envelope, hopped into a rickshaw and mailed it at the post office.

He then went back to his bed. New York. Who knows? It could happen. The United States. America. Where the deer and the antelope play, where seldom is heard a discouraging word and the sky is not cloudy all day . . . David drifted off to sleep. When he awoke, it was late. He looked at his wristwatch. It was 8 p.m. He had to leave the house, get out, go somewhere, anywhere. His mother was driving him mad. He decided to walk over to Brian's home. To tell him that he had applied for the job in America. He knew Brian would have come back from work. He hoped he would be at home. Beneath Brian's bedroom window, he yelled, 'Hey, Lull-ooh!'

Brian's head popped out of the first-floor window. 'Yeah, come up, come up, and stop calling me by dat dam name.'

David laughed. 'Lull-ooh' was Brian's pet name, it meant loose character. David's pet name was so obscene and complicated that an effective English translation of the Marathi version is impossible. Roughly, it involved his mother's private parts and a bull elephant raging with the heat of its hormones. It transgressed the line of conventional obscenity. How it came about is also best left alone.

Before David could speak, Brian patted his shoulder and said: 'You applied for dat job? I knew you would. Who knows, luck by chance bleddy, you will get it, men.'

'Yeah, I did. Thanks, men.'

'If you do get it, send me a ticket. I want to meet American girls. I heard dat they are fast. No tension.' They both laughed.

'If you meet my mother,' David warned him, 'don't stop to talk, she will . . .'

'Oh about last night? I guess she heard you vomiting, ha ha . . . you have to learn to hold your liquor, men. Bugger, you do dat every time you have too much to drink. Want a drink?'

'Sure,' said David, 'just one small peg.'

They sat on Brian's balcony in Pali Village and talked of America. Salt Peter was passing by on his way to the junction; he invited himself to the balcony.

Below, a sow was grunting gently, leading her litter home.

'There are so many Indians in America,' said Brian. 'If you do get da job, dey will help you settle in. We Indians stick together. I heard dat there is dis place called Jackson Heights in New York, bleddy looks like a street from Bhendi Bazaar I heard, bleddy strong masala smell, saris drying outside houses, dirt and all, minus da pigs. Like home, ha ha.

Yeah, men, I heard dat. No tension. You should get dis job, after all you are a war correspondent and you have also been an editor and dat's exactly wot dey are looking for.'

Salt Peter said: 'Ah-ray, home is home. All other places are shit, men. Peter likes Pali Village.'

They ignored him.

Salt Peter said he could not understand this lust to go abroad. 'Why put up with bleddy Arabs and foreigners and shitty food, men? Peter will stay here and live here and die here in Pali Village. Wot is less for Peter here, huh ... tell me, men, wot is less for Peter? You go, den you come back ... you can never really leave Pali Village. Peter knows. Your bleddy bloodline is in da Bandra gutters, men. You cannot really go anywhere. You will always remember and long for da Pali Village. Bleddy remember Salt Peter said dat.'

They ignored him.

'We will see, men,' said David, finishing his drink. 'I had better bleddy go now. My mother is acting like a tin-pot dictator.'

As he made his way home, David muttered, 'There has got to be a way out of here.'

Bloodline Bandra

7

WHAT HAPPENED IN the country or the city did not matter to the villagers. Fat Jemma's affair with Andrew Cut Throat, who was also sleeping with Hairy Hilda and her daughter Dirty Maud, mattered more. Here everybody knew everybody, and so they knew what everybody was doing. Oh, and everybody had a nickname. If you did not have one, you did not belong. Mad Thelma, Tommy-Eat-Shit-A-Lot, Mario da Pig Killer, or 'Wot can poor Stupid Sissy do? He is a dut-tee bugger. The swine gets tight, and den wallops her proper. Doesn't even go to church on Feast days.'

Gossip sustained, nourished and entertained. Where else in the world would three randy teenage girls, whose hormones went into sudden overdrive, get branded as the 'The Heat Gang'? The whole village, including the girls' parents, followed their sexual exploits. You would have to be born here, to understand what sustained the village. They knew that their language and diction were an acute bastardization of the English language, they accepted it as an imperfect cultural heritage bestowed on them. 'Wot to do? We are dat way only.' To outsiders who heard it, village talk had a quaintness that was distinctive, and even the harshest critic had to smile when he or she heard: 'You know wot, men? I am doing with my wife every night, sometimes two times, men, nothing happening. She cannot get pregnant at all. Apply, apply and no reply, men. Shee baba, I am bleddy fully fed up, men!'

There existed another side too, a dark, black side. Silent knife fights at midnight. Blood. Cracked skulls. Ripped flesh, drunken eyes. Once hit, the man must fall, and the cops arrive on cue, after the ball, always. Tommy Sexus with a naked woman tattooed on his penis. Suddenly Sexus died. Nobody asked any questions. He used to drive a Patton Tank during the Big War. A good-looking six-footer. Anglo-Indian. Mothers used to watch him. Daughters too. He must have gone to hell. And Draco, the Razor. The cops were funked. Those feral eyes flashing. I will RIP you. Black night, drunken hiss and ha! Where are your guts now? Look . . . look . . . look on the floor. Draco, the man demons prayed to. They found him one night, guts on the floor, flies in his open mouth. His razor protruding from his slashed throat. Another killing. Damian Dada ripped a man one night in a drunken haze. They took him away to a jail far, far away. The killer's spouse moved in with the dead man's wife.

The non-Catholic perception, that the Macks were genetically engineered to drown in alcohol, was never really debated or contradicted. 'Bleddy Jesus drank at da last supper. So . . . and den, remember, he changed water into bleddy wine, men, so . . .' East Indians were nurtured gently into alcohol from their raw, unwashed, barefeet days. On Feast days, it was customary for male guests to dip their index finger into their glasses of ninety-nine per cent proof illicit liquor, doused with Duke's soda water, and give young boys 'a small taste'. Mothers watched and smiled as Uncle Tommy Fodya and Uncle Jimmy Lafda and Uncle Gusteen Bejakhali administered the omnipotent festive offerings. By the time seven-year-old Gabrial Nan-Cut-Tie and the other boys had finished sucking the alcohol-dipped fingers of the benevolent uncles, they were floating. The boys, jello-legged and tipsy-brained, hot-footed around; dancing, prancing, rolling their eyes at the young girls. They feigned big-bugger mannerisms like tilting their heads to the right, ever so slightly, and running their fingers through their hair before slurring opinions no one asked for. The alcohol gave them gumption. Today they were mannish boys, ready to rumble. And fathers affectionately patted the heads of their wobbly young sons and cautioned: 'Baba, now don't bleddy run here and there and fall down!'

On Feast days, Catgut Willie made the rounds. William De Souza got the name Catgut after he began boasting that he made his own 'gee-ta strings' from the guts of real cats. He would trap stray cats at the Pali Market, he said, put them in a gunny sack, bring them home and boil the cats alive. He then extricated the intestines, cured them in his kitchen with ash water and a solution of sulphur dioxide and hung them in his bedroom to dry. He told them that he used the large intestines of bulls, which he bought from the slaughterhouse near the Bandra railway station, as bass strings. Children were fascinated with his guitar strings and, when Catgut was not looking, they would sidle up to his guitar and gently rub the strings. He said that his wife Grace, whom the villagers called 'Disgrace', did not mind the pungent odour and understood that real musicians in America did this to 'get that special warm sound'. Women in the village despised Disgrace. They said the thrusting pelvic movements of her walk were suggestive of a disgusting indecent sexual exhibitionism that whispered promiscuity. It made grown men stare and finger the old bone buttons on their crotches. They said her 'fok-fok walk' took young boys by their hands and led them to secretive, steaming wetlands. It amused Catgut Willie. He licked his whiskers and smiled. Catgut

Willie would visit 'house to bleddy house' on Feast days, entertaining the villagers. First a drink, then he would pick up his Höfner 'gee-ta' from the floor, fish for his Fender plastic plectrum which he pronounced 'rectum', and launch into crowd-pleasers. The villagers loved Catgut Willie.

Sometimes at parties, when his hand was in the back pocket of his jeans, searching for the elusive plectrum, someone would sneer: 'Why you scratching your bleddy arse, men, in front of everybody?'

And Catgut would retort, 'Bugger, I am just looking for my rectum!' and everybody would laugh. When he finally retrieved the pick from his back pocket he would mumble: 'Wot would you buggers like to hear, men?'

Someone would say: 'Sing dat bleddy Jim Reeves song, men, you know da one dat says "Put Your Sweet Lips"', but Catgut was a rocker and he would thump into Hank Williams's *Jambalaya (on the bayou)*. Catgut Willie never did unravel Hank Williams's Mount Olive accent and Alabama twang, and so he sang:

Goodbye Joe, me gotta go, to me oh my oh
Me got to go, go, see my Jer-ah-me yo
Pick it up, say good sup and be-gay-oh
You son of a gun we will have big fun on the by-oh
Jam-bo-laya, caught a mit bhai and a fila gumbo
Cause tonight I am going to see my Jer-ah-me-oh
Pick it up, say good sup and be-gay-oh
You son of a gun we will have big fun on the by-oh

The garbled, lyrical incomprehension coupled with Catgut Willie's wrong chords meant nothing to the villagers. They were not aware of the original lyrics and nobody had actually heard the Hank Williams version anyway; and when Catgut began '*All day all night Maryanne*', the men clapped, the tipsy women swayed and sang the chorus and the drunk little children danced; they loved Maryanne! It was Feast day, a time for brandy in the tea.

'Wot da bleddy hell, men, come on, Catgut, sing another one just like da other one,' someone would holler, and Catgut would start: '*This land is your land*', a Woody Guthrie classic. Uncle Boo, who usually made up the rhythm section, banging on a wooden chair, also provided a cackling high harmony that could resurrect the dead. Catgut's finale was usually his famous medley. '*Show me the way to go home*', followed by '*I-I-yippee-yippee-I*', and then a sizzling Trini Lopez version of '*If I had a hammer*' would sling into a Pali-Mexicano '*La Bamba*'. Uncle Boo attacked the chair in demonic fury, like he was beating his cheating wife ... Par la-la-la-la, Bamba ... Par la-la-la-la Bamba ... whack, whack, whackity, whack ... Bra Bra Bamba ... That cacophony of nonsensical lyrics could make Pali Village jump, and when Catgut Willie ended with '*Down by the river side*' the air turned wild, the women shrieked and everybody jived the feast away. And then Catgut Willie would have one last drink for the road, pick up his guitar, shove his 'rectum' into his back pocket and leave. Willie was a cool cat, he let the children finger his strings and sip from his glass. 'Wot da hell men, it is bleddy Feast day.'

The *laissez faire et laissez passer* latitude that Pali villagers lived under was flabbergasting. Neither logic, deductive or inductive, nor reason could penetrate it. Taking a daily shower was not a necessity. 'Come on, men, go bleddy wash your face and let us to be going.' Washing your face they believed was the deodorizing picker upper that freshened and cleansed you. Body odour was never a problem. 'Put little Pond's Powder, men, on chest and rub little underarms and you'll smell bleddy okay.' Hygiene was never a priority. The washing of hands with soap after going to the lavatory was a rarity. Nobody talked about it. It was part of the damaged zeitgeist of Pali Village.

Contradictions to their social mores were met with derision, and scathing village wisdom. 'Ah-ray, bugger, shet up, men, don bleddy try and teach your grandfather to suck eggs, okay!' Someone once asked Uncle Boo politely, why the Macks called non-Catholics 'Dal-Bhat Buggers', but referred to dal as 'Doll Curry' when it came to food, and called Mahim 'Maim'. Uncle Boo sneered, cleared his throat, spat phlegm in the dirt, scratched his crotch with vigour and explained: 'Ah-ray, halcut, we are dat way only. Why for you asking such bleddy stoopid bleddy questions, men? Saala, pee-pils are dying all over da world every day, pee-pils are having no fud to bleddy eat and you asking about bleddy doll curry? What is bleddy wrong with you, men? Ask something important, okay?'

There were no determining social scales that could weigh the eccentricities and label them insanity, not in Pali Village. village elders whispered to teenage boys that wearing underwear would restrict the growth of the penis, and, more importantly, they cautioned it seriously affected 'da angle of da dangle', which they swore was crucial to a man's ability to satisfy a woman. And so, only the very old men wore underwear that their wives 'stitched' at home.

The villagers often mixed facts and purported facts, and it was impossible to decipher just where the truth lay. Halcut

Hilda talking to Jadi Steamboat: 'Dat bleddy Virginia, men, I am not knowing wot to say? Has five children and people are still calling her Virgin, and everyone knows she sleeps here and there with every bleddy man, and now I heard she is talking behind my back.'

Jadi Steamboat was an enormous woman, and sailed around the village in her housecoat, dispensing sarcasm which she believed passed for wisdom. Rumour had it that her blubber flowed free and easy under her housecoat, unhampered by underwear. From bow to stern she was a formidable piece of hull. No one could tell where her neck, breasts and stomach began or ended; it was all a rolling river of fat flow.

Her husband, Hubert Pariah, suffered her existence in silent misery, waiting for Jadi Steamboat to die in her sleep of a heart attack, or even a severe stroke that would incapacitate her. His wishes were never granted, despite his desperate pleas to Saint Anthony and Mother Mary. In desperation, he had done what no Pope-fearing, Catholic Bandra bugger would do. He bought a coconut, crept into a Hindu temple on Carter Road, and made an offering to Ganesha. Hubert Pariah begged the powerful elephant God, known as the remover of obstacles, to put his mighty foot on his wife's fat throat and smother her until she was dead. He woke up the next day in feverish anticipation and looked at Jadi Steamboat heaving in her sleep. When she awoke, Hubert Pariah decided that the gods, both Hindu and Christian, were not on his side and seriously began considering running away from home. He was forty-eight years old and had been married to Jadi Steamboat for fifteen long, childless years. But he knew he had no place to go. If he hid out at his cousin's place, she would eventually find him and drag him back home, so he stayed, and went to work at Parle, the biscuit factory, the next day. Hubert Pariah was a bitter man who baked sweet biscuits for a living.

Jadi Steamboat puffed on. 'And Hilda, bleddy let me tell you about dat swine Kali Stella, she is also talking behind my back. God knows wot she would do if she was five shades lighter. As it is, men, you cannot see her in da night time. Ahray, shee baba, wot to tell, men? Her father is a bleddy, dutty bugger, grandfather was worse, men. One day her bleddy grandfather, bugger is dead now, three o'clock in da afternoon, sun was bright, very hot, men, you know how it is, Hilda, bleddy he went to da well. Dat was the same day dat Pawleen died, remember, po thing, and he's taking bath, men, at da well and he is showing all these young girls his dutty, bleddy private parts. My gosh, these girls are not even married, men. I don't know wot to tell you, Hilda! Those po things, they were just looking and staring, men, in shock. And her bleddy swine father is now showing his things through da window of their house. And when I told Kali Stella dat, ah-ray baba, she is bleddy coming to fight with me, saying dat my tongue is black and I am a liar, and she is saying dat I am saying dat Harry Homo is going to leave dat bleddy wife of his. Hilda, you know me, men, I never will be saying something like dat, never. Shee Baba, I don't know wot to say? No wonder God made her so black. She is bleddy just talking lies, men. I should just . . . straighten her black face, bleddy make her walk proper after dat, da bleddy black fat swine. I told her, her father is bleddy sick, men, da bugger should go and see Doctor Care.'

When the halad fatki ointment failed, and Khimad, the

Bloodline Bandra

hot, spiced, illicit liquor drink could not soothe, when the sucking leeches refused to lower the gauge of rising blood pressure, and when Saint Jude, patron saint of hopeless cases, was on vacation and his tardy assistant failed to respond, the patient was taken to Doctor Kehar Singh, whom the villagers called 'Doctor Care'. The name seemed medically appropriate and the good old doctor did not appear to care anyway. When Neville Navsaker, beloved husband of Kali Stella, began experiencing stomach cramps, his wife snorted: 'Ah-ray, bugger, told you not to eat dem bleddy chillies. Why you don't bleddy listen, men? One to be eating is fine, two to be eating fine, but five! No wonder your stomach is paining, and all dat bleddy grog you are drinking... Bleddy now why you making noise like a pregnant woman? Serves you right.' Stella's instant diagnosis was that Navsaker's stomach had to be cleansed. She poured three tablespoons of castor oil down his gullet, and Navsaker, in his own words, 'shat full bleddy stomach out'. The pain persisted, and two weeks later neighbours advised Kali Stella that she should take Navsaker to Doctor Care. And so they trudged to the dispensary a mile from the village. Doctor Care, after inquiring about the symptoms, performed a quick examination and decided that Navsaker was suffering from a case of common flatulence.

He asked Navsaker: 'Have you had any movement today?'

And Navsaker said: 'Yes, yes, Doctor Care, morning I went to bazaar, and den I bleddy walked fast to Hill Road, men...'

Doctor Care held up his hand and smiled; he was used to village ignorance about general practitioner jargon, still he used it because their unschooled answers amused him. 'When

I asked about your movement,' he explained, 'I meant, have you gone to the lavatory today?'

'Oh, yes, yes,' said Navsaker. 'I went at five o'clock in da morning, den again at ten o'clock, I felt stomach making grumbling noise, but second time, nothing bleddy came out.'

Kali Stella asked, 'Wot is dis faa-lat . . . thing dat you are saying about, Doctor Care?'

'Flatulence means farting,' the good doctor explained. 'You just have a lot of gas.' The doctor turned to Navsaker, who was twisting in pain: 'Here, take this mixture; one dose three times a day, take this yellow tablet in the morning and this white round tablet at night, you will be fine.'

Three days later, Neville Navsaker lost consciousness and was rushed by taxi to Bhabha Hospital. He was dead on arrival. The next day an autopsy identified the cause of his demise. Stomach ulcer.

Kali Stella said: 'It was time for Navsaker to go to bleddy Jesus. What could Doctor Care do? When Saint Peter rings your bell in heaven, you have to bleddy go.'

The doctor attended the funeral. He cried as they lowered Navsaker into his grave. As he turned to leave, after sprinkling the coffin with a handful of dirt, he thought he smelt something rancid. He thought somebody had farted. Ironic, the good doctor thought, very ironic. A silent flatulent goodbye for good old Neville Navsaker. May his bleeding ulcer now rest in peace. Kali Stella was right, the good doctor thought. His diagnosis could not have triumphed against the call of the divine. That night, Doctor Care turned to his dusty old medical books and looked up gastrectomy surgery. He shook his head in the dim light of his bedroom and

Bloodline Bandra

whispered: 'These villagers drink too much, that is their problem, surgery would not have helped him.' Then the good doctor laid his head down to sleep. He had to get his tired old body ready for another day of medical malpractice.

But things were changing even for Doctor Care; his patients had diminished and the young people from the village would refuse to be seen by him. They demanded that their parents take them to Holy Family Hospital where the doctors were rumoured to be competent. A metamorphosis was on and the elders complained that the 'bleddy village was not wot it used to be'. The younger men and women were leaving the village, and travelling far, to foreign lands. When they returned to vacation in the village, they acted like big buggers, contemptuous of their rustic roots.

8

A MONTH AFTER he had sent his resumé to New York, his mother handed him an envelope with American markings. He opened it. David smiled.

Watching him, his mother asked: 'Wot dat, David baba?'

He looked at her silently. 'I am leaving for America as soon as I can. I have been offered a job there.'

His mother who had wanted him 'to go abroad' put her hands on her knees and slowly lowered herself on to the small green sofa. Her face crumpled and she began weeping. His father, hearing her sobs, walked into the living room with a drink in his hand.

'Why for she bleddy crying, men? Wot da hell have you done now, men?'

David said, 'I am leaving for America, soon, very soon.'

His father walked to the sofa and sat down close to his wife. He looked down at the scuffed, dented floor, silent.

David turned and headed for his room. He did not understand their reaction. He was all they had. The 'why don't you go abroad?' litany was for public consumption. It was to demonstrate that their son had what it took to 'go out there and make it'. Without him, they would be an old childless couple, their future behind them. He was their sounding post when things went silent. His mother needed to worry about his drinking and smoking, his inability to hold on to a steady relationship, his clothes and food and a million other things. These were the reasons for her existence. Now David was going away, far away. Her life, as she knew it, was over. David's father had his clerk's job in the railways, a few friends, his newspaper and his limb-loosening, brain-numbing illicit country liquor. After twenty-five years of marriage, their union had disintegrated into a tolerance that was accepted with resignation. And now the reason for their tomorrows was going away.

'It's not far away by plane,' he said. 'I will send tickets, and you'll can come and visit me.'

He heard his mother crying as he shut the door to his tiny room. He went to his window, looked at his village.

'Adios, Amigo,' he said to the dirty lane. 'I will not miss you.'

The village seemed at peace. It was a silent night. Even the pigs were quiet. He pulled out the letter again. Yes, the job was his. He could journey to New York in two months. The editor, Manu Laxman, had asked David to call him, Eastern Standard Time.

'Have to tell Brian,' thought David. 'Bleddy bugger will be happy to hear this.'

David's mother had stopped crying by the time he emerged from his room. She was standing before the crucifix and rocking her thin, frail body. His father, watching television, was muttering to himself. When David's mother was troubled she prayed in Latin, a language she did not understand but it was once the language of Rome, and she fervently believed that the Lord preferred Latin as a means of spiritual communication. Her Catholic priest had told her that.

Oremus
Sancte Petre
Ora pro Nobis
Sancte Paule

Ora pro Nobis
Sancte Andrea
Ora pro Nobis
Miserére nobis
Glória Patri, et Fílio, et Spirítui Sancto
Dóminus vobíscum
Et cum spíritu tuo
Ahhhh-haaaa-men

David's father ignored the praying; he was reading a newspaper and muttering about the decline of human civilization. 'I will be at Brian's place,' David announced. His father started to say something, then grew quiet and lowered his eyes. One day, David would regret the fact that he had not stayed home that night. He would wish that he had talked to his mother and father. He would wish that he had tried to understand the sadness his departure would bring. But he couldn't think through the euphoria of an American acceptance.

Brian was home.

David lifted both hands towards heaven. 'I am going to the promised land,' he yelled. 'The Land of the Free.'

Brian was genuinely happy for his friend. 'Let's go to da bar around da corner,' he said. 'Bugger, dis calls for a drink dat is a drunk.'

David talked to Brian's mother, father and brother. He told them that he was going to New York City. They were all excited.

'Hey, David baba,' teased Brian's mother, 'come back with a gori American girl, men. Bring a nice one back. Fair and lovely. Ha! Wot fun dat would be. Bleddy, da whole village will be talking.'

It was only after the fourth drink that David's mind began to grasp the enormity of the change that was about to hit him. He sighed, a little fearful. 'Wonder what America is really like,' he whispered.

Brian was raising his glass. 'America,' they said in unison.

'Say hello to Chief Drinking Bull for me,' Brian joked, then said very softly: 'David, when you come back to visit, don't act like a bleddy big bugger, okay.'

You had to be born a Catholic in a village like Pali to accurately decipher what Brian really meant. It literally meant a hundred things. Like, don't act like you are better than the village folk. Remember where you came from. Just because you have money, it does not make you a better human being. Don't say you cannot eat goat's stomach anymore. Don't ask for toilet paper when you go to the lavatory. Don't carry a bottle of purified distilled water everywhere you go. Don't speak with a 'fashionable' accent. And please do not call papads 'papadums'. David and Brian looked at one another. David nodded. There was nothing more left to say.

The next day, David quit his job and began saying his long goodbyes to colleagues, friends and relatives. On the weekend, he walked to the end of Bandra, a place called Land's End. There sat the Castella de Aguada, a crumbling Portuguese fortress built in 1640. This was his favourite place to get away from it all. He climbed through a window in the rock, up a steep grassy incline and walked onto a flat surface that once upon a time had housed cannons. He heard the sea crash into the rocks below. He watched the sun set; the clouds were on fire over the Arabian Sea. A seagull glided like an apparition and settled just yards away from him on the dilapidated wall. Bird and man looked at one another. Then the bird turned to its left and plunged from the wall. He then looked at a huge cloud, flecked with crimson and shades of metallic grey, sailing slowly towards the setting sun. Behind him, the harvest moon was rising in a darkening sky. This was the month of September; the native Americans believed that this was a good month. David looked at the now fading horizon. The wild, wild, west was somewhere out there, beyond that peaceful imaginary line on the Arabian Sea.

Days and nights began telescoping into one another. The time was coming when David would leave. The sorrow of his mother, the feigned indifference of his father, the good wishes of his friends, and the uncertainty within himself churned in his gut. He wanted to leave India – he had prayed to leave India – so why was his exhilaration tinged with fear and sadness. What if the United States was not the America inside his head? David thought: 'Will it be twenty years before I return? Will my mother be dead when I come back? Yes, I like Rock 'n' Roll. No, I do not know what a "Pig in a Blanket" is. Yes, I have heard of John Wayne. No, I am not familiar with the name "Old Brown of Osawatomie". Yes, I know what deodorant is. America, free and brave and beautiful. They say you can get anything there, be what you want to be.' David smiled.

November first was two days away: the day David was to leave his home and country. He had called Manu Laxman, the editor and owner of *Asia Times* in New York. His soon-to-be boss had told him that everything was arranged for his arrival.

'David, this is crazy,' said Sharon Hill, an American girl with whom David had become acquainted in Bombay. 'They are offering you 150 dollars a week. You cannot live on that in New York City. You have to pay for an apartment, utilities . . .'

'What is "utilities"?' David asked.

Sharon smiled: 'It is different there, David, besides the rent you have to pay for electricity, gas, heat . . . I am an American, I know. Please don't go. These Indians in America do this all the time. I know. What they want is cheap labour. The moment you ask for more money, you will get fired and another Indian will take your place.'

David looked at her silently. This was absurd. His new boss in New York had assured him that he would do well, and there would be more money soon.

'I will take my chances,' he replied. 'I will look for another job, once I get to New York.'

'That is not possible,' Sharon had replied. 'The H1-B visa that you will be getting requires you to work for the specified company alone. As an alien, you have to be sponsored by another company if you want to change jobs; and let me tell you, it is very tough because no one wants to sponsor you. If they do, they do so on their own terms. You will be sold into slavery. Believe me. I know what I am talking about. They will not sponsor you for a Green Card, because they think the moment you get it, you will leave to find better employment. David, you are walking into a trap.'

David smiled. He patted her on the shoulder. 'You really don't know us. We Indians stick together. I'll get by.'

She shook her head in disbelief and dismay. 'Don't say I never warned you,' she replied. 'You should think about it, Cheech.' She called him Cheech sometimes because with his thick walrus moustache, David did look like a young

Cheech Marin from the Cheech and Chong show. David thanked her, hugged her, said goodbye and walked away saying he would keep in touch.

The next evening, he said goodbye to his mother and father and the small crowd of village people who had come to bid him farewell. His father remained stoic. As his mother wept and recited the rosary, David put his arms around her and swore that he would visit in a year's time. She slipped a slender silver chain with a Saint Christopher's medal around his neck. She kissed him on the cheek, sobbing. David hugged her, shook his father's hand, trying not to cry as he walked out the door. He smiled at his friend Brian who loaded his suitcases into the taxi. He got in. His mother walked up to the taxi and pressed the handkerchief she was using into his hand. It was wet with her tears. He touched her forehead and shoved the moist handkerchief into his shirt pocket as he got into the taxi.

David did not look back. He lit a cigarette. 'International Airport. Air India,' he said to the taxi driver.

'Going to Dubai?' the taxi driver wanted to know.

'America,' said David.

The taxi driver launched into stories of American passengers he had ferried around Bombay city. David watched poverty go by as they passed the hutment colony on the way to the airport. Suddenly, he felt alone.

'Don't forget India, eh,' said the cab driver as he arrived at the airport. David smiled. He checked in, walked to his gate and waited to board. The PA called his flight. He boarded, stashed his small overhead bag, got into his seat and shut his eyes. The novel he had brought along lay on his thighs. He had a window seat. He rested his head against the plastic and tried to imagine America. A woman was arguing with the flight staff. A man wanted to know which imbecile had placed a bag on his seat. The slam, slam, slam of overhead bins began to irritate him. Somewhere, a child was weeping. David could hear the father unsuccessfully trying to calm the little girl. David touched the handkerchief in his pocket. Emergency instructions about flotation devices and oxygen masks, welcome from the airline and the jumbo was leaving Indian soil. A mighty thrust and she was up in the air on her way to London. A two-hour stop, and then on to John F. Kennedy.

BOOK II

1

DAVID WAS STANDING on American soil. The editor had sent one of his employees to meet David. He had a cardboard sign with David's name. He said his name was Gurcharan Singh. 'Call me Gary,' he said, gently combing his long beard with his right hand, a pensive look on his face.

'God, he looks like Jarnail Singh Bhindranwale,' David thought. 'I wonder if he has a disposition to match!' Gary had a quiet intensity underlined by a silent brooding intimidation. His eyes were deep and dark. The turban and beard seemed linguistically out of step with a name like Gary.

'They cannot say my name proper here,' he explained, 'so . . .'

David thought, Arnold Schwarzenegger still retains his name, so . . .

Gurcharan Singh had been a major in the Indian army, so he said. Now here he was, Gary . . . shooting for a Green Card. He explained his role in the newspaper: 'I am collector,' he explained.

'What is a collector?'

Gary smiled. 'My English is so-so,' he apologized, 'but I am learning every day, new sentence. See, I am making rounds, the Indian and Pakistani businesses, the ones who advertise in newspaper and I have to be collecting advertising money every day. Many, they not pay after advertisement comes out in paper. I shout at them, make big noise, make nuisance every day, then they pay. Some never pay at all. What to do? The Indians and Pakistanis are like that only.

Sometimes I have to get rough and tough. Every day, that is my job, nine to five.'

He had slipped into the newspaper by accident. He was visiting friends in New York and met Manu Laxman at an Indian birthday party at the Pink Elephant Tandoor Restaurant. Laxman had been impressed with his background, said he needed a man like the major and offered him a job with the possibility of a Green Card somewhere down the line. Sponsored by the newspaper, he had applied for an H1-B visa, which Gary had to pay for, and here he was. It had been four years; Gary was still waiting for his Green Card. He shook his head. '*Bade dook de gal hai. Bade dook de gal.*'

'So why didn't you just go back home to Punjab?'

'Long, long story,' Gary whispered, 'complicated.' Gurcharan Singh was running away from something. The newspaper was his refuge, 'till few things change here and there back home'.

David sighed. He pondered the veracity of Gurcharan Singh's tale of being a major in the Indian army; it didn't sound like a straight-shooter story. He did not know what to make of the mystery that was Gary Singh. Still, it was good to be met by another Indian. As the cab drove to Fifth Avenue, Gary talked. The newspaper was a hellhole. What was David doing here? People were fired every day. The chances of David becoming an illegal alien were very high. Gary talked softly. The owner and editor, Manu Laxman, was a bloodsucker, a womanizer and a man whose morals matched the stink of an Indian public toilet. He treated Indians like chattel. The employment ads that he placed in India were a smoke screen. He needed outside blood constantly. The

Indians from New York knew his reputation, so he had to fool journalists from India into coming to America.

Gary smiled at David sadly. 'You will be finding out soon.'

'Where are we going?' asked David.

'Oh,' said Gary, now beginning to enjoy himself. 'The boss has asked, take you to office, he wait for you.'

A knot began to form at the pit of David's stomach. Gary's monologue had filled him with fear, which he tried hard to suppress as he looked out of the widow of the sedan.

The taxi stopped on Fifth Avenue, opposite the Empire State Building. David looked up, fascinated. This was one tall structure. He had heard about this building all his life. Now here he was. They crossed the street, David dragging one big suitcase, Gary helping with the other. They took an elevator up to the fifteenth floor. Doors opened. They walked to the newspaper office. And there was his new boss, Manu Laxman, in the flesh. He looked amiable. David thought his face resembled the Indian actor, Dilip Kumar. He held out his hand, smiling. David liked his firm handshake.

'Welcome to America,' he said. 'I know that you are going to be happy here at *Asia Times*.'

Behind them, Gary had grown extremely quiet. He informed Manu Laxman that he had to leave for home and departed without looking at David. His new boss put his arm around David's shoulder and said: 'I have to attend a banquet. Make yourself comfortable here.'

'You mean you did not book some sort of room?' David asked, amazed.

'This is a comfortable office,' Laxman said, smiling. 'The carpet is soft. You will sleep well here on the floor. Turn out the lights before you sleep, okay? There is a bathroom in the office. I will see you tomorrow at nine o'clock. Tomorrow we will try and settle you somewhere.' With that cryptic welcome, Manu Laxman left the room.

Jet-lagged, his brain hazy, David looked out of the office windows. It was beginning to snow. He stared at it, watching the flakes float down. The heating in the office had been turned off for the night. It was getting cold. David looked down at the street below. It was almost midnight. Traffic flowed like molten lava in the Promised Land as snowflakes fell silently. He pulled out two sweaters and a woollen blanket from his suitcase, and looked down at the threadbare carpet. As his body began to shake, David closed his eyes, pulled on the sweaters, wrapped the blanket around his body and lay curled on the floor.

It was early morning, Gary was gently shaking him awake. David was disoriented. Where was he?

'David bhai, wake up, go to bathroom, have wash. In half an hour, work starts.'

David's mouth opened involuntarily. 'I need to sleep,' he blurted out.

Gary's voice was genuinely sympathetic: 'Work today. You say "no", he get anger, say "go now", will fire you. That is the way here. He very bad man.'

Half an hour later, the staff began arriving. They all looked at David as if he were an approaching disease. Later, David found out why. If David was the latest addition, someone was going to lose their job soon. That was the way it worked here.

An hour later, a smiling Manu Laxman walked in. He summoned David to his office. 'We are behind deadline,' he explained. 'I want you to start taking charge of *Asia Times*. I am going to fire the current managing editor. You will be the new managing editor. You will get more money when that happens, but until then, you will earn a reporter's salary. I want you to learn all he knows in three weeks. He might not want to help you and I don't have the time to teach you. How you do it is your problem. Find yourself an apartment. Till then you can stay in the office. You can go to a hotel, but why waste money you don't have? I will let you stay here in the office. Save some money. Rough it out for a short time and you will be alright. Don't complain. This is a tough town. If you can make it here, you can make it anywhere. I have to leave now, have to take care of some advertising business. I will see you later.'

David walked out of his office in a daze. The managing editor would not even look at David when he introduced himself. He knew the game. If he let David succeed, he would soon be jobless. He was going to try and get David fired before his own head rolled. There was no other way. David's first writing assignment was to rewrite three articles stolen from the *Times of India*. The managing editor smiled. 'He wants this by five this evening.'

David went to his assigned computer. He tried talking to some of the staff; they shied away like he was a leper. Out of the corner of his eye, David saw the major and the managing editor laughing at him. He went to work. By 5 p.m., he was done. Manu Laxman was back. He glanced through the articles.

'You are very good,' he said. 'I will leave the heat on today, so you do not freeze. Go get something to eat. There are many places around here. This is Fifth Avenue. Journalists from India will kill to work here. I am going to get your status changed from a tourist to a H1-B visa. Maybe one day a Green Card. No problem there. Work hard, one fine day it will pay off.'

David nodded. He had nothing to say. Not one of the sixteen employees had spoken to him. He had heard the whispers though, as they discussed his plight. By 7.30 p.m., the office was empty. David sat on the floor and his mind went berserk. The fax machine spewed paper. An unpleasant sound. He walked to the window and looked out at New York City glittering with bright lights.

The next day, the situation got worse. Manu Laxman's 'floor supervisor' was a dragon in heat named Annapoorna Roy Choudhary. She preferred, she said, to be called 'Anna'. She was a buxom, nut-brown Bengali seductress, with Jagger lips, a Mumtaz figure and a silver nose ring that glinted. Her knowledge of the publishing business was pathetic, her understanding of journalism non-existent. She claimed she was an artist. Anna was there to 'keep people in line'. She was his beautiful, well-groomed, attack bitch; he was her illicit, part-time lap dog. They both believed that a person should be broken down, after which, the fragments had to be moulded to fit the newspaper's style book. A jackal and a hyena, they worked well together. Somebody once overheard Manu Laxman complain that his wife was sexually conservative in bed. Anna, he said, did it all and enjoyed it. And she was a great professional asset to him. She helped him run the paper with swastika efficiency. She didn't mind that he was married. From mediocre secretary, she was now second in command.

Asia Times was a weekly newspaper. It employed ten men

and six women. A retired journalist, Sean O'Reilly, who had once worked for *Village Voice*, came in twice a week to write a column and supervise the pages. He swatted away Anna's bully tactics viciously. 'Fok off, woman,' he said. 'Don't ye tell me how to do me bloody job.' He said he worked here for a pittance, because 'it gave him something to do' and it paid for his fags and an occasional pint. 'So take your Halloween mask someplace else. Go scare the little Indian boys.'

She had mumbled something derogatory about white people and walked away. Anna was fortunate that the quick-tempered Irishman did not understand Bengali. They could not intimidate him with the usual firing squad method. He was a US citizen; he was not on an H1-B visa. They could not frighten him with 'You will become an illegal alien once we withdraw your work papers, so watch your mouth'. So great was Anna's humiliation, she let the incident pass without lodging a complaint with Manu Laxman.

2

LAXMAN AND ANNA were a double-barrelled attack that kept everybody in a constant state of enhanced fear. Show weakness, they believed, and the employees would 'take advantage'. They stole news features, defaced them until they were unrecognizable and fed them to 'the Indians living abroad'.

If advertisers were playing hard to get, Manu Laxman screamed at his sales representatives. Told them they were scum; threatened them with the illegal alien line; told them that after all he had done for them, this is what he got, shit, which was what they were giving him. Why could they not get the advertiser to play ball? They were not good enough, they were stupid, incompetent Indians. And they wanted to make it in America. Ha. Is this what he was paying them for? 'Now go out there, get that bastard to give us his advertisement. Don't come back and tell me that you fools could not get it. Do you people want to go back to your slums in India? Eat dal and rice forever? Now get out.'

Anna's ways were subtler. She would call the target into her office. Then in a soft, hissing voice ask: 'This page that you designed, look at it; tell me what is wrong. Don't look at me, you fool, look at the page. Tell me ... now ... I asked you to do this; I gave you a scribble of how I wanted it. Why are you so ignorant? I mean, why can't you follow simple commands. You have an ego problem? Is that it? Do you have an ego problem, or are you an incompetent page designer?'

When the art director meekly informed her that he had

followed her scribble, she tore the page and, in a demonic rage, flung the shredded paper violently into the wastebasket. 'Don't insult me. I have been in this business for fifteen years. I do all the work here, help you people out and this is what happens . . . this is what happens. I want you to redesign this page, go ahead do your own thing and then let me see.' When the art director asked for another scribble, she laughed. 'Who is the art director, you or me? Go, I want that page here on my desk in half an hour or do yourself a favour, get yourself another job. Don't tell me you are leaving, just go. Let's see how you get another company to sponsor you for your work papers. You will be back here in twenty-four hours with your tail between your legs, begging me to take you back. Now go, kill yourself, you are no good to anybody anyway. I have other things to do besides wasting my time talking to you. Go. And hey, if you want to file a charge of discrimination against me, or against the paper with the US Equal Employment Opportunity Commission, go ahead . . . see what will happen to you. Yes, someone once did. He lost everything, and finally he had to go back to India. All I am asking is for you to do your job well. If you cannot do that, is it my fault? Do you think I like screaming at you all like this all the time? Now, get out.'

Anna could be cold and biting as an Antarctic winter. Once, the female sub editor, who also doubled as a proofreader, overlooked a misspelled word. The word 'antagonistic' had appeared as 'antognostic'. Anna summoned her to the office. She stared at her silently for a full minute. The proofreader lowered her head, looked at the floor. Anna whispered, venom made a hissing sound: 'Dooo yooo know why you are sitting here in front of meeeee?' The proofreader was silent. 'Answer me,' she screamed suddenly. 'This is what I want you to do. Go out, buy a magnifying glass, buy two, no, no, buy three. One for each of your blind eyes and one for your stupid brain. Then read the paper and tell me what is wrong. Now get out, your face is giving me a migraine. I don't know which gutter you people come from. Out, out . . . Be back here in fifteen minutes.'

For those who dared to buck the system, a pink slip shot out at them. Over and out, and that was that. They maintained and contained their employees by keeping them hanging on the hook of the H1-B visa, renewing it year after year. 'What did these people think this is? Mother Teresa's ashram?' They did not seek efficiency. They demanded abject servility. Acquiring replacements for shattered employees who left or were fired was never a problem. It kept wages at a minimum and the newspaper never missed a deadline. They reasoned it was good to have new blood every so often. It brought in fresh ideas and different approaches that were great for the newspaper, and it did not give anybody a chance to settle down and feel a sense of entitlement.

Several weeks had passed. It was 8 a.m. David was looking out of the window. He heard a soft scared 'hello' behind him. He whirled around, as if electrocuted. The soft voice said: 'Don't be scared.' David recognized her. It was the graphic artist who designed pages in the layout department.

'My name is Anjali,' she said. 'You have to promise me that you will keep what I tell you a secret . . . Repeat this to anybody and I will be jobless in an hour's time. I am going to trust you.'

David thought he was going to cry. This act of kindness overwhelmed him.

'I just want you to listen. That's all, Ach-haa?'

David nodded, a lump forming in the pit of his stomach.

'I have read your articles,' she said, 'you are a great journalist. Unfortunately, sometimes even people like you make mistakes. Coming here was a mistake. This man is a monster. Right now, he has you where he wants you. You have left your home and career thinking that New York and a job in a high-rise on Fifth Avenue will bring you your American dream. You have no money to go back. You do not want to go back in shame, no, no. I know what that is like. Here, we all know what that is like. He knows that we know. You cannot get another job on the visa that he is going to get you, unless another company sponsors you to work for them. That rarely happens. American newspapers will not hire you without a Green Card. You are stuck. He is going to underpay you so you cannot leave. We all work long hours here when it's deadline time. If you ask for overtime, you are fired. If you get sick for more than a day, you are fired. So please do not fall sick.'

David laughed bitterly. 'I do not have control over that,' he said wearily.

She pretended not to hear him. She had to finish speaking before another employee walked in. 'He plays one person against the other here. People whisper in his ear all the time, hoping to be in his good books. Hoping to keep their jobs. Arrey, David . . . it's like the Gestapo. He knows everything that happens in this office. *Everything*, okay? He plays on religion. You will find out. Even the Hindus are divided here. He just loves these divisions. Always look busy. If you have finished an article, act like you are still working on it, okay? He believes that if you sit around even for a minute

Bloodline Bandra

you are wasting his time and he will cut your salary. Personally, I am trying to get another job. Everybody here is in the same boat. The two advertising space seller girls are sleeping with him. If they do not, out they go. I wonder what his wife is like, sometimes. Nobody here ever sees her. He also has a son and daughter. One of the advertising girls, I heard, is younger than his daughter.'

David looked at Anjali in sheer disbelief.

She nodded. 'You will find out. Ach-haa, my advice is try and find another sponsor. What else can I say? Once he fires you, and you cannot get another sponsor, you automatically become an illegal alien. That is a terrible word. A terrible state to be in. He knows that. David, he relies on cheap labour; this is how he gets it. He drives a big Mercedes, you know. Think you can sue him? Ah, David, no way. He has the money and time. He has the power to get you deported back to India. Did he promise you that he would get doctors to look at you if you got sick? That is a lie. If you do not buy medical insurance, you will be in deep trouble. And right now, you do not have the money for that. Ask him about the doctors that he promised you. See what he says. On the poor salary that he is giving you, he expects you to pay rent on an apartment, utilities, food and drink, and don't forget your travel expenses and God help you if you get sick. He does not care if you die, okay, he'll simply get another Indian.' Then Anjali gently touched his hand, looked him in the eyes and said: 'Don't let the dog get to you. Remember you are a great journalist, okay?' She touched his shoulder. 'Ach-haa, baba, good luck.'

David looked at her waist-length hair and thin back, clad in a green kurta, walking away from him. Not once had the name Manu Laxman materialized from her breath. This was fear. Plain, pure fear. A mute black rage began filling David's abdomen. He could feel thick, bad blood gurgling in his veins and flowing in spurts to his throbbing heart. He had fleeting thoughts of somebody killing Manu Laxman. Maybe death will come by accident, he hoped.

That day, David worked, plagiarizing more articles. He tried talking to the managing editor, who politely told him he had no time. Manu Laxman ignored him. Anjali ignored him. They all ignored him. He assumed that they liked the managing editor and saw David as a new threat to their existence. It was a bitch fight they did not want their dog in. David needed time to access the semantics of the weekly paper. Manu was now aware that the managing editor knew of his imminent dismissal, he knew that David was going to learn nothing about the inner workings of the newspaper. David knew that too. So what was Manu's game plan? A week had passed. After work, David usually walked up and down Fifth Avenue. He needed to get away from his gulag opposite the Empire State building. He thought of his village often, and here on Fifth Avenue he began longing for the dirty streets of his Pali.

*

Dear Mama,
I am working and living on Fifth Avenue, one of the richest, grandest places in America. From my apartment I can see the Empire State Building. In fact, I am opposite this great building. I am fine. The job is great. Everybody here is so friendly and helpful. My boss is good to me. He tells me that soon I will be managing editor of the newspaper. Then, I will be making more money. I will be able to send

you some nice-smelling expensive perfumes from Fifth Avenue. New York is a wonderful place.

There are many interesting places to see, big museums and parks and great food. There are many Indians living in New York, they all seem very busy. Give my love to Papa, Brian and everybody else. Do not worry about me. I am fine. I will try and send you some money next month. You can write to me at my office address. I have a nice small apartment. My house does not have a post box yet. The landlord tells me that in a month he should have the box installed. Then you can write to me at my home address. I will write another letter soon.

How is Papa? Please give him my regards and tell him I think of him often.

Love,
David

*

He signed and sealed the letter and felt no guilt about his fabrications. Something had died in his soul.

3

LOOKING AT THE sophisticated store windows, assessing the crowds and hating the cold, David felt like a beggar. Standing outside the stores, he felt poor and forsaken. Bergdorf Goodman, Saks Fifth Avenue, Lord & Taylor, Tiffany & Co., Louis Vuitton. One cold Sunday, he walked through the imposing doors of Saint Patrick's Cathedral, on the east side of Fifth Avenue between 50th and 51st streets in midtown Manhattan. Its neo-Gothic style and impressive stained-glass windows fascinated David. He walked between the mighty columns and into the nave of the church. There, he genuflected and knelt, and tried talking to God. The face of Manu Laxman appeared disembodied, circling the cross and laughing. David walked out. He tried talking to a Pakistani taxi driver he met outside the Path station on 34th street. The driver was parked next to Macy's, waiting for a fare. David asked him if he knew of any jobs that were available.

The Pakistani, whose name was Akbar, asked him: 'Got Green Card, boss?'

David said that he was on a tourist visa.

Akbar asked him to go home. 'No use,' he scoffed. 'You go home, back to the Bombay. What you doing here, working for mad dogs? No good, I say, no, no, no . . . you go home.'

Working for an Indian, the Pakistani stated, was like working for a rabid slave owner. The Pakistanis were a better race of people, he said. The Indians were the cause of all the problems in Pakistan; ask the Bangladeshis, he added. They would tell him the same thing. Then he said something that made David realize the schism that existed between the Pakistanis and Indians in New York. 'If you be from the Pakistan, maybe I help, maybe, Insha'allah. Corner Candy store, in Flushing, Queens, needs people. But . . . you . . . my friend . . . my boss is from Lahore, he does not like too much people from the India. Nothing personal, bhai jaan. See, I am solid American citizen, still find it hard. Driving cab, night and day. And you . . . No use, my friend. You must be going back to the home.' Akbar looked at David with some sympathy but there was also that inner hidden feeling of superiority. 'You can stay in the America,' Akbar said, laughing openly. 'Marry the American woman. Auto-maa-tick Green Card, bhai. Auto-maa-tick . . . tee-kate for the America.'

Affronted and irritated, David turned around and walked down 34th street, watching the street vendors peddling spurious goods, turned right at Bryant Park and walked to Fifth Avenue. He went into the New York City Public Library situated on the corner. He needed to read *A Midsummer Night's Dream* to get away from the reality of his existence. He needed to be under the light of a moon in a fairyland. Convince his mind that his body was going through a bad dream. But David could not concentrate. His mind jumped from complexity to perplexity to blankness. He walked out of the library and shuffled to 42nd street and Park Avenue. He stopped to buy cigarettes from a booth manned by a Pakistani. When the man asked him where he was from, David's reply was instantaneous: 'Portugal. From Lisbon, Portugal.' He walked into Grand Central Station, sat on the steps leading to the bars on the first floor. He loved this place. The mural of stars on the ceiling. The Zodiac depicted backwards. The patch of dark on the impeccably restored ceiling. Why was that there? he wondered.

A young Japanese girl was playing the cello for dimes. She was exceptional. David had a friend in Bombay who played the cello. He was familiar with the technicality of the instrument. Nobody was listening to her. The cellist was playing fragments from two concertos by Joseph Haydn in C Major and D Major. David watched her arm. Her pronation was masterful. Up bow, down bow, her wrist seemed to not move at all. Incredible. She did a double stop, later a collegno, where she used the wood of the bow to play. David watched, fascinated. She noticed him. Smiled. For once, David forgot his miserable world and watched her perform. He loved classical music. The music was punctuated by overhead calls: 'Train for White Plains leaves from Track 22'. Somebody dropped a dollar bill into her open cello case, someone else criticized the music as 'a slow drone upstream', a woman said to her companion that she was great, someone wearing a born-to-be-wild T-shirt laughed. A cassocked Roman Catholic priest sauntered by, smiling. The cellist heard it all, watched it all and suddenly switched to *Eleanor Rigby* by the Beatles. The irony was not lost on David. They looked at each other and smiled with their eyes. When she was done with Lennon and McCartney, she gracefully laid the cello down and began packing to go. David approached her and dropped a dollar into the open case.

'If I could afford more, I would give it all to you,' he said quietly. She smiled and looked at him.

'Thank you. I am glad you enjoyed the playing.'

He held out his hand: 'I am David Cabral.'

She held on to his palm. 'My name is Hatsumi Nakamura,' she said softly. 'I play here every Sunday afternoon.'

David looked at her. She was beautiful, mysterious . . . he

wondered what she did when she left Grand Central Station. Does she play at other places? Meeting this woman was a ray of sunshine that had penetrated the opaque dullness of his existence. Somebody had acknowledged that he was alive. David said that he would like to hear her play again and asked whether he could come by next Sunday. 'Hey, it's a free country,' she joked. He waved goodbye and walked out at the 42nd street exit. Hatsumi. David loved the sound of her name. Just 'Hatsumi' seemed incomplete, when he added 'Nakamura', her name danced; and later, when he discovered what 'Nakamura' meant, it all made sense in a strange mystical way. They were both, David Cabral and Hatsumi Nakamura, village people.

With music on his mind, David had a sudden vivid memory of the 'goo-mut' of his Pali village. It was an earthen pot with a large mouth over which was stretched taut the skin of a monitor lizard which the villagers called 'gor-phad'. The goo-mut was first lightly warmed over an open fire, then usually placed on the knee of a drunk, who perched on a stool and bitch-slapped the skin rapidly and viciously with both hands, one hand at a time. The sound, amplified by the pig-belly of the pot, rocketed out of a smaller open mouth at the other end. The goo-mut was played during East Indian, seven-day weddings and frequent drunken revelries. It was always an accompanying instrument to a drunken voice shouting traditional Koli-Marathi songs. The East Indians believed that you could not play the goo-mut well when stone-cold sober. 'Not bleddy possible, men, no, no. You have to have at least two or three bleddy good drinks before you began pounding the living daylights out of the lizard. The alcohol enhanced the sensibilities of the player and lent a searing heat and passion to the sound he then created. There was no arguing this sacred dogma scripted in the fisherman's bible.

Lyrically, the songs are simplistic ditties, most certainly thought up by brains pickled with rot-gut booze. Still, they reflected the East Indian society and times, and remain a testament to their lifestyle. The more opprobrious the refrain, the more the cheers.

Consider this:

Around her neck is a golden chain,
Whose daughter is this?
Her mother is black, her father is black,
Whose daughter is this?

Or the Morning Mantra:

It's early morning, the wind is blowing
Ah-ray, why you standing at the door?
It's early morning, the wind is blowing
Ah-ray, why you standing at the door?
Chun, Chun, Chun, My pig has run away
Wonder whose house he's gone to?

And then, a simple gesture of love, straight from the clenched fist.

From Mumbai I will bring you sweets
From Mumbai I will bring you sweets
If you don't eat a few
I will beat the hell out of you

And the smooth sexual serenade:

Open da door, Mary open da door
Cum on Mary open your door
Your thighs are so white
Hot and full of spice
Cum on Mary open your door

And the goo-mut dances, alive and wild. Alcohol and lizard skin. A super-shaman's dream tools. The *Axis Mundi* is a shamanistic term, it means the connection between heaven and earth. When the goo-mut played and the alcohol raged, the East Indians dropped through a black hole, and there, for those fleeting moments, their space–time jungle stomped in the fourth dimension. And they danced, right hand held aloft, holding a curry-and-snot-stained handkerchief, waving it in the air, urging the drunk who pounded the earthen drum to sing another one just like the other one.

The goo-mut was, and still is, an important musical instrument for East Indians. He tried having a conversation once about its popularity and the response was so sulphuric, he flinched. 'Wot men, you like dat Beet-oven bugger, or wot? You becoming a bleddy homo or wot, men, shee baba! Wot is wrong with our East Indian music, men? Wot be so wrong, you tell me? Bleddy, read one-and-half books and you think you are become prime minister, huh? So you went to college, so wot? Bleddy idiot bugger!' He smiled now as he thought about that long-ago exchange.

Outside, New York city was doing what it did best. Anarchy was break-dancing out on the streets, people walked with searing intent. Everyone was hurrying to a definite focal point. A people with a purpose, buzzing with a chutzpah that could not be duplicated. David began walking towards Fifth Avenue past the public library. The thought of going back to an empty office riled his consciousness. He walked into Houlihan's at the base of the Empire State Building and ordered a double shot of Jim Beam. The warm liquid made him feel good. His thoughts were of Japanese cellos and girls with faraway eyes.

Then the current managing editor of the newspaper walked in with two of his friends. David scowled, emboldened by the drink in his system. The other man saw David and made his way across.

'Hello, my name is Ravi Malhotra,' he said. 'I owe you an explanation and an apology.'

David held up his hand, palm facing Ravi as he sat down.

'I am going to explain. It is simple. I have read your work. You are a great writer. The problem here is, if I let you get away with learning the nuances of the paper, I will lose my job. I cannot afford that. I don't need to explain what kind of a man Manu Laxman is. I am really sorry for the predicament that you find yourself in. I have been promised another job, but till that happens, I cannot let you take my place. I hope you understand that. It's nothing personal. It's a fight for survival. The reason he wants me out is money. He intends to pay you half of what he's paying me. I know that. There are other reasons, but they are not important. He knows that you are qualified to run the newspaper. So, I am going to do whatever it takes to prove that you cannot do the job. I have to demonstrate this to him. It is going to make you look like an imbecile, but I have to do what I have to do. It's the only way I will survive.'

David looked at him silently.

'I wish,' he continued, 'we could have met in better circumstances. Oh, by the way, I used to read all your reports from Israel. If you look at some of the back issues, we, meaning I, rewrote your articles, put my name on them, and the paper used them. I am telling you this because you will find out anyway, someday. I was just following orders.'

David smiled, shaking his head in disbelief, pure contempt showing on his face. His silence unnerved Ravi. He knew what David was thinking. Ravi accepted the fact that he was a hack. David understood. The two men shook hands, not looking into each other's eyes. Ravi Malhotra went to the bar and joined his friends. David went back to Jim Beam.

He decided to have another drink. Ravi and his friends were sitting at the far end of the bar. David walked up to the bartender and ordered another round. The television over the counter was on. An Indian face was explaining ancient Indian philosophy and how it worked in conjunction with modern Western reality. David decided to listen. He had read the Upanishads, the Bhagavad Gita, the Ramayana and Mahabharata. He found the stories fascinating, the philosophy redundant and the morality hypocritical. But that was his personal view. David freely admitted that he did not understand the depth of these great books. What this man was trying to explain could be interesting. The female interviewer was reviewing the guru's resume. Apparently, he was born in India and was now an American multi-millionaire, had helped billions of people around the world and written numerous bestselling books. Impressive. The interviewer, a bottle blonde with a heart-shaped, botoxed face and eyebrows plucked to a degree of perpetual amazement, was asking him well-researched questions.

'How do you apply ancient Indian philosophy to the modern age of anxiety, so that it works in everyday American life?'

The guru began speaking words of wisdom. His accent was pseudo-American. His gestures expressive, his tone professorial. 'I am all about the non-economic fulfilment of existence on our mother, planet Earth. I may have wealth and money, and there is a difference there; but that does not matter, not really. I shall visit that later. See, you can get rid of negative emotions if you listen closely to the sounds of your being and learn to interpret that language. With this particular theory of quantum mechanics, you can heal body and soul. This wave-particle duality brings energy. The theory is abstract but the healing is real. Once you understand the macroscopic properties, it is easy.'

David could not believe the splashing swine-slop he was hearing.

'The Vedas, as you know, are the oldest sacred texts known to all mankind. You know we have the Rig Veda, Sama Veda, Yajur Veda and the Atharva Veda. I would like to inform my viewers watching this segment that they may not be aware of this, but there exists myriad older Veda manuscripts in parts of Nepal. These belong to the Vajasaneyi tradition. I discovered this just a week ago. Scholars state that they come from as far back as the eleventh century. My next book is going to deal with that subject. But, coming back to your question, anxiety in today's world is a manageable problem. You have to look at the word and its concordance. When the atma, that means soul, fuses with the kundalini, great things happen . . .'

The blonde asked the guru to hold that thought as the station cut to a commercial. The guru disappeared from the screen. A man appeared in an advertisement selling miracle hair-growth products. David's mouth was wide open in absolute amazement. Obviously the guru was smart, a marketing genius. You can sell shit, just package and market it well, someone had once joked. The guru, David told himself, was living, breathing proof that this was possible. David downed his drink, left the bar and crossed the street to his mansion of depression on Fifth Avenue.

Later, he inflated the small blow-up mattress and pillow he had bought. He changed into his kurta-pyjama and lay down his head, weary, depressed and slightly intoxicated.

4

IT WAS A glorious morning. Manu Laxman was at the office whistling a happy tune. He walked around, surveying his minions, issuing orders and praising the girls from the advertising department. They had done a great job, he said. Sure, he helped a little at getting that advertising campaign, but he refused to take all the credit. He was just glad that Patel Sweets and Treats, the largest Indian confectionary business in New York, was going to be running three advertising campaigns in the newspaper. It had not been easy, but as Manu Laxman always maintained, 'In the end, hard work always pays off.'

Patel Sweets and Treats did not really want to advertise. So Manu Laxman arranged a meeting with the owner. He smiled as he told the owner that if Patel Sweets and Treats did not advertise in Manu Laxman's newspaper, the newspaper would have to run a health article exposing where Patel Sweets and Treats got their cheap raw materials from. Yes, yes, yes, the newspaper was aware that the raw materials were manufactured and packed in the slums of Dharavi in Bombay. And, of course, there was that little problem called 'child labour'. These poor little children, bone thin, in tattered clothes, working under old asbestos roofing. Some of them might be suffering from cancer already. You know about the effects of asbestos, don't you? I mean your sweets taste great and the colours are appealing, but . . . are they FDA approved? And that asbestos . . . mesothelioma. Takes the aroma away. Leaves a bad aftertaste. The colouring for the sweets was spurious, cheap stuff made under appalling hygienic conditions. Raw sewage in open gutters flowed right outside the little factory in the Dharavi slums. If analysed, the colouring could prove to be mildly carcinogenic. The Food and Drug Administration in America would love something like that.

His chief reporter, Dolly Khanna, had finished the article, it was ready for publication. The paper's special correspondent in Bombay had contributed by tracing consignment destinations with road transport companies and shipping offices in Bombay; and, of course, they had photographs showing the manufacturing plant in the slums. Terrible, just terrible.

It would not be an easy job for Manu Laxman to persuade Dolly Khanna to kill the story. We have a free press, you know. These journalists have ethics, you know. Manu Laxman had absolutely no idea, but Dolly Khanna had been working on this story for the last six months. Shocking. He was not aware of what went on in his own newspaper. Still, he could try and persuade her to drop the whole thing. Just horrible. This whole business. Leaves a sour taste in the mouth. Send Dolly Khanna a box of sweets, thanking her, you know. Live and let live, I always say. So how about advertising in *Asia Times*! And if nothing was proved, Patel Sweets and Treats could sue the newspaper, but by then, the damage would have been done. Manu Laxman told the owner that he did not really want to cause any problems, but times were hard and debts were high, and really all Manu Laxman wanted was a lousy 10,000 dollars for each campaign that would run in the newspaper. Patel Sweets and Treats was a multimillion-dollar wholesale business. The 30,000-dollar fee he would charge them was pocket change for a company so rich and respected by the Indian, Pakistani, Bangladeshi and Caribbean Island population in Canada and the United States. His customers were the same people who read Manu Laxman's newspaper, he told the owner of Patel Sweets and Treats. The campaigns would triple his sweet business. Recently, according to government statistics, the readership of the newspaper had jumped to an impressive 200,000. As an incentive, Manu Laxman promised the owner that he would talk to a top Hindi movie star about being a spokesperson for the company. He would also run a couple of advertorial rags-to-riches features in the business section on the owner himself. Imagine.

His advertising girls would meet with the owner tomorrow. They would have the necessary papers that had to be signed. 'Thank you so much for your business. We really appreciate this. In the end, we Indians in America have to stick together, you know.' Manu Laxman, clad in an impeccable Armani suit, walked out smiling, humming an obscene old sea ditty about toothless old sea dogs frigging in the rigging because there was bugger-all left to do.

Manu Laxman, born in Bombay, looked at his staff of assorted Indians with contempt. He was not Indian, he told himself, not really. He had left the land of his birth far behind. These fools did not realize what he had to go through to keep them employed. All they wanted were Green Cards, and then, the next day they would leave him. People are ungrateful, fickle, cowardly and covetous. It is much safer to be feared than loved. How true. Wonder who said that? I came from nothing. Now I have built all this. Nobody handed me a dime when I was starving in this country. This is a business here, not a dharamshala. This typical Indian

Bloodline Bandra

mentality, that if you are an Indian I have to help you, makes me want to throw up. And then, they will stab you in the back if they get the chance. That is typical Indian too.

And that David Cabral, Manu thought, was another pathetic case study. He has to prove himself worthy. Maybe I can keep the current editor and David as well. It will help to keep the competition going. Keep them both on their toes. Cut some salaries and this could be financially viable. David is a good journalist but can he manage and motivate people? Is he a good editor? Is he an 'ideas person'? We have to find out. Editors are like priests and nuns. Although they are dedicated, they need to be transferred and moved out every five years, otherwise corruption sets in. The shuffle is important. New blood is always good.

Manu Laxman's eyes swept over his empire on Fifth Avenue. He gazed at his people and retreated to his cabin where he gently took off his heavy imaginary crown.

5

SUNDAY MORNING ARRIVED on a darkening January cloud. Alone in the office, David thought of God and a hanging feeling of being forsaken overwhelmed his being. He tried praying. The futility of his existence transformed his conventional prayers to a litany of helpless begging.

David looked up and around him. The clock on the wall said it was 11.10 a.m. This was his bedroom, amid desks and chairs, computers and soiled used papers lying on the floor. The trashcan was not far from where he slept. He had to get out. David brushed his teeth, dressed in layers and took the elevator down to the ground floor. He walked out onto Fifth Avenue, turned right and kept walking. Snow flurries came floating out of nowhere like surreal, wet face powder. The numbing cold felt good. He was walking towards the New York Public Library and Grand Central Station. He thought of Hatsumi Nakamura, the Japanese cello player. She had told him that she played in Grand Central Station on Sundays. He drifted right, towards the magnificent station, then stopped and walked back up Fifth Avenue, head tucked into his coat. He wanted to talk to her, to touch her hand, and listen to her music but his hopelessness made him turn away. David was jolted out of his thoughts when a man accidently walked into him. He flinched and looked up, and for the first time, David registered the busy sounds of the city. In the midst of men dressed in black suits and women in black coats, he watched flashes of colour mingle with the street flow.

Here, a six-foot woman with flaming red hair and eyes with a hallucinogenic glitter, sucks on a cigar. There are three-inch gashes painted into each corner of her mouth, creating a spooky clownesque smile. Must be a Broadway queen. A whore, maybe. There, a bearded old man, withered by self-abuse and time, is talking to himself. Tattooed urban prophets paint graffiti depicting their communications with the almighty. A billboard advertisement says: It's better in the Bahamas. David looks around. Two homeless men wave at him. He smiles. Tourists with expensive cameras look wide-eyed at the skyscrapers. Their eyes light up with anticipation, their gestures very, very polite, not wanting to ruffle the notorious impatience and mythical temper of resident New Yorkers. Manhattan is in a state of lull, many of the working men and women are in their homes, recuperating, getting ready for Monday's assault.

David thought, unlike most Indian cities, New York has a distinctive, cocksure swagger. As he sauntered down Fifth Avenue to Central Park, the wind flashed, the colour of concrete and jungle sounds pounced from skyscrapers. Foreign accents rolled with the shadows and the constant murmur was a soft echo of what this hardboiled city was all about.

If you can make it here, you can make it anywhere; this is Noo-York baby! I'm good. Dylan's playing The Garden tonight. He be the man. You said what? Sabah el-khayr. Gut Danke. You wanna come with me, I'll make it worth your time, I'm good, you'll see, what you gotta lose man? Qui n'a point argent en bourse ait miel en bouche. You're my nigga, we be brothers, now don't be dissin' me, ya hear. Dig this honkey, Parisian bitch. You wanna walk or talk, I said? Capitalistic Pig, she said! If it were not for the Americans, the French would be speaking German right now. Know what I mean, Guido! Come on, give daddy some sugar, honey, I love you. Après l'amour, le repentir. Nice rack. That's a straight booty call, dog, don't you be giving me no jive. Señon Márquez Qué le paró en el ojo? Tell it like it is, pimp. I remember when a dollar was a dollar! More bang for the buck back then. Fuhgeddaboudit! Got some loose change for a veteran? You tawkin' to me? This country does not give a shit. No wonder the A-Rabs hate us. Which way to Times Square? How many blocks? What is block? I am from India, sir. Not fully understanding this block business. How much for these sunglasses? How much? Much too much expensive. Will purchase it for two dollars. That is one hundred rupees in Indian money, sir. Lot of money, I say. Yes, we always bargain, part of Indian culture. We have a great culture. Come Smita, let us to be going now. Please don't call me that. In India we show respect to the elders. Alter schützt vor Torheit nicht. Yes, I am English. Yes, I love New York. Get outta here. No, I don't want a baggi, mate. Hey Paki, Jinnah on down to your own country. Sand nigga. Now as I was saying, she stuck out her tongue with a thick barbell and then proceeded ... ahaaaaaaaaaaaa ...... wish you were there. Who died? NO! Really? NO! You really mean seventy-two virgins will be waiting for you? Come on man, you be putting me on. Es una broma, right? Can I come with you? I need a virgin, just one, man. Have not had one since I came to the States. Will kill for one right now. My computer crashed; died. Oh wow. Oh wow. Oh wow. My hard drive needs some software. What?

Are we talkin' sex now? Yea, I am an illegal alien from Syria, so? I have contributed to the American dream; ask my first born, my son. E-mail him; it's the only way to talk to him, through cyber space. Is this a great country or what? Who you calling a wetback, gringo? I ain't no wet back, moo-cha-cha. I am Catholic. The Pope is from Crack House? Fungool. Not Crack House stupid. The Pope is from Krakow. Fesso. Achtung! We are a peaceful religion. Don't say anything bad about it. I will kill you. Now do you need some

Bloodline Bandra

hard-core Nazi Hitler Youth Porn? These police sirens, they are the national anthem of New York City. Dig it, baby. Get your ass down to the village tonight, that's where it's happening. Welcome to the Big Apple, on your far right, holding a .38 revolver is Christine Chubbuck . . . It's live T.V.

Crap game on sidewalk. You don't need Vegas. Come on, come on, man. Black man selling shiny wrist watches from a big briefcase. Made in China. Just like the original. Ten-year warranty. Five-year guarantee. Any problems, write to the company. What's the problem, Honky?

. . .

David looked at the homeless men and realized that they were the happiest human beings he had seen since he had come to New York City. They were laughing and slapping their thighs. Pure joy. Satisfaction in the moment. And they had nothing. No money, no home, no families. Nothing. Just some cheap alcohol in a torn brown paper bag. His eyes moved to an oriental girl. Their eyes locked, and he looked away quickly. Here, staring translated as rudeness and sometimes aggression. She reminded him of Hatsumi. How her sculpted fingers moved in ballet postures, performing flawless pirouettes on four strings. David wanted to go see her but looked at his watch and knew that he had missed his chance this Sunday. He walked back to his inflatable mattress and lay down thinking of Pali Village and all that he'd left behind.

6

THE NEXT MORNING, David was summoned into Manu Laxman's office. 'So, let's see,' Manu Laxman said, 'I am going to give you an assignment. Between June 1987 and February 1988, there was a gang that operated in Hoboken and parts of New Jersey. They called themselves "The Dotbusters". They used to attack Indians. Now it seems trouble may be starting again. I have heard through the Indians living in Hoboken that a different gang is now targeting the few Indians there. They are looking for Indian women who wear the bindi on their foreheads, or anybody with an Indian name or surname. This can be big news. Let's hope that they begin attacking the Indians, and then we will have a great story. Here is what I want you to do. I want you to go to Hoboken and try to get in touch with some of the old gang members. Some of them must be around. I want you to find out why they hated the Indians. What were their reasons? You are used to danger. If they attack you, well that is part of the story, eh! They are not going to kill you, not today, don't worry. Let's see how good you are. You have two weeks to file this story. Now go.'

David began researching. July 1987: Jersey City. The Dotbusters published a letter in the Jersey Journal: 'I'm writing about your article during July about the abuse of Indian people. Well I'm here to state the other side. I hate them, if you had to live near them you would also. We are an organization called "Dotbusters". We have been around for two years. We will go to any extremes to get Indians to move out of Jersey City. If I'm walking down the street, and I see a

Hindu, and the setting is right, I will hit him or her. We plan some of our most extreme attacks, such as breaking windows, breaking car windows and crashing family parties. We use the phone books and look up the name Patel. Have you seen how many of them there are? Do you even live in Jersey City? Do you walk down Central Avenue and experience what it's like to be near them: we have and we just don't want it anymore. You said that they will have to start protecting themselves because the police cannot always be there. They will never do anything. They are a weak race, physically and mentally. We are going to continue our way. We will never be stopped.' Newspaper reports from 1987 stated that the Dotbusters comprised mostly of Spanish teenagers.

David thought: 'There is something amiss here. I thought Cyrus Merchant was killed by a white supremacy group.' He walked to 34th Street and took the Path train to Hoboken. He had another lead. 27 October 1987, Gold Coast Café, 9th and Willow Street, Hoboken, New Jersey. A murder had occurred. David was good at working a story. He was an 'instinctive' reporter and tracked the smell of a lead with his gut, aided by his experience. He did not have a car. He bought a cheap, second-hand, rusty bicycle for ten dollars at a garage sale on River Street in Hoboken and 'was good to go'. He pedalled from Hudson Place to Washington Street, passing 38th Newark Street, where the old Clam Broth House used to be. He looked at the peeling, hand-shaped neon sign, perched above the corner of Newark and Hudson streets.

Marlon Brando, Frank Sinatra's mother, Natalie Della and Woodrow Wilson. They used to dine here and, of course, ol' blue eyes too. He pedalled to the *Hoboken Reporter* on

14th and Washington Street and asked to meet the chief reporter. David was lucky. The chief reporter was on his lunch break and had half an hour to spare. David white-lied his way about who he really worked for. He knew that if he mentioned his current newspaper, the chief reporter would lose interest. David said that he was working as the New York correspondent for *Der Spiegel*, Europe's biggest magazine. He pulled out his war correspondent press card. It worked. The chief reporter was duly impressed. David was on familiar ground. Journalist-to-journalist. He told the chief reporter what he was looking for. The chief reporter said that he had heard stories that thugs in Hoboken were beginning to target Indians again; he told David that he had some old contacts who might know where these men lived. Although it was possible that they might have all moved away, who knows.

'Give me a day, and I'll call you.'

'I will come back, the day after tomorrow at your lunchtime,' David said. The chief reporter said that he should have some news by then.

When they met again, the chief reporter said, 'I have good news and bad news. First, the bad news: my contact says that all but one have moved out of New Jersey. Whereabouts unknown. The one man who is supposed to be in New Jersey has no permanent address but there is a lady who might know him. I have her address, and lord willing and the creek don't rise, maybe you'll be able to get to him.'

He handed David an address on Central Avenue, in Jersey City Heights. The chief reporter said, if your paper needs a stringer, give them my name. David said he would do that, thanked him profusely and rode away.

Bloodline Bandra

He chained his bicycle to the stand near the Hoboken Railway Terminus and took a taxi to Central Avenue. When he got off, David noticed that it was a Hispanic neighbourhood. He thought about the death of Cyrus Merchant. It took him half an hour to walk to the address he was clutching. He knocked on the door of the basement apartment and waited. The door was yanked open and there stood a Spanish galleon in full sail. Her body was enormous. He moved his eyes to her face and decided that he had never seen a woman so obese, unkempt and ugly. She snarled at him in Spanish. David just looked at her, fascinated by the apparition.

Then, speaking softly and slowly he said: 'I am looking for a gentleman. I believe you know him. He might have come into a little money.'

She started to speak, halted and said: 'Moan-ee!'

'Yes. Mo-Nee.' He whispered the man's name.

She scowled.

To show that he was a man of honour, David produced a twenty-dollar bill and gave it to her. 'For your trouble,' he said. 'I need to talk to him. Just five minutes.'

The woman scowled and took the money from David. He breathed easier.

'He is good plumber,' she explained. 'Good work, he does ... but too much drink, much too much, hombre. You come night-time. He be here, okay?'

David could not believe his luck. The woman had fallen for the oldest trick in the book; entice an informant with news of a small windfall and the rest will follow. He had expected to chase this story for a good week before he even got a lead. This was going better than he had hoped.

He got back to Hoboken, stood at the edge of the west bank of the Hudson River and looked out at the skyline of New York city. Impressive. He looked at the old dock. Now all that remained were pilings of the once-thriving waterfront shipping industry. Tough stevedores had worked here. This used to be the mafia's workshop. From here, contraband was shipped, received and then injected into New York city. Young World War II soldiers had shipped out from here to fight 'the Krauts'. This was a place where many stories started, some without end. David walked to Hoboken terminus and bought a hotdog and coke, wishing he could have a beer instead. He unchained his bicycle and rode to Monroe Street. He managed to find 415 on Monroe, tucked between 4th and 5th Streets. His anticipation turned to disillusionment; this was where Frank Sinatra was born. There was nothing there. Not even a structure. He stared at the emptiness. If the city of Hoboken cared enough about Frank Sinatra, why had the city fathers not protected Sinatra's birthplace? It made no sense. Disappointed, he rode back to the Hoboken train terminus, chained his bicycle and walked into a bar on Washington Street. He checked his tape recorder and ordered 'Jack on the rocks'.

David worried that the man, after all these years, would not talk. Jose Ruiz, aged sixteen; his brother, Robert, eighteen; Orlando Justin de Jesus, eighteen; and Pedro Padilla, seventeen, had all been convicted of the murder of Cyrus Merchant. The trial was a sham, according to the Indian community. A fifteen-member jury panel convicted three of the boys of aggravated assault. They were sentenced to ten years at juvee. The fourth was convicted of simple assault, a crime punishable by a maximum of six months in jail. Cyrus Merchant sustained a fracture above the right eye and three fractures beginning at the back of his skull, he died four days shy of his thirty-first birthday.

David finished his drink, paid the bartender and began walking to the corner of 9th and Willow Streets. He lit a cigarette, thinking of Cyrus Merchant. When David got there, he stared trying to recreate the murder in his mind. It seemed impossible, with the noise, people's laughter, children crying and the general tumult of everyday Hoboken. He pictured the dying man, his blood congealing on the street, being beaten brutally by teenagers just because he was Indian. If someone here taunted him with a racial slur, David decided that he was going to fight. As he walked back, a group of seven Hispanic men were walking towards him on the sidewalk. They were laughing at something and talking amongst themselves. David refused to move out of their way. Instead, he maintained a steady course and walked right into them. They parted to let him through, still laughing at whatever they were discussing. He walked into another bar. Jack again on ice, and then one more for the road.

When he finally knocked on the door on Central Avenue again he was feeling that old adrenalin pumping. He expected the Spanish galleon. The door cracked open, black eyes peered out at him and then the man pulled the door wide open. He looked to be in his early forties, short-sleeved shirt, Levi jeans. Short and stumpy, with tattoos of naked women on both arms. He spoke good English with a Spanish accent.

'Welcome sir,' he said. 'Margarita told me that you would be coming. How did you hear that I did plumbing work?'

David walked into the small cramped living room. On the left wall was a framed picture of the infant Jesus. Beside it was a picture of Our Lady of Guadalupe. The man saw David looking at the pictures.

'You Cat-oh-lick?' he asked.

David nodded. He hoped that Margarita would not be around, she could complicate this meeting.

In answer to his hope, the man said: 'Margarita had to go to her sister's place in Union City, I had to go too but since you were coming I decided to wait for you.'

David thanked him, and then decided to double check: 'Your name is Orlando Justin de Jesus?'

'Si, si.' He looked amused. 'What is the problem with the plumbing at your house? Margarita said something about moan-ee?'

David looked him in the eye and said: 'Sir, I am a journalist. I came here to write a story about you.'

The man looked confused. 'Me. Story. What story?'

David told him.

He laughed and said, 'You have the wrong man, señor. I have never killed anybody. I would have liked to have killed my ex-wife, but no sir . . . you have the wrong man.'

I should have known, David told himself bitterly, this was not going to be easy. Then he thanked Orlando, apologized for the inconvenience and walked out. He knew then that the chief reporter had deliberately misled him. Dead man's curve that led to a blind alley. Now what?

7

FOR THE NEXT nine days, David walked all over Central Avenue, in the Heights in Jersey City asking for Jose Ruiz, Robert Ruiz, Orlando Justin de Jesus and Pedro Padilla. Nothing. Dead air. Dead ends, and more curves that led to blank walls. His research had told him that these men had lived on Central Avenue. Someone must know what happened to them. The story deadline was approaching. Manu Laxman would be disappointed. David had talked to so many people that by now he was a familiar figure. The junkies, winos and unemployed who lazed on the sidewalks of Central Avenue every day knew what he was looking for.

David was standing outside the liquor store when a white woman approached him.

'Looking for action, boss?' she said, smiling.

'No,' David said flatly. 'No money.'

She looked at him and said: 'I know where Michael de Jesus is.'

Astonished, David exclaimed: 'What? Who is Michael?'

She smiled coyly. Extended her hand in the universal gesture of asking for a bribe.

David was not falling for this. 'I don't want to know,' he said, 'and I have no money.'

She smiled, withdrew her hand, placed her hand on his shoulder and said: 'His brother's name is Orlando. I know why you are looking for Orlando. It is because of that Indian boy who was killed?' The way she said it, her words were both a simple sentence and a loaded question. 'Do you work for the police?'

David laughed and shook his head. 'No, I am a journalist; I just need to write a story, that's all.'

'And why should he talk to you?' she asked.

Irritated by her question, David answered: 'I don't know, set the record straight. Tell the truth for once so that he can rest in peace.'

The woman was silent.

'Look,' he said, 'I will pay you, once you put me in contact with Orlando Justin de Jesus.'

Now David looked at her closely. Her flabby rice pudding face had seen better days. A bad dye job rested on her skull like an abandoned bird's nest. She wore a short skirt, long brown boots and a heavy sweater. The pupils of her grey eyes were dilated. She looked like a dead-end junkie in a snuff film, searching for a vein and wishing that the tourniquet around her arm was twisted around her neck. David was expecting nothing but another hustle.

'I will take you to him,' she said. 'I know him well. He is the one you are looking for.'

'How much?'

She smiled. 'Fifty bucks.'

David was Indian, bargaining came naturally. 'Twenty-five. I am not made of gold.'

'Oh, I can see that,' she said sarcastically.

'Let's go.'

Fifteen minutes later, they turned between North Street and Patterson Plank Road near a park. She cut left and, asking him to wait, walked to the door of a town house. David could not see who was on the other side of the door when it opened. He saw her talking, gesticulating wildly. Suddenly, she turned around and beckoned.

Bloodline Bandra

David moved fast to join her. Instinct told him that he was looking at one of the men who had killed Cyrus Merchant. He held out his hand and introduced himself. The man shook it, his face expressionless.

The first thing he said in a thin nitrous oxide voice was: 'Are you an Indian?'

'I am from Goa, a small island off the west coast of India. I am Portuguese by heritage. I was born in Vasco da Gama.'

David's white lie may have saved his life. The man looked at him intently.

'Come on in.'

David excused himself, turned to the hooker and gave her the money. She brushed past him, kissed the man on his cheek and walked out. David was silent.

'This is my brother Michael's house. My name is Orlando.'

David made no effort to hide his relief. 'I have been looking for you all over town.'

'I know, I heard. Central Avenue is my town. It is no accident that you are here. It was I who sent her.'

He looked at David in absolute silence. Outside, a police or ambulance siren wailed and then faded. The silence returned. Orlando turned around, as if in pain, walked into the next room and came back with a bottle of Tequila and two shot glasses. He poured. They drank. David stayed silent. There was no other way to do this.

Orlando was small, almost fragile. His five-foot-nothing frame bordered on anorexia, his small, black pig-eyes were set in a tortilla-flat face and his thick, back-combed hair ended with curls at his scrawny neck. In other words, nondescript. David thought he was cold, shifty, the kind of coward who found his spine only in a mob situation.

'Why?' Orlando asked. The grit in his voice appeared to bounce off the walls.

'It is for a German magazine. Not many people in America read it.' David thought of offering him money and decided that it would not work.

'Why?'

David answered bluntly. 'Sir, there is some news that this anti-Indian thing could be starting again. I just want your story of what really happened and why. It could stop someone from being killed . . . again.'

'Why should I believe you? I should just ask you to leave.'

David pulled out his war correspondent identification card. 'I have seen death, Sometimes, it can be stopped if people have the courage to speak out. Forget the story; personally, I just want to know *why*. Was it just because he was Indian?'

Orlando poured two more shots. He drank his in one gulp. David shook his head, indicating that the liquor was getting to him.

'See, I do not want to go to jail again and you do not want to be dead.'

David could not think of a suitable rebuttal.

'Let me tell you, chacho, about Indians. I have worked for many, in Jersey and in New York. They do not trust anyone, even their own people they treat like dogs. I have seen this. And, dios mio, hombre, they are tight with their moan-ee. They do not even like to pay minimum wage, that is why they employ so many illegal people. I worked for them because then I had a drug problem, and they pay under the table, but never mind that! And when they want

Bloodline Bandra

to talk about you in front of you, they start speaking in that Indian language. That is rude, chacho! One guy I worked for, he owed me money, said I will give moan-ee tomorrow. His mañana never came, he never paid me. I lost three weeks' pay, brother, three weeks! He told me: "Tomorrow I can get ten Indians to do what you do." And he laughed at me when I said I would sue him, he said his brother was an attorney, and he would swear that I stole moan-ee from him, and his Indian employees would all swear that too. Most of the Indians working for him were illegal, some were on temporary visas or something, I don't know, and they were all scared of the boss. What is wrong with these people? They come here for a better life, ha!'

David ignored him.

Suddenly Orlando exclaimed, 'I will do this interview, one condition.'

'What condition?' David had a feeling this was going to hurt.

'How badly you want this story?' Orlando asked. 'Are you willing to risk a little . . . give a little . . . make it happen . . . eh, chacho!' David had no idea where he was going with this. 'I will do the interview if you deliver a small package to a friend of mine who lives in Queens.'

Now David knew. His heart began pumping blue funk into his blood stream.

Orlando was talking. 'Through the years I have given just one interview after I got out of the Big House, and I did not tell them everything. I have done my time. They cannot touch me now, so I can talk, but there is a price tag. The police in New York city are watching me. I need this package delivered tomorrow. It's simple. I give you the package. You deliver it and get your story.'

'What happens if you refuse to talk to me after the package has been delivered?'

'This works two ways. I will give you the interview because if I don't, you can go to the police and make trouble. There is nothing that you can prove anyway. They will want to know why you accepted this deal in the first place. And I am a man who keeps his word, chacho.'

'And what if I am arrested?'

Orlando lifted his shoulders in an elaborate shrug. 'Then you get arrested, hombre, I don't know, call your mother. What do you want me to do? I have my alibi, just in case . . .'

David said he would think about it and be back in half an hour. Orlando nodded. Blood rushing through his body, head swirling with thoughts, David called the office and talked to Manu Laxman, who seemed glad that David had tracked down the source of the story.

When David began explaining the deal, though, he yelled: 'I don't care how you get this story; do what you have to do. I really do not want to know.'

David replaced the receiver and walked back to Orlando. The address and package were handed over in silence. Orlando pushed open the door. 'Call me when you are done. Ask for Speedy Gonzalez. If I do not get the call, I will not be here. If all goes well, I will be here tomorrow at noon and I will talk to you about what really happened on 27 October.'

8

DAVID LEFT WITH the merchandise wrapped in red paper, which he carried in a cheap, black crocodile-skin imitation briefcase. He walked through Central Avenue, disembodied. David was travelling uptown on the F train to Queens. He could feel the pores on his face sweating. Instinctively, he wiped his face, feeling bile swirling in his abdomen. He looked around furtively. No one it seemed was watching him. He tried to analyse some of the faces. Did they look like undercover Narcs? What does a narcotics officer look like anyway? He had this overwhelming desire to get off at the next station and begin running. 169th Street, Jamaica seemed like the Far East. David closed his eyes, tried deep breathing. What would his mother say if she saw him now? How would his father react? David forced his mind to think of a sea of long, green grass, swaying in the wind, an abode of tranquillity. A homeless man boarded at the next stop. He was panhandling. Singing Christmas songs and exhorting the commuters to feel a sense of the Christmas spirit. David opened his eyes, looked at the man and half decided to give him the package. But as the panhandler passed him, David sat still, wishing he could smoke. The next station was his. He stood up, grabbed the chrome handrail and slid his way to the door. The train stopped. David got off, expecting to be arrested. People walked around him. David stood still, unable to move.

A police officer on the platform was watching him and began walking his way. Rigor mortis set in. David watched the twin 9mm semi-automatics moving towards him. He felt vomit rising as his bowels threatened to soil his underwear.

'Are you alright, buddy?' the cop asked. 'Do you need some help?'

Some hidden reserve of strength gave voice to David's vocal chords: 'I . . . I am alright, I have a stomach virus . . .'

Then the unthinkable happened; David vomited on the platform. Now people turned around to stare. The police officer helped him to a bench on the station.

He stumbled, stuttered, 'Thank you, thank you . . . I'll be okay, thank you so very much.'

The officer stayed with David as he gulped in air and cleaned himself with his handkerchief. Five minutes later, he smiled at the officer, told him he was alright, thanked him again and walked out of the station, sweating like an Eskimo in an Indian summer.

Outside, he lit a cigarette with unsteady hands. He asked a woman for directions to Saint John's University and walked to the corner of Homelawn and Hillside. Finally, the Q30 bus to Union Turnpike and Utopia Parkway arrived. David got off and went searching for Brown Beck Apartments. It took him fifteen minutes to find it. He took the elevator to the tenth floor, apartment 102, and rang the bell. A middle-aged Hispanic woman with huge earrings and hair slicked with gel over her forehead, opened the door.

'Yes?'

David pointed to the bag. She nodded. David asked to make a phone call. She led him into a small kitchen on the right and pointed to a red wall phone. He dialled the number Orlando had scribbled.

'Madre Tierra Restaurant and Bar,' a voice answered.

David asked for Speedy Gonzalez.

Orlando came on. 'Yes.'

'It's me.'

Orlando was silent. David handed the phone to the lady. She listened to Orlando for precisely three seconds. Did not say a word. She handed the phone to David.

'Good,' said Orlando. The line went dead.

David gave her the briefcase, and felt his flesh and skin disintegrate as his skeleton scampered out of the apartment.

Back on the street, he lit a cigarette and felt his blood begin to circulate once again. When he finally got back to the office, it was dark. The office was deserted. He noticed a strange smell as he undressed. When David tugged his underwear off his body, there was a dark brown stain on the white cotton fabric. He showered and lay on his mattress.

The next day, David headed back to Orlando's apartment on Central Avenue. He didn't expect the murderer to be there, so it shocked him to see a smiling Orlando sitting outside his brother's home on a small wooden stool. They walked into the living room and Orlando reached for a bottle of Captain Morgan's spiced rum.

'A celebration, hombre, a celebration,' he exclaimed exuberantly. 'I never thought that you would do it, Papi. I never dreamed. Ah . . . well . . .'

David thought about asking him what was in the bag. He knew that he would not receive an answer; there was no sense in trying. 'What was in the bag?' he asked anyway.

Orlando smiled. 'Mexican jumping beans, *amigo*, ay dios mio.' He laughed until tears rolled down his cheeks. 'What was in the bag? What was in the bag?' His thin voice was crackling with delight. '*El Diablo* was in the bag, señor.'

David waited for Orlando's self-entertainment to subside. Eventually his laughter gave way to chuckles, and after he had sipped Captain Morgan he grew quiet as he pondered his promise.

'I told you that I would keep my end of the bargain, amigo, I will.'

He finished his drink, offered one to David and poured himself another. David excused himself, went into the bathroom and switched on the recorder in his small duffel bag. He flushed and emerged from the bathroom, wiping his hands on the seat of his pants. Orlando appeared to be growing mellow and at ease with Captain Morgan at the wheel.

'I am going to talk, hombre. Just listen, Papi, okay. No talk from you, chacho, or I will forget. You ask questions later. I just want to say this: after today, I do not want to see you again. Si?'

David nodded.

Orlando grew very quiet. His eyes were moving ever so slightly, his tongue protruded between his teeth and licked his lower lip, but his body was as motionless as a Russell's viper in long grass. 'I remember that day, hombre. I will always remember, the night of 27 September 1987. First, let me tell you how I used to be. There was a rage within me, because I was uneducated, could not speak the English language well, Papi, and did not have dineros to dress like a gringo. I was ghetto, amigo, ghetto as the baddest, badass rapper there is. I needed to prove that I was somebody. I became a tough guy. It was something that I could do. I am not a big man, but I fought dirty. Splinters of sharp metal at the ends of my nails, rusted spikes on my shoes. And I began

Bloodline Bandra

hanging around with a really tough group of chicanos. We had nothing to do with the Dotbusters, nothing at all. We were not a real gang, know what I mean? The Dotbusters were a bunch of redneck white boys from Jersey City who hung out at street corners in the Heights and Hopkins Avenue in Jersey City. They were the ones who bashed Kaushal Saran, the Indian man. I am glad that he survived his coma.

'I did not know his name then, the man who died, I know it now; Cyrus Merchant just happened to be in the wrong place at the wrong time, Papi. We never had no fight against Indians amigo, ever. Anyway, here we were drunk, about ten of us. Three girls and seven boys, just horsing around, talking on 9th Street and Willow Avenue in Hoboken, when one of the girls noticed a bald Asian man and his white friend walking past. I remember looking at him. He was bald, no eyebrows ... weird, like he was an alien, man. The girls started teasing him. Just having fun, chacho. Calling him baldy and glow head. Then one of the girls, who was drunk, walked up to him and nudged him in his hips with her body. He shoved the girl and that's when the trouble started. The girl began abusing him in Spanish. She said to him "*mira canto de cabron*". Called him a piece of shit or something like that. We began moving towards the two men and this Cyrus Merchant put up his hands in karate fashion. Si, the way his body was positioned we knew he could fight. There was construction going on opposite the street, we picked up bricks. His friend was trying to pull him away, but Cyrus Merchant stood his ground. I don't know who threw the first brick, but after that, a shower of bricks struck him, and he went down. As he was attempting to stand, we swarmed all over him, kicking, jabbing. There was blood, lots of it. His friend, the white boy, lay in a corner, someone from our crowd must have put his lights out. We left. The next morning we were all arrested. They told us that Cyrus Merchant had died. Four of us were charged with his murder. The rest you know.'

Orlando let out a long resigned sigh. 'My life changed after that Indian man died. Jail was no fun, amigo, but that is something that does not concern you. I never really wanted to kill that boy.'

David asked, 'Once Cyrus Merchant was on the ground bleeding, why did you continue hitting him?'

'Liquor, señor. That's why, chacho, that's why! We were all really drunk and did not think he would die. It was not a racist thing and we were never in the Dotbusters gang.'

'Do you feel that you have to make it up to the Indian community for what you did?' David asked.

Orlando shook his head. 'No. What is done is done, señor. The man lost his life. It is over. I do not want to talk about this anymore, amigo. You have to go now. Just one more thing, I have heard that there is a gang in Edison that is planning attacks on Indians. I don't know how serious they are, but if you deliver another package for me, I will contact them and see if they will talk to you, off the record, of course. *Ah pues bien*, let me know, we can do business together, chacho.'

David stood up, looked him in the eye, shook his hand and left.

The next day, David wrote the feature and handed it to the managing editor who read it and passed it on to Manu Laxman. David was satisfied that he had written a good article. In the evening, Manu Laxman summoned David to his office. In his left hand was David's article. David looked at the publisher and his blood ran cold.

'This is garbage,' Manu Laxman was saying. 'I cannot publish this material. The Indian community will crucify me and advertisers will pull their advertisements. What are you trying to do? This man should have been repentant, he should have at least said that he was going to make amends to the Indian community for what he did. This murderer—'

David cut in: 'You wanted his story, and that's what I got for you.'

'What kind of third-class journalist are you?' Manu Laxman screamed. 'Can't you direct an interview? Slant the questions the way you want the story to go?'

David realized that it was useless trying to argue.

Manu Laxman looked at David's article, which he was waving in his left hand. He transferred the sheaf of papers to his right hand and then moved his arm to his wastepaper basket. In slow motion, David saw Manu Laxman's fist open as his disgraced work began a surrealistic journey into garbage and humiliation. He turned around and began walking out of Manu Laxman's office.

Manu Laxman's snarling sarcasm stuck a dagger in David's back: '*Muchas gracias*, for nothing, señor.'

9

IT SEEMED LIKE a long, long time ago that he had been a respected journalist, whose intuitive nose for news and writing skills were admired. Now he was being told that he was a hack who was not worthy. And his own people were doing this to him. He began to hate Indians with a passion that he did not want to rationalize. David had nothing but hate to cling to. He felt that this was his psychological sustenance, a controlled burn that built a firewall around his psyche and kept the flames from jumping the fence of his present reality. But here he was dead wrong, because one day this crimson rage would lead him to the daunting periphery of murder.

He sat at his desk, his mind and body in a state of paralysis. The office watched. Somebody sniggered. David sat immobile for two hours until everyone had left. In a blind daze of self-pity, anger and desperation, he left the office and began walking towards Central Park. He could hear someone talking to him and the terrifying realization dawned that he was talking to himself. David saw two homeless men sitting on a bench. He could hear them laughing. He stopped.

They looked at him suspiciously and one of them said, 'Heard you talking to yourself – loudly.'

David was scared to speak but he didn't want to appear like a madman even to these men who looked homeless. 'I am new to this city,' he said.

The one who looked like a dirty Santa Claus grunted: 'So what do you want?'

'Nothing.'

Dirty Santa Claus laughed, slapping his thighs. 'Urban

isolation,' he said, 'that's what it is, urban isolation. I guess you are just lonely and you need someone to talk to. You have to learn to deal with it, here in this city. Once you do that, you will become a New Yorker.'

'I have seen you guys before,' David explained. 'I just wondered what it is that makes you so happy.'

Dirty Santa Claus turned to his friend. 'Why are you so happy?' No answer. He turned back to David and said, 'One gradually attains tranquillity of mind by keeping the mind fully absorbed in the self by means of a well-trained intellect and thinking of nothing else.'

Why was this American bum quoting the Bhagavad Gita? Who was this man? Was he insane? A psychopath? A philosopher? Or just another Westerner bitten by the bug of far-out Indian mysticism? Of the 700 verses in the Bhagavad Gita, why had he chosen those lines? What if they were insane? What if they attacked . . . knifed him? He thought of his parents receiving the news. His friends learning of his demise and the way he died. Was this his karma that had led him here or was he overreacting?

People walked by. Joggers with earphones ran to different drumbeats. David felt safe for the time being. He got off the park bench and pretended to stretch. The two men ignored him while they fished for fries in the brown paper McDonald's bag. The whisky bottle lay on the grass covered by a tattered scarf. Dirty Santa Claus twisted the seal off the bottle, drank deeply and passed the bottle to his companion. Their eyes glazed with tears as the alcohol bit into their guts.

Dirty Santa Claus passed the bottle to David and held out his hand. 'Sir, my name is . . . Bond, James Bond.'

His companion suddenly convulsed with laughter. David smiled.

Godfrey Joseph Pereira

Dirty Santa Claus stayed serious. 'Would you like to be shaken or stirred, sir?'

His companion doubled up on the bench like he was in the throes of an epileptic seizure.

'Aw, I'm just kidding,' Dirty Santa Claus said. 'Sit ye down, have a little sippa. I am not trying to be condescending, just having some fun. Laughing helps crow's feet, I am told.' He squinted at his companion, who went into another epileptic fit.

David drank from the bottle hidden in a brown paper bag. The liquor swirled, warm and sweet through his stomach. He could feel his paranoia begin to leave. David raised the bottle to his mouth and drew a man-sized gulp. His eyes began to water as he passed the bottle to Dirty Santa Claus's companion who had retreated into a meditative silence. The bearded one answered David's questioning eyes.

'He does not really like talking to strangers. Just leave him be.'

David nodded.

'I never in a million years thought that you would drink from this bottle,' Dirty Santa Claus said. 'Most people tend to kick us to the curb, it's something I have grown used to. I mean, I wouldn't want to be associated with me either. And that's alright with me. We will continue this conversation when I have the time.'

Dirty Santa Claus and his silent friend burst out into loud laughter. David began walking away, thinking about urban isolation. And his anxiety returned.

David thought of home, the little things; past gestures of inconsequence now appeared warm and inviting. He missed his mother. He missed his friends and the surety of their

Bloodline Bandra

brotherhood, the warmth of home, the polluted Arabian Sea and the smell of swine faeces in Pali Village. David began to cry, gulping air. Walking back to the office, he heard Bosco Big Stomach's voice: 'Do you have da bleddy guts to stay and fight dis? Or do you crawl back home to da village with your bleddy tail cut off?'

Back in office, he wrote Brian a letter.

Dear Brian,
I hope that you are fine and all is well. Can you believe it's been nine months since I've left Pali? I like my job and the people I work with are great. The publisher has told me that I will be the chief editor of the newspaper soon. I am really excited. I like New York. It is a fascinating place. Last night, I went down to Greenwich Village. It is on the west side of lower Manhattan. Brian, it is a crazy place. I have never seen so many freaks in one place. Men dressed as women and women dressed as men and sometimes I could not tell if it was a man or a woman. Freaked out, man. What is wrong with these people, I don't know. But, it was fun. I remember we used to talk about the village in Bandra and wonder what it was like. Now I know. I wish you could see this place. There are bars and restaurants, and musicians playing on the streets, and the whole place is crowded like Bhendi Bazaar and the bars stay open till dawn. Lots of tourists. I walked to the corner of MacDougal Street and Minetta Lane and had a drink at a place called Cafe Wha?. Brian this is the place where Jimi Hendrix and Bob Dylan and Woody Allen started their careers. Bleddy fantastic just to be here. Some local band was playing, I forgot their name.

I then asked somebody about the recording studio that

Jimi Hendrix created and walked to Electric Lady Studios, at 52 West on 8th Street in the village, just to see it.

You know something, I found out Jimi Hendrix recorded his last song here and then he flew to London on an Air India flight. This was his last flight, on Air India. Three weeks later, he died. Anyway, the Electric Lady Studios is not an impressive building, a dirty brown colour, the studio is on the ground floor. I don't know what I expected, but I just stood outside trying to imagine Jimi Hendrix playing inside. I know that you like his music.

What is happening back in our village? Anything new? Any new bands? I also went to Washington Square Park that is at the foot of Fifth Avenue. I will tell you about it in the next letter.

Say hello to everyone for me. I have written a letter to Papa. I am sure he got it. I know he does not like to write. Tell him I am fine and I will call.
David

10

DAVID WANTED TO see the two homeless men again. The men intrigued him, especially the one who looked like Santa Claus. It was their happiness that had first made David stop and stare. He had looked at them, seen they had nothing and wondered what the story of their decline was; and yet they seemed so happy ... Had they chosen to live like this because society had overwhelmed them? The Sanskrit term sadhu, or good man, refers to people who are renunciates, people who have chosen to live their lives on the periphery of society so that they can follow a distinctive spiritual path. What was the story of these two homeless men; and why did one of them spout lines from the Bhagavad Gita? Perhaps they were dharma bums, lost in the groove of a mantra that had been hip a long, long time ago?

David was walking in the Bowery, in the southern portion of New York one Sunday morning. He liked walking in the city; it took his mind away from the vacuum of loneliness he felt. And then, there sitting on a bench on Delancey street, their possessions piled into a stolen Target cart, David spied the two homeless men. David knew that the founder of the Hare Krishna movement, A.C. Bhaktivedanta, Swami Prabhupada had lived in the Bowery in 1966, and now, here were the two bums with a possible India connection. It all seemed so mystical and strange.

David heard the bearded bum shout something in what he thought was Sanskrit to a pedestrian. The duo laughed at the man's terrified reaction. He approached them, said hello. They ignored him.

David sat on the bench and asked, 'Was that a saying in Sanskrit?'

The bearded man, without looking his way, asked, 'Who wants to know?'

David could sense their hostility. Before he could answer, the other bum snarled, 'Go away.'

David began shuffling his feet. A long minute passed. David stood up, waved a half goodbye and turned to leave; and then the bearded man said: 'Yes.'

He whirled around. Now David was confused. Did he mean 'Yes, that was Sanskrit', or was he asking 'Yes, what is it you really want?'

The bearded man smiled. 'We'll talk at some later date, boy. Right now I have some paperwork that I have to finish.'

They roared with laughter. David decided to leave.

A new week began. He waited for people to show up at work. But they would not look at his hunched figure. Finally Dolly Khanna approached him.

She smiled. 'I would like you to cover this story. The Indian ambassador to the United States is giving a press conference at the United Nations. I'd like you to cover it. This is a straight feature. Just report what he says. It's simple. The press conference is set for 12 o'clock today. I have made all the arrangements. You can get your clearance pass from the lobby.'

He thanked her, picked up his note pad and pen and headed for First Avenue. It was 9.30 a.m. David decided to walk to the east side of Midtown Manhattan. At the United Nations building reception, he told the girl manning the desk that he was there for the press conference that the Indian ambassador was scheduled to give at noon.

The girl looked at him in amazement. 'Yes, sir, I have your name here but you missed it, sir. The press conference was scheduled for nine in the morning today. You got the time wrong, sir.'

David felt his veins popping like frozen pipes. Dolly Khanna had misled him. She must have been working in tandem with the managing editor, Ravi Malhotra. He struggled to maintain his composure as he heard himself thank the receptionist. David turned around and walked out of the United Nations, slowly, like a cripple. He did not know or care where his feet were taking him.

Madness had come to David Cabral. He chain-smoked, talking to himself. New Yorkers looked at him askance, he thought. David walked on. Even through the opaque darkness of his depression, David finally began to see the reality of his situation. He knew he had to get back to the office. Had to face the humiliation, scorn and criticism. There was no way out. He was in the heart of a dystopian horror show.

David realized that he was close to Washington Square Park, which was at the foot of Fifth Avenue. He began walking back to the office, shame on his shoulders, and failure on his mind. He was losing the game. When he got back to the office, he headed for Dolly Khanna's desk. She looked up at him. David's face was a death mask. His body was quivering like a bowstring after the arrow has departed.

'The time that you gave me was wrong,' he said.

She looked at him and smiled, displaying uneven teeth. 'I left the invitation on your desk yesterday,' she said sweetly without blinking. 'You forgot to take it. It's not my fault.'

'There was no invitation on my desk,' he said firmly.

She pointed to the desk. He walked over to his desk, and

there was the press conference invitation. He looked back at her. Her head was partially concealed by her computer. David felt a sick, sinking feeling, bile began churning in his stomach, he could feel the sour taste as he swallowed hard. Dolly Khanna was now standing beside his desk.

'Manu will have to be told about this. I have never in my life seen such unprofessional behaviour. If you did not want to go, I could have given this assignment to someone else.'

'You know that is a lie. You know that you told me of this press conference only this morning. You know you told me that it was scheduled for noon. You know that you placed that invitation on my desk after I had left for the United Nations. You know that.'

She smiled. 'I think you are losing your mind.' She patted him condescendingly on his shoulder and walked away.

David turned around to look at his colleagues. They appeared busy working. He knew that they were all listening.

Manu Laxman emerged from his office, crooked his forefinger at David. When the door to his office was closed, Manu Laxman motioned for him to sit down. Anna was there, smiling. David began speaking. Manu Laxman held up his hand, demanding silence.

'I had great plans for you,' he said, his voice furious, his contempt devastating. 'You have let me down. You have let your colleagues down and more importantly, you have let this newspaper down. I gave you a great chance. I invited you here, to New York, Fifth Avenue and look what I got in return, I could have—'

David spoke now, not caring about interrupting Manu Laxman's monologue. He tried to explain what had occurred.

The contempt in the boss's voice deepened. 'Why would

they all be against you? What reason do they have? What you say does not make sense.'

David knew that it would be spitting in the wind to try and explain. He walked out of Manu Laxman's office and returned to his desk. He had lost the battle and the war. He wished he had the courage to confront Manu Laxman and his two-bit whore.

That evening, when everyone had left for the day, David went to the bathroom. He felt a strange sensation in his bowels. David looked down into the bowl. He had begun to pass blood. Fear descended on him instantaneously. He needed to see a doctor and he had no medical insurance. The only person he could turn to was Manu Laxman. What if I am dying? What has happened to me? Trembling, he curled into a foetal position. David could see his body, dressed in a grey suit, hands clutching a rosary and the priest sprinkling holy water on dead skin. The laments of his parents and friends, and the villagers shaking their heads in grief. 'Bleddy, he should have died here, at home. For wot did he leave? For wot? Look, wot happened, poor bugger?' One last prayer and the body is moved into the moist, brown hole in the ground. Everyone cries as his body is lowered. People who loved him throw dirt on his coffin and leave. Finally, the grave diggers fill the grave with soil.

The next morning, bleary from pain and lack of sleep, David walked into the office of Manu Laxman. He explained what was happening to him. He begged Manu Laxman to keep his promise that if David fell ill in New York, Manu Laxman would arrange for a doctor to see him. The company, Manu Laxman had once assured David, would pick up the tab. For once, Manu Laxman relented without scorn or an outright refusal. At precisely 3 p.m. that day, a man walked into the office. David watched the reedy, thin individual from the corner of his eye and he had a feeling that something was amiss. Then Manu Laxman and the thin man walked over to him.

'This is Dr Patel.' Manu Laxman introduced them and left.

The good doctor was a doddering man in his seventies, with watery, rheumy eyes. 'How do you do?' Patel said.

He had a heavy Gujarati accent and he smelled of stale sweat and sour curd. His face was lean and long, his hands shifty as they scratched his short nose. His suit was bottom shelf, Salvation Army, and David noticed that there was dark dirt under his long fingernails.

'Manu told me you have backside problem. I will do examination.' And then he stunned David: 'Let's go to bathroom.'

David's mouth opened . . . he began stuttering. 'But, but, but . . . I thought we would go to your clinic.'

Dr Patel smiled. 'No clinic . . . come, you come now.'

David's body sagged. The whole office was pretending not to watch and listen. He stood up and walked to the bathroom in the corridor. Dr Patel ordered him to drop his trousers and bend over. He looked at David's anus area, spread his cheeks and inserted a finger into his anus.

After a five-second examination he said: 'You have big haemorrhoid. If bleeding not stop, maybe surgery. Could be something else, though. At this stage, who knows? My advice for you, buy the medical insurance. Otherwise, I say to you, you are going to be facing many, many troubles, okay?'

A couple of men had walked into the restroom; they

stared in amazement and disgust and muttered to themselves. David felt violated. He hurriedly pulled up his underwear and trousers. Dr Patel, he noticed, had not bothered to wash his hands as they emerged from the bathroom. He wiped his finger on his Salvation Army trousers and walked towards Manu Laxman's office. David could feel shame slicing through him. He stepped out on to the fire escape to light a cigarette. He thought of Dr Patel, his uneven English and filthy demeanour. David looked at his hands, trembling from shame, humiliation and fright. He looked up to the grey, foreboding skies, wishing God could see him now and offer pity and consolation. He hoped he would die in his sleep before the sun filled another day with misery.

When he got back to his desk, there was a note taped to his computer screen. 'You Are FIRED. Please Vacate This Office Tonight.' He looked towards Manu Laxman's office. The light was turned off. Manu Laxman had left the building. The rest of the staff pretended not to notice. No one cared to say goodbye as they left for the evening. Finally alone, he began to weep and rail against God and mankind.

BOOK III

1

THE PHONE SHRILLED. It was 10 p.m., someone was asking for him. A male voice. The voice at the other end seemed far, far away. Once again, the voice asked for David, and finally he heard his defeated voice, soft and weak. 'Yes, this is David.'

'My name is Martin. I heard that you were in New York and working for this newspaper. I know you are a friend of my brother. I just called to say hello. How do you like New York? How are you doing?'

David had no intention of sharing his misery, but the levee cracked, the pressure destroyed the floodwall. Martin was yelling at him, David realized. Through the turmoil of his tears he heard: 'Stop talking. What is the address you're at?' David answered. Martin was speaking: 'Pack your bags. Wait there. I will pick you up in an hour.' He could not believe the fortuitous timing of Martin's call.

That is how David, shattered, broken and bleeding, landed in a dank basement apartment, off 168th Street in Jamaica, Queens. Descending into a basement apartment was a new experience for David. It was not like the hutment dwellings of Dharavi, or the congested boxed-in tenements that dotted the city of Bombay like smallpox indentations. There, you could walk out of your doorway and see the sky. Inside the basement apartment, David felt like a large rat in a hole. The short flight of cracked concrete steps led to a minuscule area. A dead naked bulb hung on a shredded wire. To the left was a flaking wooden door, to the right, a spider sprawled in the corner, waiting and watching. Inside was a thirteen-foot space with a shower stall, commode and cooking platform at the far end. There was one small, cracked, dirty, window for air. Rusted pipes that gurgled lined the ceiling.

For David, this was paradise. Martin helped bring David's luggage in and introduced him to his girlfriend. David bowed low, telling Veronica how glad and thankful he was. Martin smiled and patted David's back.

'Welcome to our house, bugger. We don't have much but this is home.'

Gratitude brought tears to David's eyes.

Veronica hugged him. 'It's alright,' she whispered. 'We are here now. Nothing bad is going to happen to you, relax.'

Martin pointed to the overhead pipes. 'If the landlord has dysentery, you will get no sleep. Every time he flushes, you hear the sound of music.' They all laughed.

Later, when Veronica was in the bathroom, David confided to Martin: 'I have a bleeding problem. I have a haemorrhoid.'

Martin nodded. 'Use Preparation H, it is an ointment. It will soothe the problem, until you see a doctor. I used to have that too. I used the ointment and the bleeding stopped. You can buy it over the counter at any pharmacy. Bugger, don't look so bleddy worried, you are not going to die.'

Martin was from Bandra. His brother, Lionel, a journalist who worked for a big Bombay film magazine, had told Martin that 'David, the journolist', a friend of his, was going to be in New York, and Martin had tracked David down to the newspaper, just to say: 'Hey bugger, how you doing.'

Martin still talked like a 'Bandra Bugger' and Veronica like a 'Bombay chick'. They made David feel at home. David looked around the basement. There was one mattress on the floor and a plastic wardrobe. They were dirt-poor by

American standards, but they had chosen to share that dry-bread-and-water poverty with him. That night, David got drunk on good American whiskey. He related his story in New York to them.

'What's wrong with the Indians in America?' David asked Martin. 'The Indians in India are not like this!'

Martin smiled; he had his own stories. 'Something happens to them. I don't know what. The bleddy buggers become bleddy animals; they forget the main things of life. Forget where they came from.'

After a great meal of fish curry and rice, David thanked them again. He lay on a small, clean, paper-thin mattress near the door and went to sleep, warmly embraced by Jim Beam and a small heater that groaned. That night he dreamed of the village and the soft, warm womb of his home.

In the morning, Martin and Veronica awoke at 6 a.m., got ready and left for work. Martin worked as an accountant for a shipping company and Veronica was a secretary at a small insurance agency. Their offices were on the West Side on Columbus Avenue in Manhattan. Martin worked from 9 a.m. to 5 p.m., and Veronica, from 9 a.m. to 5.30 p.m. Martin usually waited for her to finish, and then, they both travelled back to Queens.

Martin said, 'Get some sleep, bugger, tonight we'll talk about getting you some work, or something or the other to do. Bugger, don't be embarrassed. I am glad that we are around to help you; otherwise, God only knows what would have happened to you. Don't be worried, yaar, no problems. See you in the evening. Fish curry is in the fridge.'

After they had left, David drifted back into slumber. It was late afternoon when he awoke. He thought about all that had happened since Manu Laxman had fired him. He knelt in the basement apartment and thanked Jesus Christ. Once again, the miraculous hospitality of Martin and Veronica brought tears to his eyes. 'There are some good Indians in America,' he muttered, as he stepped outside the door, climbed the short flight of stairs and lit a cigarette.

That evening, when Martin and Veronica returned home, they began talking about strategies for getting David some work. He was still on a tourist visa and getting legal employment was out of the question. Martin and Veronica had Green Cards and David felt a twinge of jealousy when he thought of their privileged status in the United States. He needed to get sponsored by an American company to get a legalized H1-B visa, so that he could work in the United States. The moment his visitor's visa expired, he was going to be just another illegal alien.

David had five months to solve this dilemma. Martin suggested a temporary measure. 'Try and find some work. There are thousands of kiosks all over Manhattan that are mostly owned by Indians and Pakistanis. Walk around, ask if they need help. I will also try from my side, okay? Buy the Indian papers, look at the "Wanted" advertisements. You never know, something will turn up, not to worry.'

The next day, David trudged through Fifth Avenue. Most of the Indians and Pakistanis were dismissive, others were rude, while still others spoke to him with patronizing attitudes that were designed to humiliate.

'It is difficult without a Green Card, no?' Then, there was: 'Can't you see I have customers? Go away.' Others just laughed in his face. 'Sorry, I am really sorry for your situation, ha, ha, ha ... but what do you want me to do? Get into trouble for hiring an illegal alien, eh!' And finally, the icing on the cake: 'You have a tourist visa. Well, since you cannot work, why don't you do what tourists do, see sights and then go home. Bye, bye.'

It was Christmas Eve, four months without work, and over a year since David had left Pali Village. David, Martin and Veronica went to Midnight Mass and David begged the Lord for a job. They talked about Bandra, reminisced about Bombay and remembered old friends and enemies. They drank to good health, long lives, freedom, liberty and the pursuit of happiness. David called Brian, talked to his parents and told them that he loved his job. He told them that New York City was the most fantastic place on earth, especially at Christmas time. He described the big store windows all dressed up and the Salvation Army Santa's with the red buckets for alms. When he hung up, he felt disconsolate.

Martin and Veronica continued to encourage him, telling him that he would get a break. David had grown to love them but he could no longer believe their assurances. One evening, as David came home despondent from another job-hunting forage, Martin stood before him, smiling, 'showing all thirty-two teeth'. He held an Indian newspaper published from the Flatiron on 175 Fifth Avenue in Manhattan at 23rd Street and Broadway. And there, on page six, in a small box was an advertisement for an Editor/Writer for the newspaper *India InTune*. 'Apply in person between 9 a.m. and noon,' it said. This was great news. David immediately gathered up his writing samples and resumé. Tomorrow morning, he would be at the newspaper's office, 9.30 sharp.

There was a soft knock on the door. Martin opened it. A short squat man with a short stabbing-knife in his right hand came hurtling in. He pushed Martin back, snarling. Veronica screamed as Martin tried to grab the knife. Martin yelled at David, asking him to call the police. Veronica was hysterical. David ran out, found a pay phone and dialled 911. 'Man with knife . . . man with knife,' he stuttered, gave them Martin's address and ran back to the apartment. David stood outside, shaking with cold and fear. Inside, he could hear screaming and smashing, and then came a loud thud. The screaming continued. Three voices in a theatre of terror. The police arrived, sirens screeching. Instinctively, they grabbed David, twisted his arms behind his back and slammed him hard on the hood of the police car. The hood was hot, it seared his face. David squealed like a stuck pig. The police were frisking him, screaming: 'Stay down, stop moving, stay down, down, down . . . Knife, where is the knife?' Their hard hands were all over his body. Guns were pointed at his skull. David felt like he was being raped as their groping hands fingered his crotch area and the crack between his buttocks. He began crying. Somebody was yelling: 'Where is the weapon? Where is the weapon?' They released their choke-hold on his neck and David screamed: 'Man with the knife, inside the house, inside house, in-si-deeeee . . .' He was babbling, shaking, screaming . . . people had stopped to stare, passing motorists rubber-necked as they slowed down. The cops, guns drawn, still held David as two of them ran down the short flight of steps that led to the basement apartment. Suddenly, there was quiet. David thought that his friends were dead. Minutes later, the cops emerged with the squat knife-man, his hands behind his back in handcuffs. The police now let go of David, and he rushed downstairs. Martin was holding Veronica. They were both shell-shocked, unhurt and alive. David looked at the left wall. A fist had gone through it and there was broken glass all over the apartment.

After Martin and Veronica had filled out the necessary paperwork, the police apologized profusely to David and drove away. Later, after they had cleaned up the apartment, Martin went out and bought a bottle of Scotch.

Martin smiled. 'This calls for a bleddy drink, men.'

Veronica, still shaken, apologized to David, thinking that this was all her fault.

'That swine with the knife,' Martin explained, was Veronica's ex-husband, Francis, an Indian, born in Byculla, Bombay. They had divorced because of his anger issues and his penchant for prostitutes. 'A disturbed Catholic boy' is how Martin described him. This was not the first time they had had to deal with his fury. Francis wanted Veronica back, and his drunken deduction was that Martin should die. The hole in the wall was his failed attempt to punch Martin.

'I managed to knock the knife out of his hand, so the bugger tried to punch my head off. I moved, his hand went through the wall, and I managed to land some nice shots to his kidneys. Ahaaa . . . like they say here, shit happens. And like we say in Bandra, pour another bleddy shot men.'

David laughed nervously, his hands were still trembling.

2

DAVID COULD HEAR the backbeat of his heart as he entered the Flatiron building. The owner of *India InTune* greeted him warmly. 'Call me Achyuta,' he said. David handed him his file and waited, afraid to breathe. The publisher put on his reading glasses and went through the file. Finally, he looked up and smiled.

'Your experience is great. You could be just the man I am looking for, but I need a few clarifications, if you do not mind, okay?'

David's throat turned dry. He nodded.

Achyuta pointed a finger at him and said, 'I know you used to work for Manu Laxman.'

The coil in the pit of David's stomach unwound with a snap, he thought he heard gurgling noises in his gut.

Achyuta laughed. 'Don't worry. I know the story. It was not your fault. I know the full story, okay?'

David began to breathe normally again. He wished Achyuta would stop saying 'okay'.

'I have had twenty-five applicants for this position. You seem to be the best choice. I like your writing style and your credentials are impressive, but . . . what is your status?'

David said it straight: 'I need to be sponsored.'

Achyuta nodded. 'I will sponsor you, but there is a price to pay, okay? You will have to work for minimum wage. I am being upfront with you, okay? No medical benefits, okay? . . . There is a small room, right here in the office that you can use for free. It has a decent bed with a small kitchen and bathroom. You are a bachelor, you will survive. And then, if everything goes well, who knows, I might sponsor you for a Green Card, one day, okay? This is a weekly newspaper. It's easy. Now do you want the job?'

David did not hesitate. 'Yes, I will take it.'

Achyuta smiled. 'Start next week, okay? Here is the spare key to the office.'

David said, 'Okay.'

That evening, David discussed his job with Martin and Veronica. 'I don't have a choice,' he explained.

Martin thought that this job would give David time to explore other possibilities. That Sunday evening, he drove David and his belongings to the Flatiron building – David's second home-office.

Achyuta walked in at 10 a.m., all smiles. His jet-black hair gleamed from liberal oil application. His small mouth with a pencil-line moustache on the upper lip seemed to be constantly pursed, sniffing for food or hidden predators. When he smiled, his extremely large teeth jumped out like beacons against his dark skin. His pseudo-American accent was curried with a distinctive Keralite twang. Like Manu Laxman, he trusted nobody, especially his fellow Indians. 'Keep them all at arm's length, okay?' was his sullen motto.

David felt like a knife had been inserted into an old scar. He was glad that Achyuta had offered him a job the same way a field slave was satisfied that he was now a house slave. He could leave and return to India, but he couldn't bear the thought of returning home a failure. So he stayed, looking at his shackles, despising what he had become, hating the people who had power over his existence.

'You will do what I say without any stupid questions, okay?' Achyuta was saying. 'This is not a charity place.

There is a time clock near the door. You are Number One. When you come in or leave for the day, just punch the Number One button. It is simple. You shut your mouth, do your work and we will be okay. If I am not satisfied, you will be fired, okay? There is no overtime and all that nonsense. You work till the work is over, okay? Remember that I am going to sponsor you. Make you legal. Be happy. You may think that you are a big reporter and all, but here, you are just my employee.'

David began to wonder where the other employees were hidden.

Achyuta answered his unspoken question: 'There is one other employee besides you. He makes the pages. Between the two of you, you will bring out this newspaper, okay? This is not the *New York Times* or *India Today*, okay? You are going to be a copywriter. You will be rewriting stories that are published from other newspapers and magazines. Just rewrite them so that we will not be sued, okay? In this damn country, everybody sues, so be careful, okay? Just fill the pages with decent stuff. Now that you have seen the paper, you know. We have movie gossip, politics, Indian cooking, etc. There is lots of stuff on the internet, okay? Just have the paper ready for the printers every Thursday night. Simple, okay?'

David heard the door to the small office open and a short, fat man walked in. He looked like a clown with a sad face painted on him. His gait advertised tragedy.

Achyuta introduced him to David. 'This is the page maker. His name is Deepak.'

David held out his hand, which Deepak grasped weakly. There were no words, just a silent communication between the damned. Dead-fish eyeball met open-eyed comatose sight.

'Deepak knows everything about the paper, he will fill you in,' Achyuta expanded. 'I have to go now, see about some advertising. I will see you tomorrow, okay? Before the evening is done, I want four of the political pages ready, okay? I will check them out in the morning. Deepak here knows what spaces have to be kept for the advertisements. Proofread the pages, correct the mistakes, before you set them on my desk, okay?' Having said that, Achyuta adjusted his cheap suit, picked up a leather briefcase, slicked his thin moustache with his right thumb, muttered 'okay' to no one in particular, and walked out.

David looked at Deepak, smiled and said: 'Okay.'

Suddenly, Deepak came alive. He laughed, slapping his thighs. David discovered that Deepak was from Bangalore and had also worked for Manu Laxman. His story of the American Dream was the same as David's. He had been fired by Manu Laxman, and now he was stuck with Achyuta, a monster who had his life in a sponsor death-trap. He had been working with *India InTune* for two years.

'Where do you live?' David asked him.

Deepak lowered his eyes and said: 'The poor side of 125th Street in Harlem.'

Through Deepak, David learnt that Achyuta had a temper that made Attila the Hun seem like an altar boy. Achyuta lived 'somewhere in Manhattan', was married and often brought his Malayali friends over to the office at night to drink and watch pornographic movies.

Once the two men were done exchanging misfortunes, they began to work. David skimmed through the latest Indian newspapers, picked out newsworthy features and rewrote them. From his computer, he sent them to Deepak's machine.

Once Deepak made the galleys, he organized the lengths. 'You need to cut five inches of this one,' he would say, and David would quickly snip five inches away. So it went. Cut and paste, cut and paste. They worked fast. It was 11.30 at night when the proofed pages were laid on Achyuta's desk. Deepak said goodnight and headed for his poverty. David, too tired to even walk down to a street-food vendor, lay on his bed and slept hungry.

The next day, Deepak turned up at 9 a.m. 'Business pages today,' he said briskly.

Achyuta walked in at noon, looked at the pages on his desk and smiled at David. 'I tell you, you are good. I like what I see. We are going to make a great team, okay? Your headlines are beautiful, the photo captions wonderful and your copy is very, very, good.'

David thanked him.

Achyuta hung around the office for the next four hours, making cajoling calls that begged for advertisements, citing astonishing assertions about the high circulation of *India InTune*. Deepak and David worked in mute harmony. Achyuta left early, saying he had a doctor's appointment. He explained that he was beginning to get headaches that were gradually becoming more frequent, and that yesterday he had vomited.

Before Achyuta left, he had asked for David's personal information. 'My attorney is going to apply for your H1-B visa tomorrow, okay? Soon you will be a legal employee of *India InTune*, okay?'

David nodded, wondering why he did not feel elated.

It was 3 a.m. when they finished working on the pages. David had bought some canned food and beer in his lunch break. After Deepak had left for the night, David ate out of a can of tuna, downed three beers and went to bed. This was to be his routine day after night after day. He called Martin and Veronica and told them that he was alright, and would see them in a couple of weeks when he had the time. At the end of three weeks, Achyuta declared that lagging advertising revenues meant that he would have to delay David's paycheck. At the end of the fourth week, he handed David and Deepak 200 dollars each in cash. He smiled and promised them more 'financial gains' when the advertisers made good on their promises. He had more good news for David. His H1-B visa was being approved by immigration. But David felt no happiness. Later that night, he wrote to Brian.

Dear Brian,
Hope you are okay. How are things at your job? Thanks for your letter. Brian, I have been offered a great new job. I am now working for another newspaper. My office is at the famous Flatiron building at 175 on Fifth Avenue. The salary is better. I now have a new apartment in Queens; it is small but nice. I am in charge of the newspaper. My boss respects me as a journalist and I am sure that I can make this newspaper into a good successful publication. The newspaper is called India InTune. *I have been walking around the city, it is a great big melting pot. People from all over the world live and work here and there are many places that have an interesting history. Last week I went to Washington Square Park. It is a place where musicians come to play and hang out. It is quite a cultural centre in New York. I was talking to an old musician and he told me that this place was once a big graveyard. He said that there are over 20,000 bodies buried underneath this park. Once upon a time, this place was the graveyard of thousands*

of homeless people. In the nineteenth century there was a big yellow fever epidemic and the city buried all the dead here. It is kind of eerie. But New York has an energy that is addictive. Times Square, with its lights and crowds, makes me think of Bombay; it makes me think of home. How is everyone there? Salt Peter and Small Tree Big Fruit and Tommy-Eat-Shit-A-Lot. I hope that they are all fine. In a strange way, I miss them all. Remember we used to talk of the great art museums? Well, Brian, I have been to them all. I went to the Metropolitan Museum of Art and the Whitney Museum of American Art and the Guggenheim Museum. I have seen the masters. It is fantastic, Brian, I wish you were here. We could walk all over the city and see the fantastic architecture. Yes, the buildings in New York, like the Flatiron building, are like museum pieces. Most people don't even notice it. Despite all this, I miss Pali Village sometimes. But I guess this is my destiny.
    David

On many Sundays, David walked through the city, hoping that he would see his homeless 'friends'. They seemed to have vanished into the New York haze. For months, he would look, scouring the nooks and crannies where the forgotten huddled, but they were gone. One evening, when walking in the small mid-town plaza at 520 Madison Avenue, he heard that laugh and he knew it was them. It was easy. All he had to do was follow the sound of their happiness. They were sitting in the park, sharing some joke that only they could decipher.

    Dirty Santa Claus looked at him and said: 'How ya doin' son? Watcha be wanting now?'

David answered: 'You both seem so happy, considering...'

'Considering we have nothin.' How can we be happy when we got nothin'?'

David nodded.

Dirty Santa Claus smiled. His friend had gone silent as always. 'Maybe someday, sometime, we'll speak of it, huh?'

David looked at him. His nicotine-stained moustache was ragged, his beard, wild and unkempt, but his eyes twinkled. He looked like a man who knew a secret and was not willing to share because he thought that the rest of humanity was not worthy.

Suddenly, Dirty Santa Claus said: 'Tell me about yourself. I don't want to know where you came from or what your name is. What are your fears? What makes you happy? Where are you going?'

David talked. The bearded man listened like a good teacher.

When David fell silent, the other man said, 'You seem to have trouble with your own kind; but there are bigger issues, if you want to think about it. See that wall over there? It is part of the Berlin Wall. It is twelve feet high and twenty feet long. It was brought here in 1990. Yes, that is the infamous Berlin Wall that had divided Germany. It is a reminder of many things. The artwork on the wall was done by German artists Thierry Noir and Kiddy Citny. I like looking at it. It takes me back. That colour is a language I understand.'

David asked: 'Was that Sanskrit that I once heard you shout to a passer-by? And why did you do it?'

The bearded man grew pensive. 'I don't know, sometimes I yell out gibberish, just for fun.' He now looked at David and said: 'There are people around the world who think that living in New York and America is like living at the centre of the universe. But they are wrong.' He pointed to the Berlin Wall. 'There are walls here in America that keep people segregated, just like that one did. There are black walls and white walls and brown walls and there are grey walls whose construction nobody understands. These concrete walls do not mix and merge. And those walls have internal fractures, no one can see them, but everybody feels the pain. Do you know what I mean?'

David nodded. He noticed that the bearded man was no longer talking like a country bumpkin and this intrigued him. He said, 'You are clearly not an uneducated homeless man. An ignorant bum.'

Dirty Santa Claus smiled, turned to his silent friend and said: 'It's time. We have to go.'

Where were they headed, David wanted to ask, but he decided to hold the question.

The silent one seemed to have come out of his stupor. He looked at David, squinted and said: 'We'll see ya when we see ya.'

Dirty Santa Claus began pushing the Target cart and then they were gone.

Monday morning, the phone call came. Deepak answered it and handed the phone to David. It was Brian. David heard fragments. Mother. Intensive Care. Holy Family Hospital. Heart Attack. Doctors say dying. David. Come home. Mother asking for you. Wants to see you. Crying for you. Praying she will see you. Before her eyes close. Come home, David. Mother dying ... David, Mother ... eyes, close, forever. Home, David ... home ...

He talked to Achyuta.

'If you leave now, immigration will not let you back into the country. Your H1-B papers are being processed and you can't leave until you are approved. And if you leave, I cannot hold this job for you, okay? The choice is yours to make, okay?'

David wanted to talk to his father, but his home in Bandra had no phone, so he called Brian the next day. Said he could not come. Said he hoped that his mother would get better. Said to say hello to his father and mother. Said he was sorry, but . . . Said that he felt terrible, but . . . David heard a gentle click. Brain had disconnected.

Three days later, the office phone rang. It was Brian. Olive Juliana Cabral had died with her eyes wide open, staring into the distance. Salt Peter had said that she looked like she was waiting for somebody. Everybody knew who that somebody was, and nobody dared whisper his name. Sitting limp in his chair, the first thing that came to David's mind was his mother's baking.

Mother is baking a cake in the warm kitchen. She is happy. It is Christmas Eve. She is reading from a Polson Butter-stained 'Cake Book'.

16 oz soft butter
10 2/3 oz sugar
7 eggs
1 pinch of salt
16 oz flour
1 tbsp baking powder

She gently slides the cake into the preheated oven, 350 degrees Fahrenheit. After sixty minutes, the cake is golden brown, she pulls it out.

'My mother is dead.' He heard his own voice, lost, tremulous. 'My mama died.'

Deepak's hand was on his shoulder. David could hear sounds of sympathy. He walked out onto the fire escape and chain-smoked. There were no tears, just a deep empty void.

David called Brian, talked to his father. The old man was brain-dead with the shock of losing his wife. 'You need to come home, David baba,' he cried. 'You need to bleddy come home, men.'

Then he began to sob, mumbling garbled gibberish into the line. Brian was taking care of the funeral arrangements, and promised to look after David's father, and said he had to go to arrange for David's family grave to be dug. He asked if there was any way David could come home. David cried, said no and put down the phone. David thought of his father. He knew that in his own strange way, his father loved his mother. Guilt spiralled into mocking forms as his mouth spewed cigarette smoke into the polluted New York air.

When he got back to the office, David worked with frenzied abandon to finish the page quota for the day. By 9.30 p.m., the proofs were on Achyuta's desk. Deepak hugged David and left. David walked to the nearest liquor store and bought a bottle of Napoleon Brandy. He got back, lay on his bed and thought about his mother, his father, his friends and the acidic reactions of people when they discovered that he was not at the funeral. The biting alcohol blasted through his empty stomach like a mainline hit through an open vein.

At 11 p.m., he heard the office door open. David walked out to the main door and saw Achyuta smiling.

'Just came in to see a few movies and have some drinks with friends. You can go to your room; we will not disturb you, okay?'

David just said 'okay.' He didn't consider telling Achyuta

that his mother had died. The publisher did not give a damn. David needed to shelter the little dignity that remained in him. He refused to beg for sympathy from a man he now considered sub-human.

He sat there in solitary confinement as alcohol numbed his grief. Outside, Achyuta and his friends were having a great time. Their muffled laughter and the first soft moans of the pornography they were watching floated in. Flesh slapping flesh, the obscenities, the heavy, laboured, short breaths, the long, guttural moans. He tried to focus on his mother, but the heavy breathing and slurping invaded his grief, violated his sadness and the visions of his mother flashing through his mind. David buried his head in his pillow and wept silently, helpless. He tried to sleep, but the sounds of rolling flesh and the guttural moaning of women kept him awake despite the alcohol. David began to get sexually aroused. Shame descended on him.

Bloodline Bandra

3

HATSUMI SAT AT Grand Central Station, playing an interpretation of '*Bloodstream sermon*' as people walked past her. Her next piece was whatever was on the Top of the Pops. Somebody threw her a dime. People rushed by, burdened by the baggage they carried, hurrying to catch the next train. David watched her movements as she played, and finally walked up to her. He came up behind her and touched her elbow as she stopped to take a break. He hoped that she would be happy to see him even though he hadn't made an effort to see her. She looked pleased to see him. When she asked where he'd been all these days, he said he would explain everything over a meal. Hatsumi said she was done for the day, and began packing up her instrument. David offered to take her to Jackson Heights in the north-western section of New York city. Jackson Heights was the Little India of the Big Apple. Hatsumi liked the idea. As they walked towards 74th Street, David could smell curry on the streets. He had travelled here many times to eat some authentic Indian food. As he was guiding Hatsumi into one of his favourite restaurants, the Jackson Diner, David remembered his previous visit to Jackson Heights.

He had been surprised to see his homeless friends sitting on the curb on 74th Street, outside a restaurant. They were friendly this time.

'We be in your part of town,' the bearded man said. 'Oh, the smell, that glorious smell.'

David offered to buy them lunch. Instead of walking into the Jackson Diner, he steered them to Mumbai Express.

Midway through the meal, David noticed a tattoo on the bearded man's right arm: *Kalo Asmi Loka-ksaya-krit Pravardho, Lokan Samartum Iha Pravattah.* The journalist in David jumped out of his skin. He stayed silent, while the two men gnawed on the mutton bones. He had seen these words before. 'Now I am become Death, the Destroyer of Worlds.' These were the words Oppenheimer had said after the test of the atomic bomb.

Dirty Santa Claus asked, 'Why did you stop by us anyway? It's unusual . . . strange . . . you have been trying to talk to us for some time now. We do not, as a rule, associate with strangers, but I realized that you were from India . . . yea, all that talk about which tribe you were from was just a joke. I have an India connection, never been there, but it is tattooed on my soul. My name is Martin Chevalier. Call me Marty.'

Marty wiped his curried hand on his stained shirt and extended it to David as if he wanted to shake his hand. David realized that Marty had dropped his street accent.

'You think I'm a bum, right, but I used to be one of the professors of Theoretical Physics for Advanced Study at Princeton, after the Second World War.'

David thought he was joking. He looked away so Marty would not see the amusement on his face. But, David knew the significance of what Marty was telling him. He knew who had headed the Advanced Study Department at Princeton after the big war. In 1947, Julius Robert Oppenheimer, Father of the Atomic Bomb, head of the Manhattan Project, had accepted an offer to take up directorship of the Institute for Advanced Study in Princeton, New Jersey. David realized that Marty had worked with history. If what he was saying was true . . .

Bloodline Bandra

Marty looked at David and nodded. 'This is not a story that I concocted, I don't know why I am telling you ... maybe the Indian connection ... Yes, he was my friend, till the day he died at his home in New Jersey.'

David sat there, stunned. He glanced at Hank who appeared to be in a trance.

Marty noticed David watching Hank. 'His mind moved to a parallel universe after his sister committed suicide.'

David grew very still. He looked down at his hands and noticed that they had a visible tremble. This was incredible.

'It feels good to share this with somebody sometimes.' He showed David the tattooed Sanskrit writing on his right arm. The Bhagavad Gita was his Bible.

'This is history,' David said. 'Why don't you write a book? It could make you a rich man. You don't have to live like this!' Intuition told David that he had just mouthed a pragmatism at the wrong time, in the wrong place, to a stranger.

Marty reached for the glass of water. 'This is what I choose,' he said with a chuckle. 'Sure, I can be rich, but I will have to be corrupt, understand?' Marty recited lines from the Bhagavad Gita, lines that Robert Oppenheimer had once taught him, a long, long time ago.

Marty looked at David. 'Now you know.'

Hank was still lost in the maze of his semi-consciousness. David stayed silent. Words seemed shallow and unnecessary.

Marty turned to Hank who was tugging at his sleeve. He passed him a fork and asked David: 'What are you doing here, so far away from India?'

David began talking about life back home in Pali Village. He explained what he was doing in New York and told him how he had met Hatsumi Nakamura.

'Your friend, she is Japanese?'

'Yes, from Yokohama.'

'You know,' said Marty with a smile, 'Hatsumi means "the beginning of beauty", and Nakamura means "in a village". Looks like your villages have met; you just might be on to something there, son!'

David laughed and said that he was not aware of the meaning of her name, but the village part sounded great. As if on cue, Hank and Marty stood up, and began walking out of Mumbai Express. David raised his right hand, palm open to wave goodbye. He wondered where they would sleep that night. David thought about following them. He wanted to ask them if they would like to be interviewed for a feature, then he shook his head. Marty would never talk about his past and his choices that led to homelessness. Never.

Now he was here with Hatsumi, sitting in the Jackson Diner. The conversation drifted to her life. She told David that her work papers were sponsored by the Mizuho Corporate Bank; she worked in the Scarsdale branch as a teller, an interpreter and provided general help to Japanese clients who had difficulty speaking English. Her English, she explained, was good because she went to an American school in Yokohama. Her parents wanted her to learn the language. David told her about Saint Andrew Catholic School, where English was the language of instruction, and that his grasp of Hindi was poor and his pronunciation was abhorrent and laughable.

They went back and forth with their life stories. She was working in Yokohama as a teller when the offer to go to America was made. At first, she declined the offer, but when they told her that she would be working in New York, she

Bloodline Bandra

agreed, because that's where the Juilliard School of Music was. Her parents begged her not to go, saying that New York was full of gangsters who carried guns. They wept when their only child boarded the plane. She said she talked to her parents twice a week, and visited Yokohama every year. David was surprised to learn that she had been in America for four years. David told her this was his third year and the only good thing that had happened to him was meeting her. She blushed.

She talked about Japan, its quaint culture, her quiet father, her over-anxious mother, her happy growing-up years and her music. David noticed Hatsumi's eyes come alive when she spoke about her music. She had started playing the cello at the age of five. Now she was twenty-two, waiting to get into Juilliard. Her music, she swore, was the soul that gave her existence meaning. They talked, flirted, touched hands, their nervous fingers lingering, then pulling away. They left Jackson Heights happy and satiated. David felt free for the first time since he had arrived in New York.

And then, three Sundays later, it happened. They had met at Grand Central and decided to walk across the street to get some coffee. David sat smiling as he listened to Hatsumi's anecdotes about her work in the bank and stories about her Japanese clients. David told her that he worked in a third-rate newspaper and was trapped in the job because he couldn't go home to India defeated. Hatsumi said she understood his need to 'save face'. David talked about Manu and Achyuta, stories that alarmed Hatsumi. She reached across the table and held David's hand. His body visibly relaxed as he shifted the conversation from his work to his best friend Brian back home in Bombay. As they sat huddled in the coffee shop, talking, David wanted to lean over and kiss her. Her hand was still on his. Then Hatsumi asked for the cheque, suggesting that it was time to leave. He carried her cello as they walked out to the street. She asked David if he could help with a paper she had to submit to Juilliard on the use of a seven-note diatonic musical scale. David was thrilled at the thought of spending more time with Hatsumi. He hoped she would invite him to her apartment. As they walked back towards Grand Central, she explained solfège syllables. He had absolutely no idea what she was talking about. He was thinking about sex. She knew. He hoped that she knew. She smiled at David. She smiles a lot, this Japanese girl, David thought.

'There is something about you, David,' she said softly, 'something I can relate to. I am not afraid that this might turn out to be a mistake.'

As they waited for the train to Scarsdale in Westchester County, the northern suburbs of New York city, Hatsumi's mind wandered to the first time she had met David. The train to White Plains rolled in. Forty-five minutes later, they got off at Scarsdale and walked to a nearby parking lot where her Honda was parked. They drove to a town house, and walked up to Hatsumi's apartment on the second floor. She smiled and kissed him on the cheek. He laughed nervously and looked stupid. David settled on the couch, while Hatsumi, walked into the kitchen and came back with a bottle and two glasses.

As they drank plum wine, David said, 'You know, I don't know where my life is going to go. I guess, I may eventually go back home to my village, hopefully with you.'

She rolled her eyes, and made a funny face.

Bloodline Bandra

'New York is a fascinating place, but it scares me a little,' he explained. 'I mean, look at people living in the high-rise apartments. They can be neighbours for twenty years, and still their acquaintance is just a head-nodding "hello, have a good day, how ya doin" relationship. I don't understand it. I mean, I read about people dying in their apartments, and for weeks nobody knows, till a rotting smell alerts the janitor or a neighbour. Back home, it's different. Everybody knows everybody, nobody is a stranger; people do things for one another.'

Hatsumi leaned over and poured more wine into David's glass.

After a few more glasses of wine, David helped Hatsumi with her seven-note paper, structuring the language, being extremely careful with the technicalities. Hatsumi announced that she was going to shower and emerged in a cloud of mellow fragrance.

'David,' she said shyly, 'I would love for you to shower. It's the Japanese way.'

David leapt out of the couch and walked towards the shower in happy anticipation. The small one-bedroom apartment came alive with subdued murmurs and sighs of contentment.

As they lay in bed, David said, 'I am scared that I will fall hopelessly in love with you. I have nothing to offer.'

Hatsumi said that he needed to live in the 'now'.

'How?'

They laughed at the juvenile rhyme.

'You have to look at life's humorous side,' she said, 'otherwise, all you will ever see is grey. Let me tell you a funny story. An old Japanese woman was visiting New York with her husband. At a restaurant, someone asked her, "How ya doin'?" The Japanese, you know, are very polite, and she felt that she had to respond appropriately to the question. She was scared of creating a cultural blunder and offending the stranger. She knew English very well and so she began telling the stranger of the stomach pain that she was having, and how she could not sleep well at nights, and how she was worried that her son back home was becoming an alcoholic, and how she was scared that someone would mug her in New York. When the stranger told her that he had to leave, the old lady stood up, faced him and bowed. People in the restaurant stopped eating and turned to stare. The stranger turned around and fled through the door.'

David's body convulsed, he shook with laughter, trying to picture the stranger's befuddled face. The conversation finally drifted to David's mother.

'I never imagined that I would never see her again. When I was leaving home, she just stood there broken, crying. I did not even look at her once I was inside the taxi. I just left her standing there. I could have said something, I could have touched her hand, I could have . . . looked back and waved once the taxi started moving, but I did not. And now, she is gone, dead and buried. I feel like a heartless, cold-soul bastard.'

Hatsumi rolled over to him and hummed a Japanese song that she dedicated to his mother's soul. Later, she talked of her journey to America, and of her parents back home in Yokohama. Like David, she was a single child, who had left home with a desire to make a success of herself in America.

'I miss being in Yokohama. It is the city of cherry blossoms, where the spirits of the descendants of Yoshibumi Taira dance the Noh Mai under the Sasanqua trees.'

David slid off the bed and walked into the kitchen to get himself a drink of water.

Early next morning, Hatsumi drove him to Scarsdale station. He took the train back to Grand Central Station, and walked to the office, wearing the memory of cherry blossoms. David wondered what marriage to her would be like. Will it work? Hatsumi Nakamura Cabral.

'Sounds entirely bleddy funny, men,' he told himself.

4

DAVID BEGAN CALLING his father every Saturday. Brian had managed to get the old man a telephone connection. Every time David called the old man he grunted that he was alright, and that he did not need any money. He would tell David that his job was fine, and that he visited his mother's grave at Saint Andrew Church every day. The conversations were short and ended with: 'David boy, when are you coming home, men?'

Months rolled by. It was late summer in New York. Achyuta's sickness had gotten worse. He called David to say that he had vomited again and had had a small seizure. He told David that his left leg felt funny. It seemed that he was experiencing a loss of sensation in his left leg and the headaches had become worse. He was going to see a specialist and would be in the office Monday morning.

'Don't forget to distribute newspapers to the Indian stores,' he reminded them. 'You people have the list. If you don't do it, I will hear about it, okay? Every store on the list has to receive a free bundle of papers, okay? I must be getting headaches because of you two.'

They had to distribute bundles of the newspapers to the Indian grocery stores dotting Jersey and New York city. The papers were available for free. Sunday was Paper Distribution Day. David's six-day work week now became a seven-day one.

He was reminded of a school in Bombay where the children of beggars were trained by slum lords to be pickpockets. The kids were proud of their skill. It was a profession ten notches higher than what their parents had chosen. It put chutzpah on the table of poverty. 'Better than begging.' You gotta do what you gotta do.

It was a Sunday afternoon. They were in Jackson Heights delivering newspapers. The smell of curry powder was overpowering as David and Deepak worked the Indian grocery stores. David's mind was dulled with the monotony of loading and unloading bundles of newspapers. He looked at Deepak, who was pointing at another Indian store, and wondered what made a man bend so low. He was terrified that he might end up like Deepak. Spineless and defeated. David picked up a bundle of newspapers and threw it into a dumpster. One less load to distribute. Deepak grunted. The so-called 'newspapers' belonged there anyway. David's name was in the paper, as editor-in-chief. He belonged in the garbage too. David explained the sad significance of his action to Deepak, who was not interested in the philosophy. He was just enjoying flinging more newspapers into the garbage dumps. Their hand-truck was getting lighter.

Deepak, now in a good mood, said, 'Our destinies are chosen by God. There is nothing we can do. I know that He is going to change my life soon. I am waiting, and if He does not do anything about me, well . . . it's life and life only. You live, you die, what else is there?'

David imagined Goddess Kali, with her tongue flashing. He saw her descending on Deepak, her gaping mouth a canyon filled with corpses. Deepak offered up his good Karma in his outstretched hands. An offering fit for the finest goddess ever created by man. He gets down on his knees, arms out, lips moving in silent adoration. He prays for salvation. She orders him to be reincarnated as a mute beast of burden.

The streetlights fluttered a feeble beginning to the night. The papers had been delivered, sort of. Deepak hurried home to a cold meal. David sat in Jackson Heights and ate good chicken curry, like his mama used to make back home. He thought, this does not feel like America. He looked at the crowds outside, and wondered about their lives and dreams. What are they all doing here in this foreign land clinging to flotsam? Was bragging that 'I live in the USA' when they go back home laden with Kit Kat bars worth this? Who's the lucky one here? The one who left, or the one who stayed behind? And really, what does it all matter anymore, anyway? Pressure in the cooker is hissing lava. Living is a numbing chore, filled with shame, regret and uncertainty.

David finished his curry and went home.

Then, one bright morning, death, that sobering, humbling, neutral equalizer, came calling at Achyuta's window. Soft knocks in the blinding white light, bearing dark news.

He walked into the office, dragged a chair to David's tiny desk, and said, 'I have a tumour in the brain, okay? The specialists say it is cancer. I think I may be dying.'

David mumbled something about feeling sorry for Achyuta. As the weeks rolled on, Achyuta began exploding at small changes or errors. David and Deepak became his whipping boys. 'What the hell are you fools doing? Here I am sick, okay, and you people are taking advantage. Get out from here, get out.' Achyuta had turned into a paranoid, sly monster that sniffed at imagined conspiracies, and then lambasted David for not following up. His screams turned personal. He began accusing David of trying to sabotage the newspaper, that he was like all the other Indians, a backstabber. He refused to pay David for a week, pleading

Bloodline Bandra

poverty, and sarcastically told David that he could leave if he wanted to. 'Where will you go, eh?' He placed a Colt .45 on the table, and told David that he liked to kill vermin.

As the days passed, Achyuta stopped visiting the office and began communicating by phone, stating that he was too sick to come to the office. Every evening, David had to report to him about what had been done, and, as usual, Achyuta heaped scorn and bile on David. And so, when the phone rang one Monday morning David ignored it. He did not want to talk to anyone, especially Achyuta, this early in the morning. The ringing stopped and started up again. He left the office, went onto the fire escape and lit a cigarette. When he got back to the office, the ringing persisted. He picked up the phone. A woman was asking for him. She introduced herself as Achyuta's wife, Kamala, and told him that Achyuta had taken very ill, and had been rushed to New York Presbyterian Hospital on York Avenue.

The woman at the hospital reception counter told him where to find the newly arrived patient. He gasped when he saw Achyuta. He appeared shrivelled, his eyes were sunken and half-closed, his mouth was lolling open, his skin the pallor of dirty mutton fat. Achyuta's countenance had been transformed into a macabre death mask.

David stared at the woman next to him. Short and anorexic, she looked like a cartoon of a human being whose facial skin appeared to be stretched to extreme tautness. Her mouth was a razor slice, and black hair hung down to her waist, twisted into a thick black rope. She was dressed in ill-fitting blue jeans and a white Indian kurta with Kolhapuri leather sandals on her feet. Her neck was bare, her expression the same. The only jewellery she wore was her wedding ring, two, small, ruby-like earrings and a tiny nose ring that looked like, David thought, an irritating glinting pimple.

'She is so bleddy ugly, men,' David said to himself, as he lowered his eyes to watch colourless fluids flowing into Achyuta. She appeared to have a mean disposition, but he tried to stay in a neutral corner about her. David went over to the other side of the bed and extended his arm in introduction. She shook his hand, her claw limp. He smelt her sour body odour, and when she whispered, 'Hello, I am Kamala,' David felt her gingivitis-diseased breath arrow through his nostrils. He held his breath and moved to the other side of the bed as quickly as politeness would allow. Kamala smiled at him, her wide eyes alive. 'Jesus, Mary and Joseph,' thought David. 'My gosh, I think she bleddy likes me, men.' David's eyes grew shifty as he looked at her, nodded imperceptibly and then quickly looked at Achyuta, pretending to study the structural anatomy of the fluids seeping into what David considered an absolute human wasteland.

After visiting hours, down on York Avenue, they said goodbye.

'I am coming to the office tomorrow,' Kamala said. 'Cabral, I am going to need you. We will run the paper. Tomorrow we talk. Not to worry, okay? Hope you don't mind, I will call you Cabral. I like the sound, okay?'

He smelt her fermenting body again as her claw grasped his wrist, pressing skin and bone and flesh, tapping a message like the Morse code of old. He knew then that this was the start of an unpleasant, complicated story. He watched her, the way a cricket player watched a googly bowled to him. 'Which way is the ball going to turn? Do I just tap it, hit it hard or just stand still?'

David heard his mouth mumble: 'Tomorrow, Kamala. Not to worry.'

He turned and walked away. David had often heard the phrase 'his blood ran cold', now he knew with precise clarity what it meant.

David lay down in his bed, curled into a foetal position and wept. He came to life the next morning the way a wild animal awakens. Instantly alert, silent, wary . . . and stalked into the shadows of the darkening concrete jungle.

Kamala walked into the office bright-eyed and ready, her claws fingering her handbag. The slit in her face now had a fine line of crimson lipstick. She said that she would call all the advertising contacts. David nodded. By afternoon, she had finished with her phone calls. She told Deepak to take the afternoon off as she had editorial matters to discuss with David. Deepak scampered off, ecstatic to have time out of the office. She locked the door and walked to David who was busy plagiarizing a news article. She sat on his cluttered desk. David could smell her.

'Cabral,' she said, 'I am going to get straight to the point, okay? You and me, we can run this newspaper, we can make money. I promise you I will raise your salary and I promise you that I will sponsor you for a Green Card. But I need your cooperation, okay?' She had Achyuta's habit of saying 'okay'. It was annoying.

'Okay,' said David.

'You can call me Kamala, okay?' she said, smiling as she laid a hand on his shoulder. She squeezed gently.

David stepped out for a smoke. When he got back, Kamala said that she had to leave and would see him when she could come to the office. 'I cannot promise you when, I have to look after Achyuta, but soon, okay? Meanwhile, the ads will all be in by the weekend for the next issue, okay? Achyuta wants you to take charge of the advertising. Tomorrow I will give you all the contacts. The newspaper has to come out on time . . . But you are very good, Cabral, you can do this. I will be in touch, okay?'

David nodded. She patted the back of his head and walked out of the door.

A week had passed, and Kamala had failed to appear. Miraculously, Achyuta recovered enough to visit the office occasionally. He told David and Deepak that they would have to take on more responsibilities; talk to advertisers; meet clients; and deal with the printing press. 'I will be keeping an eye on the two of you, okay?' Achyuta hissed. At work, David found Achyuta shooting morphine in his vein in the bathroom, and mainlining at his desk. He was addicted to morphine. To David, his black eyes, fixed in their sockets, seemed dead already. Achyuta would pass out at his desk every time he injected himself with the morphine. David felt nauseous when he saw the syringe and tourniquet, Achyuta's blood on needle tracks, the deathly grey on his face, and death in his eyes. He would sit at his desk and watch Achyuta's body slump in his chair. The fear of dying surrounded Achyuta's aura like a funeral wreath. It occurred to David that Achyuta and he resided with resignation in the same web. Both beyond the realm of absolute control. In many ways, they were both dying to live, and desperately hoping for a second chance.

David was interrupted by a phone call: Brian from Bombay. He picked up the receiver hesitantly. It was past midnight in Bombay and calls from Pali Village at this hour only brought bad news. Brian told him Salt Peter had died. A car had crashed into him, mangled his skeleton. He had died instantly.

Memories of the dead are softened by sympathy. The stupid babbling idiot that Salt Peter had been now appeared amusing. David smiled sadly, thinking about the things he used to say. When they were discussing a life abroad, he had said, 'David, oh David, you can go anywhere in da bleddy world, bleddy to any place, men; become British, American or Australian on paper, talk all pish-posh with your mouth and wipe your bum with soft paper, but you will always miss home.' David went to his window and looked up at the sky, and then the tears came. He remembered what Salt Peter had said about 'bloodline'.

'Damn it, the stupid, ignorant bugger had been right,' David thought. He recalled the many times Salt Peter had helped his mother and father, doing menial chores, satisfied with last night's curry and bread as payment. That was the kind of man he was. Now the simpleton was gone, taking his brilliant idiocy with him. Pali Village would not be the same without Salt Peter. In Pali Village, they called him an idiot, and Salt Peter, in his simplicity, considered their patronizing attitude 'a folly'. When they asked him what 'folly' meant, he accused them of ignorance. 'If you all are so bleddy smart,' he'd say, 'why for you asking me about da folly?' That was Salt Peter, ablaze in his uneducated glory. Now he was gone, and David was here, in a house in the Promised Land, in tears and sorrow, missing home, thinking about a bloodline, thinking about Salt Peter in a grave, far, far away. He whispered: 'I will miss you, you stoo-pid bleddy bugger.'

David felt drained. His mother had died, now Salt Peter was gone. Who was next? What would happen if he died here? Would somebody send his body home? He needed to get some air. He wandered the city in a haze. Drug pushers were holding a huge rally in Central Park, complaining of unfair trade practices, and the opening act was a Chinese prostitute dressed as the Dalai Lama. She set herself on fire, protesting free trade and the Chinese occupation of Tibet. Somebody laughed. David walked the streets, scowling at them.

He walked from Central Park down to Grand Central Station. Some imbecile near Grand Central held a soiled cardboard sign. 'Moother Dying. Please donate.' David looked at him and thought: 'Your mother is dying, so . . . My mother died. Nobody cared. What makes your mother so special? And, you spelt "Mother" wrong, retard! How can anybody have a compassionate belief in your cardboard sign?'

David saw a couple of Wall Street prototype flow by in tailored suits, hurrying to support the various tumbling indexes of their lives. The American dream. Two-car garage, white picket-fence, four bedrooms, deep in the vortex of debt. If it wasn't for credit, his existence would have no merit. I ain't gonna grieve, my Lord, no more.

He returned to the office, where Achyuta was reclining with a cancerous sneer spread across his face, sedated by the soothing comfort of a refined poppy painkiller, imported illegally from Kabul, Afghanistan.

'Come on, come on, you are late, is this what I pay you for?' Achyuta, stood up, started a slow weave to his office, carrying his tools of comfort. He stopped in a daze and said: 'This week, there might be a paycheck when some money comes in. Keep up the good work, okay?'

David watched the syringe in his hand. Deepak watched

him too, and then lowered his eyes to proofread a page. Achyuta disappeared into his office and slammed the door.

The next day, when David asked for his delayed paycheck, Achyuta snarled. 'You are not man enough to stand up to me. Lower your eyes and get back to work, you dog, you will get paid when I say so, okay!'

David wanted to kill him. Murder is simple if you bet your life on it. This is the trigger, the words that changed him into a fervent apostate. *In nomine Patris et Filii et Spiritus Sancti*. David was ready. For death, for life, for existing without the possibility of parole. Murder is simple if you bet your death on it.

5

BUT IT WAS Kamala who returned to the office the next day.

Later in the afternoon, after Deepak was dispatched, Kamala said to David: 'We lost two good advertising accounts because Achyuta does not care anymore. I don't know what to do. I wish that God takes him soon . . . I care for him, okay, but I wish . . .'

David looked at her. 'What you are saying is that you would like to see him dead, right?'

'Yes, okay. The Gods work in many ways, okay? Achyuta is finished with his life. He is going to die anyway, soon, okay? Why do we all have to pay for his cancer? You tell me, David. Think about it, okay? I cannot run all this without you, Cabral, I will always need you, and I really like you. We can live a good life in New York; I have some money . . . okay? Think about it . . .'

David nodded. 'Sure, okay.'

She sidled up to him and began a slow chest rub. Repulsed, he pushed her hand away and walked into the bathroom.

David remembered graffiti on a wall in Edison, New Jersey: *Real Indians stay in India, the scum floats here.* He walked out of the bathroom, pushed past Kamala and walked out onto the street. It was rush hour. Commuters were heading home. David walked into the 23rd Street subway station. A headlight appeared not far from the platform. A train was rumbling in. David looked around. Amplified sounds jack-knifed like ballet dancers. The shutter from a Japanese camera snapped, then froze. In slow motion, a guillotine appeared and began its downward free fall. Suddenly, the silence was shattered, everyday sounds came back. People were holding David. He inhaled. Somebody was asking questions: 'What is wrong with you? Why did you try to jump in front of the train? What is your name?'

David began sweating drops of warm liquid that felt like gel. He smelt himself. Real brain-stunned fear has a distinct odour, it emanates from every pore. He could not move. He had just tried to commit suicide. People were staring. A policeman appeared. Conversation with the policeman happened in disjointed statements.

Cowering, David held his navel area. He felt a cord dragging him, unwilling and screaming, back into the depths of the concrete jungle. He began walking into the city of his dreams.

Instinctively, he went back to the office, thinking about his attempted suicide and how fast it all happened. David did not want to die, but he was afraid, very afraid of what his life had twisted into. It was after hours. The office was silent.

He called Hatsumi. 'I need you to listen to me,' he said quietly.

Hatsumi sensed the desperation. 'I am here, David.'

And he told her, not caring if she decided to leave him after this.

'I want you to come here, to my home tonight. We need to be together. Stay there, I will come and pick you up.'

David sat fixed to his chair. An hour went by. The door to the office was ajar; he heard her footsteps. Hatsumi held him like a child, saying: 'I understand, I understand, I understand.' David wept. Later, in her home, they talked of living.

'What happened to you,' she explained, 'is that you got trapped by the extremes of existence. There is a middle way here, but your fear could not see it.'

David stared at her. 'I did not know what I was doing,' he said, an incredulous grit edging his tone.

'David, we are all guided, consciously and subconsciously, we are not aware, that's all. In the cycle of birth and death, your death was not to be, not today anyway, your decision to die was not yours alone. But, David, I am glad that you are here, and I am here, so don't be afraid anymore.'

Hatsumi took him by his hand and led him to bed where they held each other in silence.

Later, David ran his fingers through her hair and said, 'Why are you still with me considering what has just happened . . .?'

She smiled, touched his cheek and said, 'David, I know who you really are.'

David did not have the luxury of a day off. The next day, Kamala breezed into the office. She said that she had something urgent to discuss with David.

'I have fifteen pages to finish,' David told her bluntly. 'Deepak needs to stay.'

Kamala beckoned to David to step outside the office. They walked to the fire escape, where David lit a cigarette.

'What is it?' he asked.

Kamala seemed almost euphoric. 'Last night, Achyuta overdosed on morphine. An ambulance had to be called and he was rushed to the hospital. He is okay now, but . . . You see, he has been buying morphine from a pusher in Manhattan, okay? He is addicted. If he overdoses again he could die . . .'

David could sense danger here. She was telling him that this could be the route to murder without blame.

'It is on record that he overdosed. I told the paramedics

the truth that he was buying morphine illegally, okay? They are witness to my statement, okay? They told me that he could die the next time this happens. He comes to the office sometimes, it could happen here. You know what I mean? If you help him a little. You know what I mean? He won't even know, Cabral. He is too far gone, okay? What use is he anyway?'

David watched her silently. He lit another cigarette.

'We can make this business better, Cabral, you and me, but I cannot do it while he is in our way.'

His hand, as it travelled to his mouth to puff his cigarette, trembled perceptibly. 'I don't know,' he said, 'I really don't know.'

'Well, just think about it, okay? Promise, okay?'

David said he would and told her he had to get back to the office. Kamala said she was heading home and would call him later.

Deepak and David had forged a good working relationship, but Deepak was sharper than the simpleton he appeared to be. When Deepak had asked him 'You and she are doing it or what?' David just smiled, and Deepak drew his own conclusions. Now David decided that he had to say something to Deepak who was looking at him expectantly.

'See, Deepak, Kamala was telling me that Achyuta has been buying illegal morphine and that he overdosed last night. He could die soon. If that happens, we, you and I, will take over the newspaper. We will get more money and she says she will sponsor our Green Cards.'

Deepak came alive when he heard the words Green Card. 'Well, hope the bastard dies soon then.'

'Yeah, yeah,' David agreed.

He decided to stop talking and get back to work before he mistakenly let Deepak know what Kamala really wanted him to do. When work was done, Deepak tapped David on his chest and asked: 'Do you trust her?' Deepak looked into David's eyes, then turned and left without waiting for an answer. David slumped into his chair. That was something he had not considered. What if she was setting him up so that she could kill Achyuta and frame him for the murder? What if she had another lover waiting to move in once the dirty work was done? What if, after Achyuta was gone, she kicked him out and did what most Indians do; get cheaper labour? David's head ached with the questions. He had no answers. He decided to get drunk.

It was in the middle of his fifth drink that it hit him. David had seen Achyuta fill the syringe again, immediately after he injected himself. If he could convince Achyuta to have a second shot rapidly after the first, that would do the trick. But how? David did not want to touch the syringe because his fingerprints would stay on the plastic. Finally, David decided to tell Kamala that he would not and could not do it. Simple. If Achyuta overdosed and died, great. If not, a Green Card was not worth its weight in murder. Having made his decision, David went to sleep with a sense of calm.

6

AS THE DAYS passed, David wanted to see Hatsumi again. He called her number, got a machine. David hung up. He called again, the machine again. This time he left a message. A week passed, no reply. David wondered what had happened to her, as this silence was uncharacteristic. He thought he knew her; thought she loved him. He felt abandoned, lost and sad.

Then, suddenly there she was one Tuesday morning, saying hello. 'I had to go to Florida. I left my cell phone behind. Why don't we meet? I have been thinking about your colours, I missed them.'

'What?' asked a perplexed David.

'Your aura. I like your aura.'

'Oh!' said David. 'Thank you. I love the way you talk. I will meet you Sunday at Grand Central Station and we will see where the evening goes from there.'

They said goodbye. David blew her a kiss. He smiled. Life was good, at least for the moment. Somebody in New York city loved him.

On Sunday, David waltzed to Grand Central Station, whistling. Hatsumi made him happy. He liked her disposition, loved her attitude and wanted her body.

She was there. He stood by the ticket counters and watched her, enjoying the subtle moves her head made in unison with the right hand that held the bow. Her glistening shoulder-length straight black hair fell over her face as she bowed her head, swaying with the notes. He closed his eyes, tried to laser in on her sounds amid the bustle of Grand

Central. He thought she was playing Charlie Parker's '*Lover man*', but then she switched from the lament, leaped and went soaring into a long, deep curve; and suddenly, the resonant cello sound dropped like a stone and went spiralling down into a corkscrew, turning and twisting till it crashed.

She is really good, he thought as he walked across the station to meet her. Hatsumi greeted him with characteristic tenderness. She looked into his eyes, caressed his cheek with her palm and kissed him lightly on his mouth.

David smiled and said, 'I was listening to you from back there by the ticket counters, you are brilliant.'

She blushed, pointed to her cello case; it was full of dollar bills. She said that she would like to play for another hour as it was going well financially.

David nodded, just happy to be near her. He sat on the floor as she picked up her Brazil-wood bow, sat on her small chair, adjusted the cello and drew the bow like an archer. She closed her eyes and the base voice of the cello began singing her emotions. She looked sensual, sexy with the instrument between her legs, as she began a classical tune.

Suddenly she stopped, looked at David and said: 'I am going to play a song for us.'

As David nodded she began '*For Baby*' by John Denver. The cello moaned, deep and low and David sang softly: 'And the wind will whisper your name to me.' She looked at him, smiled with her eyes, lost in the melody of the song, whispering: 'And I'll love you more than anybody can.' David stood up and kissed her on her cheek as Hatsumi played their love song. He sat beside her, marvelling at her expertise, loving her expression changes as the notes moved her soul. People passed by, some stopped, enchanted by the hypnotic sounds. She played on, seemingly oblivious of the world around her. When she stopped, a young couple – tourists from Sweden – talked to her. They were curious. What was this young Japanese girl doing in New York, playing a cello in a train station? She smiled, talked to them. They dropped a five-dollar bill into her case, she thanked them, smiled at David and the cello sang another song.

This fascinating Japanese girl loved him. He wanted to hug her, protect her, take her away from this concrete jungle. He had this idyllic image in which he envisioned taking her away to a mountain top in Japan or India where they could sit under a cherry blossom or mango tree and listen to the sound of One Hand Clapping, while a cuckoo cooed out a rhythm.

She was tapping David on his shoulder. 'You were far away.'

David smiled. 'Yes, on a mountain top with you.'

She laughed, knew exactly what he meant. They were in sync, and they both realized how special this union was.

'Time to go,' she said.

David stood up as she collected her money and stored her cello in its case.

'I am tired,' she said. 'Would you be willing to come home with me?'

David laughed out aloud. 'Willing? My love, I would be willing to walk through the Valley of Death with you.'

She smiled and said in mock admonishment, 'Valley of Life would sound better, David.'

She told him that she had gone to Saint Cloud, Florida, to visit her cousin who had just come from Japan to work at Sea World in Orlando. She had visited Clear Water Beach, and had gone down to see the Florida Keys. 'Florida is a beautiful place,' she said wistfully, 'the sun sizzles, but it is nice. Maybe one day we will visit Florida together.'

David nodded. He told her that a friend of his lived in Kissimmee and, yes, he would like to go there one day and see Mickey Mouse. When they reached her home, David put his hand into his back pocket and fished out a small package.

'For you. I hope you like it.'

Hatsumi hugged him, opened the package like an excited child and held a small silver bracelet that had entwining hands as a clasp.

'I will wear this for us. For you and me, and the circle that we have created together. Thank you, David. I love you. You know, when invited to a Japanese home, it is customary to bring a gift; we call it "omiyage". You are also expected to remove your shoes.'

'Aha,' said David, 'I did not know that. In India, the Hindus do the same. It's an interesting cultural similarity.'

She offered David saké, and said she was going to shower and then cook. 'You know,' she said, 'everybody thinks that saké is exclusively Japanese, but saké is a 7,000-year-old intoxication from China. Saké-making implements were discovered in the Yangtze River Valley in China, about the time nomadic man settled down to agriculture. Some anthropologists believe that the only reason why the Chinese grew so much rice was to turn it into saké.'

David laughed, and told her about the Goans back in India. 'We have the feni, you know. Them bleddy Goan buggers grew cashew nuts and coconuts for the same reason.'

'That's a strange thing you just said,' Hatsumi observed.

'What did I say?'

'You said, "Them bleddy Goan buggers", that's funny talk. Do people in Indian speak English like that?'

David was mildly embarrassed. His Mack-a-Pao petticoat had slipped from underneath its English frock. 'You know what, some people in my village in India talk like that, well, most of them talk like that. It is quite quaint and funny.'

He felt this urge to share his past with her. He told her about Freddy Fakir, who was infamous for trying to teach village children morals. He worked as a clerk at the city court and was often heard proclaiming: 'Da law is da law' and 'Spare da rod'n' spoil da child'. Teenagers made fun of him: 'Hey, Fakir, your bleddy rod is hanging out, men, dat is against da law.' Freddy Fakir would smile at them, raise his middle finger and curse their juvenile years.

'Do you know how he got his name? One day, during the summer holiday in May, when Fredrick Fernandes was five years old, he asked his parents for twenty paise to buy sweets from the corner shop. They refused to give him the money. So young, enterprising Fredrick decided to engage the community to raise the necessary funds. He went around the village, door-to-door, pleading poverty, and collected the "sweet money", paisa by paisa. When his parents heard about their "beggar boy", they confiscated the meagre amount and slapped their embarrassment on the young boy's buttocks. The next day the whole village went into a raging debate. "Should da bleddy child be allowed to keep da dam money?" In the end, Fredrick and his supporters lost and then somebody jocularly called young Fredrick "a fakir". The name stuck. Fredrick Fernandes is now forty-five years old, earning a decent salary and they still call him "Freddy

Godfrey Joseph Pereira

Fakir". That is how many people in my Pali Village get their nicknames. There is always an embarrassing factual story and, by the time the village children reach high school, they have a nickname that stays through life and sometimes even gets carved on their graves.'

Hatsumi thoroughly enjoyed David's story and said she would like to hear more of that and then headed off for a shower. David sipped his saké. Half an hour later, just when David thought she had fallen asleep in the bath, she called his name in her sing-song voice.

'Sit here in the kitchen with me while I cook, so we can talk, if you don't mind.'

David picked up the bottle of saké and his glass and headed for the small, neat kitchen. She should see my kitchen, David thought, she will die. David noticed that she was wearing a slinky kimono. He could tell she was naked underneath the silk. She turned around and saw the look in his eyes.

'You are a dirty man,' she said, smiling. 'I just feel comfortable like this.'

David told her she looked great.

'You know, a kimono is wrapped around the body, always with the left side over the right, but when the dead are dressed for burial, it's right side over the left. Bet you did not know that. Can you eat with chopsticks?'

'I can hardly eat with my ten fingers, never mind chopsticks. Most Indians eat with their hands.'

'I will teach you how to eat with chopsticks. Here, hold the first chopstick with your middle finger and thumb. Then grip the second chopstick with your index finger. Hold it steady. Practise opening and closing the chopsticks. You know, before eating or drinking, it is customary to say "itadakimasu". This means, "good eating to you, I am starting to eat". In Japan, it is considered extremely rude to start a meal without saying "itadakimasu". And when the meal is over you say "gochisou-sama", which means "many thanks for the food". What I am cooking right now is yakisoba noodles. It is called gyudon, which is simmered beef served on top of steamed rice. Pass the saké, please, I need to add a little to the beef. And remember, when you finish eating, your chopsticks must be positioned across your dish or on the side. Never, never place your chopsticks in your bowl or standing up in your rice. This is done only at funerals. Now tell me something about India.'

David laughed. 'Okay, I will teach you how to talk like a Bandra bugger. Now say: "Ah-ray, baba, you coming or what, men, I am going to Big Bazaar. Why you bleddy just standing there, cum-ing or what, men?"'

Hatsumi tried; she doubled up with laughter, delivering the sentence Kabuki-theatre-style, elongating the words, dramatizing the start of each word. She pronounced 'bleddy' as 'heady'. David laughed so hard he spilled his saké on the floor and then bent low so his ribs would not hurt from his stomach convulsions.

He wiped the tears from his eyes, and said, 'Hut, men, not like that. Shee baba, I am fully fed up with you, men.'

She laughed and echoed the sentence. Her accent and delivery were a riot.

And then David said, 'Hey, I am a bleddy Bandra bugger, men, wot you bleddy want from me, baster?'

She laughed very hard as she said it; her face was red with the exertion. She pranced around the tiny kitchen, chopsticks in hand, saying: 'A-waaay, I am a heady ban-dee-raw bug-or, bled-eee, wot you want wit me bos-ter?'

They fell into each other's arms laughing and Hatsumi put her forefinger on David's lips.

'You are my *Sanko*. You are my ideal partner.'

She kissed him, long and deep and David held on to her petite, slender body with desperation, hoping to freeze this perfect moment.

'I really, really love you, Hatsumi Nakamura,' he said, as tears filled his eyes and fell on her shoulder. 'You are my anchor here, without you I would drift into nothingness. I love you.'

They relaxed on her bed. She told him she had visited a Native Indian Reservation in Alligator Alley, west of Fort Lauderdale to experience a Pow Wow and met Running Waters from the Miccosukee tribe. The old Native American told her that he drank too much 'fire water', but he said he knew the history of his people and believed that the wisdom of his forefathers lived in his body. They talked of the Great Spirit and life in this century and what it must have been like when his people roamed the prairies, free and proud. 'We talked of God,' she told David, 'and he told me something fascinating:

'He said he had walked the hollowed-out walls of the white man's institutions, learned nothing. And that there were trails of tears that led to big cities, where money trees grew and wisdom died . . . and God was a one-word question that had no answer. See, most people, before they start praying, swallow a religious laxative that lubricates their spiritual bowels, and this usually leads to verbal diarrhoea. Remember, they are talking to God, all-wise, all-knowing, all-powerful, a God who created all the infinite questions and all the complicated infallible answers. And what do people do? They whip themselves into submission, liken themselves to helpless worms, they crawl, request for pity, save a wretch like me, cry, thank, plead, beg, question, make deals, swear to reform, promise to perform, bargain for a trade, if I do this, will you do that . . . dear Lord, please mother of God . . . I am not worthy, forgive me. He said that it was a process of mental mutilation, self-flagellation that is as good as impotent expired semen. And then, when they were finished talking, they got off their knees and left. It is a case of primary narcissism. Praying, for people, is more about the 'I' than it is about forming a relationship of spiritual understanding. The American wise man explained that He is the Great Wise Spirit, He knows what the problems are, He has the solutions, don't you think they should just sit down, shut up and listen? If people today want to reach the happy-hunting ground, they should smoke the peace pipe and listen to the four directions.'

'If we go to Florida at some point in our lives,' David said, 'I would like to meet Running Waters, have a drink with him and talk. I don't hear wisdom like that in people.'

They both decided that Florida would be their first vacation together and hoped that old Running Waters did not die before they journeyed to the magic kingdom of the billionaire mouse.

David then talked about Achyuta and Kamala, said they were terrible people but he was stuck, and had no choice.

'We always have a choice,' she corrected him. 'Are we brave enough to walk that road? That is the question.'

David smiled. 'Alright, alright, Miss Know-It-All, I

surrender.' She smiled and kissed him. David told her that Marty had said that her last name translated into English meant 'in a village'. She said he was close. It meant 'village in the middle'.

'You and me,' David said looking into her eyes, 'are both from a bleddy village.'

She laughed at his 'funny talk'. It was approaching midnight; David wanted to make love to Hatsumi. Her eyes were shut, her lips parted. He caressed her stomach, and moved his hand up to her breasts. He looked at her, she was fast asleep. He marvelled at the contours of her face, watched her chest rise and fall like a calm sea and felt a sense of great belonging with this beautiful Japanese girl. He switched off the light, laid his body beside her and felt soothed by her gentle breathing.

7

THE NEXT DAY, back at the office, David and Deepak worked on pages while talking about Achyuta and their future in New York. It looked grim, dark and ugly. Around mid-day, Kamala walked in, partially supporting Achyuta, who was snarling in residual anger over a domestic dispute. She stayed silent, a look of extreme irritation on her face, listening to his rant – the way one does with a dog that barks incessantly. Achyuta headed for the bathroom while she checked the office messages. She did not look at David. Picking up the phone, she began sweet-talking some advertiser named Mr Gupta, explaining how advertising in *India InTune* would benefit his company. David heard her sales pitch and smirked. She would never be able to sell space in a newspaper.

Kamala set up a meeting, looked at David and said: 'I think you had better come with me. He was asking me questions that I had no answers to, okay?' Then, suddenly, her mood pivoted. Her lipless mouth tightened. Kamala looked at the bathroom door, noticed that Achyuta was still inside and barked: 'Cabral, I want to talk to you.'

Deepak kept his head down low, listening to everything, pretending to work on a gossip page.

David slipped on his jacket. They walked to the fire escape.

He lit a cigarette, and she said, 'I have a plan. I just want you to listen, okay? Don't talk, okay? Just listen.'

David nodded.

'Every time Achyuta injects himself with morphine, he

takes vitamin pills. I don't know why he does that, but he does, okay? In his drugged state, he always asks me to get him the vitamins. Now, listen carefully, when he does this at the office, okay, all you have to do is hand him his morphine pills, after he has injected himself, that's all. He keeps these pills for emergencies, in case he runs out of liquid morphine. He will ask for his vitamins. You give him morphine, okay, and it will happen. He will not know the difference. It is better that it happens at the office. If it happens at home, there could be problems, okay? An accidental overdose. It has happened before to him, there are hospital records.'

David was silent. He told her that he would have to think about it, it was a big decision.

Kamala's face turned dark with rage. 'If this does not happen, you will be fired, okay? You know that he is going to fire you because he knows that you have got close to all the advertisers. He wants me to take over that function, but I cannot do that, I cannot sweet-talk these fools. Sales is not my strong point anyway. I am a housewife, okay? I am offering you a way out of this miserable life that you are living. We will both be free. I know what you are thinking, that I will not need you after this has happened, but I cannot do that, Cabral, you know that, you are on great terms with most of our best advertisers, if we lose that, I gain nothing, okay? They trust you. They will pull out of advertising in *India InTune* if you are not there. You know that. So why would I let you go? This is a foolproof plan, okay?'

'I said I will think about it,' David snapped, his impatience showing. 'You are asking me to murder your husband. Why don't you just say it?'

Kamala's voice shook with emotion: 'I don't like that

word, okay? Achyuta has not much time left anyway, what is his use?'

David looked into her large haunted eyes, raised his voice and said, 'I don't want to do this. I do not want to murder your husband, or be an accessory to the murder of Achyuta, okay? If you want to do it, that is your business, your problem, your husband. I don't want to know anything about this from now on. You don't want his blood on your hands so you are asking me to do it. Fire me. I don't care. I am not a wild animal for hire.'

Kamala eyeballed him. 'Think, Cabral, think of the future, okay? Let me know, soon, okay?'

David opened the door of the fire escape. Kamala walked ahead. David slipped his fingers into the pocket of his Levi jacket and switched off the micro-cassette Sony tape recorder that he used for interviews.

David knew he had to talk to Hatsumi. He needed to bounce this off her without letting her know what was going on. He was scared that Kamala might try and frame him. David knew that Kamala needed him to run *India InTune*. He was now familiar with many of the advertisers. They liked David, trusted his pseudo-analytical theories of what *India InTune* could do for them in the long run, and Kamala would not want to disturb that arrangement. He could one day own this newspaper if he shuffled the deck with a quick sleight of hand. However, taking a life for this . . . how would he live his life after death became an integral part of his existence? A voice inside kept whispering, no, no, no . . . the lure of a settled future swayed like a tasty morsel of live bait before his eyes. David thought about leaving the tumult behind and heading home, back to Pali Village, defeated, bitter and disillusioned. By happy coincidence, a letter arrived, from Brian.

Dear David,
Yes, yes, everything is alright, men. How is your health, bugger, hope you are fine? How is that Japanese girl you wrote to me about? She sounds nice; bring her to Pali Village to see the crotch of the Far East. Ha, Ha! How is America treating you? Hope your job is fine. Made any friends? Everything is same, same. Yes, your father is still drinking. He is now a holy functioning alcoholic. Church, Work, Bottle. Our Father, Aunty's Liquor. Amen. That is all he does and of course visits the grave every day. But don't worry I am looking after him. Small Tree Big Fruit finally got married. She is still going mad with all her property problems. Now she is very unhappy. Her husband looks like a homo. Baboo 'Boom Shankar', the Barber, died, just like that. They found his ganja pipe in his front pocket with a crumpled picture of the God Shiva. He was a non-Catholic, you know. The villagers paid for his cremation. Boom Shankar, you know, had been cutting hair and shaving the villagers for thirty years. He was a charsee, but an alright bugger. He had lived as a tenant in that small room at Dominic Big Stomach's house, you know that. Ten thousand rupees was found wrapped in plastic beneath his mattress. Boom Shankar's life savings. Dominic Big Stomach that baster pocketed the money. 'Bugger's dead, men. For wot he needs it now for?' that's what he said. The Pali Village professor, Daryl Dumbo said, 'That's a classical irrefutable argument that would have absolutely no chance of rebuttal in a utilitarian court of law.' Ha! He's always talking nonsense that professor.

After Boom Shankar had been cremated, Dominic Big Stomach's tongue slipped one night, when he was drunk. He boasted that he had found Boom Shankar's money. Everyone in the village was angry. They wanted the money that they had paid for Boom Shankar's cremation given back. Dominic Big Stomach refused, he said Boom Shankar owed him rent money. Everyone called him a bloody big fat liar. They called him a swine. They said he would burn in bloody hell. Finally, Dominic Big Stomach said he was thinking of giving the money back and then somebody called his mother a prostitute for giving birth to a bastard son who had an ugly big stomach. David, the villagers complained to Father Peter. When Father Peter showed up at the house of Dominic Big Stomach, he told the priest: 'Father, what happens in bloody Pali Village is none of God's business. Go count your bloody sheeps and cows, you go now.' My gosh, can you believe that! Father Peter left shaking his head. They then called the police. One hawaldar came. Dominic Big Stomach met the policeman at the junction and gave him a fifty-rupee bribe. The policeman then told the villagers that Dominic Big Stomach was drunk when he said that he had found the money. There was no money. Boom Shankar had died a pauper, everyone knew he was a poor barber for God's sake, and the Lord would reward every villager who had contributed to his cremation, that is what the policeman said. He even gave a small speech to the villagers who had gathered around him. He told them that he was a Harijan, and he admired their Catholic compassion and love for a Barber who was a non-Catholic and had no family. He said that the case was closed as far as the law was concerned. Dominic Big

Stomach smiled, thanked God for the legal system, and cursed the villagers who doubted his innocence. What to do? And yes, another piece of news. Molly Mad Cap had been missing for three days. Somebody found her wandering in the Big Bazaar, near Hill Road, arguing with the fishmonger, telling him that Jesus had multiplied fish and given them away for free; so why was the bugger asking two rupees for his dried fish that smelt like dog shit? She said she was waiting for the Pope, said somebody had told her he was coming to the Big Bazaar, said she had something to tell the big bugger. They brought her home. She had one bag of dried Bombay ducks. She said that Jesus had given them to her. Molly Mad Cap's cousin was happy that she was home finally. She thought that Molly Mad Cap had died and gone to heaven. They fried the dried fish, ate it with loaves and Molly Mad Cap is now talking about walking on water when the monsoons come.

And somebody said that someone they knew had met Lancy Lamba in Canada. You bloody remember him? Asked him about 'The Grave Incident'. Lancy Lamba had said that he had to attend a funeral and was in a hurry. That's all. The bugger did not want to talk. The Heat Gang has broken up; the girls have decided to go their separate ways, some problem about who was sleeping with who, complicated story. And Charlie Chicken has left for Bahrain. And a new rock band is making the Bandra scene hop. They call themselves 'The Bandstand Boys'. They played at Peter Parrot's wedding. Sounded just like Creedence Clear Water Revival, these Bandra buggers, you should hear them do 'Proud Mary' and 'Lodi'. Same like bleddy Creedence, ditto. Everybody is talking about the buggers, all over Bombay. Wait till they play at the Bandra Fair in the September Garden; that will be bloody fab, men.

Send some latest music from America. When are you bloody coming home?

Write when you have the time,
Brian.

David felt the familiar pangs of missing Pali Village. Salt Peter had been right. His bloodline ran deep under the gutters of Pali Village. He missed that rustic, homey simplicity and their idiotic problems. Missed the awful smells and sounds, missed that bleddy Bandra bugger talk, but here, in New York City, lived Hatsumi.

David wondered sometimes how the two realities would morph. Bleddy, I don't know wot to do about dis, men. At some point, wot if I want to go back and live in Pali Village, den wot will bleddy happen? Will she come? Who knows, men. How will she get along with all those Bandra buggers? Yes, yes, I want to marry her and have some chil-ren and all at some point. But wot about her fadder and mudder? Wot da hell will they say about all dis, and wot will papa say about her being a bleddy boo-dist and all dat, and wot about da bleddy chil-ren, men ... imagine boo-dist chil-ren running here and there in Pali Village, everyone's tongue will be bleddy rattling full time, men. Maybe I should talk to her, I don't know, maybe. Wot if she wants to live in New York for good? All these bleddy questions coming fast, I feel like dat Socrates bugger. And how will she live, men, in Pali Village with da May–October heat, and da dirt, and da monsoons, and da ducks, and da dogs, and all those Bandra buggers, and da pigs? She says she loves me, and all dat is bleddy all very fine, men, but a Japanese girl in Pali Village? Wot if those buggers start making fun of her... you know how da stoopid buggers are, men... because she uses toilet paper and eats raw fish and all dat... and they will all be talking rubbish from their bleddy arses. Every day she can give classical music lessons in Bombay and maybe join an orchestra or something dat will bleddy keep her mouth smiling, I don't know, men. She has only once to smell dat bleddy masala Bombay duck, and she will be wanting to go back home very fast, men.

8

HATSUMI DECIDED TO take Sunday off. 'It's my Sabbath, so no cello today,' she joked. They decided to walk to Strawberry Fields in Central Park West between 71st and 74th Streets. They stared at the black-and-white 'imagine' mosaic, designed by a team of artists from the Italian city of Naples.

Hatsumi said, 'I find this ironic. This teardrop-shaped land is designated as a quiet zone in Central Park. John Lennon was a musician. There should be buskers here, musicians from all over the world, people celebrating the man and his music.'

'For music to be banned here is a travesty,' David agreed.

They met a man who said his name was Sergeant Pepper, dressed in an old army jacket, walking a black Labrador named Mary Jane. He claimed he was the mayor of Strawberry Fields, did flower arrangements on the mosaic circle, kept pesky musicians away and fed tourists lines on the Ballad of John and Yoko. David smiled and thought: 'This was America, You Can Be What You Want to Be, Yippee-I-Yay-Yeah-Yeah-Yeah!' The mayor smiled and hustled them for money. 'A Contribution for Peace,' was his panhandle line. David shook his head in disbelief and dropped a dollar into the mayor's palm.

Hatsumi was talking to some Japanese tourists who were fans of the Beatles. 'Konnichiwa,' he heard her say as they bowed to one another. They had wanted to know if she had been lucky enough to bump into Yoko Ono. David and Hatsumi sat on a park bench and talked about the tragedy of

Lennon. She said that she believed death was a mere passing phase and reincarnation for her was a reality. Buddhists, she explained, view the body as an impermanent vehicle.

David had Achyuta on his mind. 'Since we are talking about death,' he said, choosing his words thoughtfully, 'if a man is sick and dying, can he take his own life? What if someone else helped him to achieve death? Would that be morally wrong?'

Euthanasia was legal in modern Japan, Hatsumi told him. 'There are medical, ethical and legal clauses, but yes, I do believe in euthanasia, if . . . (and here she held up her palm and began counting on her fingers):

'One, if the disease is incurable by modern medicine. Two, if the pain is unbearable – for the patient. Three, there is no violence, the dying person has a right to a peaceful end. Four, the person himself/herself must request the killing, while conscious and sane. Five, the method of killing has to be humane. Six, the killing has to be handled by a doctor.'

David thought about Achyuta's situation. Morally, the only violation that stopped him euthanizing Achyuta was number six. He had heard Achyuta on more than one occasion complaining that he wished he were dead and free from his pain. But David could not tell Hatsumi of the fire that was raging inside him. He needed to make this decision alone. He looked away and then, right there, sitting in Strawberry Fields, David Cabral decided to end the miserable existence of Achyuta. She sensed the tension, asked him if he felt alright. David smiled and nodded.

'Let's go to my place,' she said, 'I have something that I want to give you.'

David touched the silver bracelet that he had given her.

Bloodline Bandra

She said that she would wear it always. He kissed her as they walked out of Strawberry Fields and headed for Grand Central Terminal to board a Metro North train via the Harlem Line to Scarsdale.

Once home, they relaxed with glasses of plum wine and ate tekka maki. Hatsumi talked to David about Japan.

'It is a nice place, and it is not a nice place.'

David observed, 'Well that's a very Japanese saying, I guess.'

She laughed and explained: 'See, for the Japanese it is nice, but for a *gaijin*, a foreigner, it can be pretty intimidating. If you live in Japan for a hundred years, you will still be considered a gaijin. The Japanese are a xenophobic race; you cannot and will never, ever integrate completely into their society, even if you speak Japanese as well as the *tennô*, which is the Japanese word for emperor. You are deliberately shunned. The average Japanese person believes that all gaijin are ignorant of Japanese customs, mores and language. They believe that gaijin are naturally rude, coarse, disrespectful human beings, and that they are all guilty of some crime that they will commit against a Japanese person in the near future.'

David said that Bandra, where he came from, was different. Sure, they had their prejudices, but they usually accepted foreigners.

She told him that the Japanese, like other societies, had their own peculiar mores. 'It is considered rude to look someone directly in the eye, cross your arms or legs, or have your hands in your pocket when you are speaking to them. The Japanese usually focus their eyes on the lower neck of the person they are talking to and try to avoid staring.'

David was doing just that, staring at her without realizing it. She laughed and poked him in the ribs: 'Lower your eyes, look at my lower neck.'

David widened his eyes, formed his lips into an exaggerated O and concentrated on her breasts. Hatsumi squealed with laughter and playfully cupped his eyes.

'Close your eyes,' she commanded.

He heard her walking into the bedroom, heard her shuffle back. 'Now look,' she said. She was holding a silver chain with a tiny locket in the palms of her hands. 'It is the Japanese way,' she explained. 'You use both hands to give a gift. Inside this locket is some of my hair, a small piece of cloth that I touched to every part of my body and an imaginary piece of my soul, so that I can be close to you, always.'

David was overcome with emotion as she placed the chain around his neck.

'You like?'

He nodded silently, tears in his eyes. They kissed, made love, cried, held each other like drifters in a wicked sea storm. Later that night, she placed the cello between her legs and played a song of passion and fire. She ended with a crescendo and said: 'Now, we can sleep.' David heard her from far, far away, caught up in the music. She noticed, he laughed nervously and said: 'Yes, that will be nice.' In bed, holding her body he felt his soul at peace. She was asleep when he turned to lie on his belly.

9

DAVID WAS PROOFREADING the 'Entertainment' section, squinting to try and decipher a line he thought was grammatically faulty when Achyuta and Kamala walked into the office. He looked up, said hello, and continued proofing. Deepak kept his head down, ignoring them. Achyuta looked calm, almost melancholy, as he shuffled his way into his sectioned-off 'Publisher's' space. He carried a small black bag. David guessed it was his medication. Kamala looked haggard as if she had not been sleeping well; she said she had to go back home. Fifteen minutes after she left, Achyuta appeared, glassy eyed, his pupils dilated. He dragged a chair and sat before David's desk. David looked up. Achyuta had tears in his eyes. David lowered his gaze, pretended to proof.

'I know,' he said, 'what you feel about me, okay? But I want you to understand that I had to become this . . . this mean, tough, nasty bastard.'

David started to protest, tried to say that he did not hate him, but Achyuta held up a trembling hand. 'Do not interrupt me, okay?' he yelled, with his usual nastiness.

David nodded, silently cursed him and wished he was dead.

Achyuta continued, his face purple with the exertion of shouting: 'When I first came to New York, twenty-five years ago, I had nothing, nothing, okay? I thought the Indian community would help. I was wrong. They kicked me down and then laughed when I tried to crawl. I started working in a restaurant as a waiter for food and a place to stay. After one year, they let me keep the tips. They promised to sponsor me, of course they didn't. I was a fool to believe them. I was an illegal alien. Not a good feeling, okay? One day I met an Indian man who had come to the restaurant to eat. We got talking and he asked if I needed a job. This fellow worked at the Port Newark-Elizabeth Marine Terminal on Newark Bay in New Jersey. Later, we met again in Newark, and he told me that he could supply me with grade-A marijuana. He used to steal from the cargo holds. Apparently, the DeCavalcante crime family had been using this port for years. They never missed the minuscule amounts that he was pilfering. We worked out a fifty-fifty deal. And that is how I began selling weed in Washington Square Park in Greenwich Village. I was famous among New York University students and the musicians on MacDougal Street. I was cool, once upon a time, okay? Made some money. Did not get arrested.

'A contact I had in the Park set me up with a prostitute who had a big drug habit. She was just what I needed. I married her and that is how I got my Green Card, okay? At that time you could get away with things like that, not now . . . Anyway, our business marriage worked, okay? She thought that I was still a waiter in an Indian restaurant; she had no idea that I was a grass dealer. She was white trash, quite nice actually, and we got along well. She said she was from West Virginia, who cares? I paid her 5,000 dollars. Two and a half before, and the rest after I got the Green Card, then I kicked her out, the whore, but she was quite a good person actually, better than most of the damn Indians.

'Then I came to work here for this paper as a delivery boy and eventually learnt the production part, okay? My boss was a wicked man, a pariah dog, born in Calcutta. If you think I am bad, you should have seen that son of a bitch. Anyway, he got sick of New York. I guess he missed his freshwater fish, rasgullas and mishti doi, who cares! The paper suffered. He wanted to shut it down and go back to his mustard oil India. I told him that I would like to try and salvage it, and so with the help of another Indian who had some money, we bought *India InTune*, lock, stock and barrel for ten thousand dollars. I met Kamala in Queens and married her. She was, and still is, a good bookkeeper and we get along okay. Eventually, we made my partner's life miserable, she cooked the books and we cheated, and he knew that we were inviting him to leave. Ha! Yes, invited him to leave. Well, I gave him some money and the paper was mine. But it has been a long, hard road filled with deep potholes . . . But, I made it what it is, okay? You may not approve of my ways, but I made it, okay?

'As the years went by, I grew a tough shell. I cheated, back-stabbed, made sincere promises, which I never kept, delayed the payback on loans . . . never paid them in the end but promised that I would do so soon. I blackmailed advertisers, fudged print order numbers and finally got *India InTune* off the ground. I had to play their game. In time, I became like them, a conniving, crooked, conman. Now it has all come to this. I am very sick, okay? The pain is so great sometimes I want to die. You are doing a good job here, you and Deepak. Kamala has to take over. She does not want to do it, but she has no choice, in time she will learn, this is the only source of her income, okay? You have to teach her and maybe she will sponsor you and Deepak for your Green Cards, maybe, okay? Keep the advertising contacts, be good to them, play their game, see that they pay, do them little favours, sometimes a free ad, okay? A good write-up. Learn about their companies, many of them are involved in shady deals. It will help you get ads from them. That is the game. It keeps them hooked, okay?' Suddenly, Achyuta winced and hit his head viciously with the palm of his hand. He placed his hands on David's desk and stood up, grimacing from the pain. He looked at David and then Deepak, silently, started to say something, shook his head violently and then headed for the bathroom. David and Deepak continued working.

Two hours later, David went into the back storage room where the bathroom was. The door was slightly ajar. He saw Achyuta sitting on the seat of the commode. His body was slumped against the left wall and the water cistern. Froth was forming at his mouth and his body twitched. David walked back to his desk and sat down. Deepak's head was lowered, cut-pasting a page. Should he call 911? Should he go in there and try to resuscitate Achyuta? Should he call Kamala? David walked to the fire escape, lit a cigarette. He was shaking. The cigarette calmed him down. He walked back to his desk and began typing furiously – an article on Hollywood and its impact on Indian society. An hour later, Deepak went to use the bathroom. He screamed in horror and fright when he saw Achyuta. David ran to the bathroom. He quickly ran back to his desk and called 911. Trembling, he told them about the morphine. He called Kamala. She was calm, and told him not to worry. David watched the paramedics, who were feverishly pumping Achyuta's chest. He was rushed to Mount Sinai Hospital on Fifth Avenue. Achyuta never regained consciousness. He was declared 'dead on arrival'.

Fifteen minutes later, the police arrived. They questioned

David and Deepak separately. From the tone of some of the questions, David figured that they had already questioned Kamala. David swore that they had called 911 as soon as Deepak discovered Achyuta's body slumped on the commode. The police volunteered no information. If they knew that Achyuta had overdosed before, they kept the information to themselves. They said that they would contact David and Deepak if they had any further questions. Deepak, nervous and distraught, went home. David walked to the liquor store and came back with a bottle of Jack Daniels. He needed Jack on a night like this. Sitting on the fire escape, he watched New York go by. He hated its momentum because his own life had come to a standstill. He lit a cigarette, watched the flame on the match slowly extinguish.

'I could have saved him,' David thought. 'I could have saved his life. I should have called 911 when I first saw him in the bathroom. Does that make me a murderer?' A voice inside him said: 'The man wanted to die anyway.'

Still, the guilt remained. David told himself that there was nothing wrong with assisted suicide. By keeping silent, he had helped Achyuta die peacefully, something the man wanted.

Sanctity of life.
Dignity of life.
Whose life is it anyway?
Do we own the copyright to our death?
Should a person who does not want to live be forced to stay alive?
Was he guilty of 'passive euthanasia'?
Did he violate the moral obligation clause of society?
Did he negate Good Samaritan laws?

Had he now committed a Mortal Sin?
Will God ever forgive him for letting a man die?
What was this degree of murder?
What would Hatsumi say if he explained his inaction?

David thought: 'I wanted Achyuta dead, that was the reason I did not make that emergency call. It does not matter if I did not help with the overdose. If I had called 911, he would be alive, right now.'

The gavel came roaring down. He felt the handcuffs click and bite into his flesh. A prison door slammed. A key turned. A sharp snap. The lights were turned off. David flinched as guilt slow-sliced through the darkness of his consciousness.

Achyuta had wanted to die. He had passed on, serene and calm with the help of medication. That's the way David tried to view his death. The Catholic in him hammered every rationalization he offered until Jack Daniels mercifully intervened and laid his body down to sleep.

David and Deepak were not invited to the cremation. Kamala called constantly, asked about the newspaper and the advertising. She told them that she was going to accompany Achyuta's parents to India to immerse his ashes in the Ganga. She would be back in three weeks. She had taken care of all the bills. There was nothing to worry about. Everything was going to be fine.

David's instinct warned him that Kamala thought that he had played a hand in Achyuta's death. If she wanted to get rid of him, all she had to do was drop a hint at the police precinct and his life would morph into a nightmare. He considered leaving New York and fleeing to India, to hide in the fishing village of U-Tan with his relatives. Even if the American police tipped the Bombay cops, they would never find him in U-Tan. He spent the next two days packing his meagre belongings and trolling the internet for cheap tickets. He had to leave before he was entangled in a murder investigation.

Deepak talked incessantly of how things were now going to get better. He conceived plans on how they were going to run *India InTune*, and how he was going to bestow on himself the title 'senior executive art director'.

David patted him on the back and said, 'Yes, we are going to have new lives. We are going to leave the madness of the past behind.'

Suddenly, like the rising sun, a question peeked out and grew bigger and bigger as it ascended. His conscience slipped on dark glasses against it.

What was he going to say to Hatsumi?

That Sunday afternoon he went to her apartment. She had called. She was down with a respiratory tract infection. David looked at her small frame under a blanket, at her almond eyes and inverted-teardrop face framed by black hair. David felt a pang of loneliness. Now that he had decided to leave New York and go back home, he was going to miss her. She asked if everything was alright because he looked 'disturbed'. The usual work pressures, he replied. He told her about Achyuta. She said that he was in a better place, and that death was a blessing sometimes. He sat beside her, gently caressing her feverish forehead. He could not tell her, not now. David said that he would stay while she slept. She nodded, kissed his hand and drifted into a deep slumber.

He moved silently into the living room. He stared at a large print of *oni* demons from the *hyakki yako* scroll. The demons had shattered the wooden crate they were imprisoned in and were now free to rape, ruin and plunder, to destroy by any means necessary. At the rear end, a fiery, demonic, loathsome figure with talons was contemplating absolute freedom and all the evils that it could do with it. It was ripping the crate apart to free the bloodsuckers still trapped. It was the beginning of their life; the end for many they would encounter. That was just the way life and death worked, as partners in a cosmic factory. There was nothing personal about it, they were just doing their job. You had no choice . . . or did you?

David stared at the print, juggling his choices. Inside the bedroom, he heard Hatsumi moan in her sleep. To live his life, never seeing her, never touching her again was an existence he could not wrap his head around. But, like they said, a man's gotta do what a man's gotta do! Finally she awoke, smiled at David, and said she was going to take a warm shower. An easy comfortableness had grown between them.

'Bleddy hell,' thought David, 'I have to leave her. I have to go.'

He thought of his friend Brian, thought of his father. He would tell them that he got homesick and had decided to forsake New York. He could tell them anything. But what about her?

She said she was feeling better after the shower. 'I dreamt of you.'

'Was I naked?' he joked. But David knew that the dream was a nightmare. He could read it in the depths of her dark eyes.

'You were being eaten alive by a vulture,' she said softly, then she stopped, looked away. 'The vulture had the face of a woman.'

Bloodline Bandra

David felt his stomach churn.

She sensed his quiet horror and smiled. 'Well, at least the vulture wasn't me! But, I can't remember the woman's face. Anyway, it was just a bad dream. People have them all the time.'

David laughed uncomfortably. 'Yeah, yeah, it happens all the time.' He kissed her lightly, told her it was alright, and walked outside to light a cigarette with a hand that had a perceptible tremor. 'Kamala,' he thought, 'Kamala, Kamala, Kamala, the bitch vulture.' He looked up at the cloudy sky, a lone hawk glided on the wind stream, circling, looking for prey. David looked at the hawk one more time, flicked his cigarette into the bushes and walked back into the house. Hatsumi was in bed reading *For Whom the Bell Tolls*.

David lay down beside her and held her hand. She marked her page and closed the book.

'I miss home sometimes,' he said, 'I miss Pali Village.'

She wanted to know what it was like back home. David told her. He talked about his father, Brian, the characters that peopled the village, their eccentricities, the rural goodness of their soiled souls and the ugliness of some of their ways.

'If I had my way I would take you back to India,' he told her. 'We would live in the village.'

She nodded, silent, and placed her hand upon her heart. He touched her bracelet, and she kissed the locket around his neck.

'I cannot promise you the same,' she explained, 'because Japanese society will never fully accept you. It is just the way they are. But I am here, and you are here and we can stay in America. I can visit Japan every year to see my parents. I could stay here if you are also here.'

David nodded, saying nothing. She sensed the tragic undertones to his sentences, felt the dread of something about to snap. 'You are scaring me, David,' she said clinging to him.

'Life is unpredictable,' David explained lamely, 'you never know what will happen.'

It was getting late. She was tired. David said he had better get going. Tomorrow would be a long day at work, they had to work on ten pages, get them ready, the deadline was approaching. She said that she would call him. David looked at her and thought: 'I am leaving, Hatsumi Nakamura, I love you. I love you. I love you. We will never see each other again.' He nodded, hugged her and walked out of the door. He stumbled to the station, crying in frustration, shame and helplessness.

It was late afternoon. The phone shrilled. David was at his computer, checking out airline tickets to Bombay. Deepak answered. It was Kamala, calling from Kerala in India. She wanted to speak to David. He hesitated, but Deepak had confirmed his presence in the office. David sighed and held the receiver to his ear. He did not care anymore. If she threatened him, he decided that he would say nothing.

Kamala was saying, 'David, I want to thank you for running the paper. I will be back soon, okay? David, I want you to know that I do not blame you for Achyuta, even if you gave him the extra pills.'

David quickly interjected: 'I did not. I did not have to. You have to believe me.'

Deepak looked at him quizzically.

Kamala was saying, 'It does not matter, David. It does not matter. I need you, okay? He overdosed. It was his fault. I

Bloodline Bandra

promise you, I will not make trouble for you because the fact is that I need you, okay? Without you the paper will close down. I know that and you know that. I cannot get another employee who knows the editorial and especially the advertisers. I have no other source of income. Please do not leave if someone offers you a better job, okay? Without you I can do nothing. When I come back to New York we will talk, okay?'

David said goodbye and replaced the phone in its cradle.

When David put down the phone, Deepak asked: 'What was all that about?'

'Oh, nothing, nothing,' David answered, 'she is paranoid, that's all. I was just trying to reassure her. No problems.'

He lit a cigarette outside and wondered what was going to happen. He thought about it and decided that he would risk staying.

Back in the office, as he x-ed out the airline website, he thought of Hatsumi. Tears of relief came to his eyes.

Deepak looked at him and said, 'Now what?'

David jumped up, slapped him on the back again and said, 'Baster, you don't know how happy I am. You don't bleddy know, men.'

Deepak shook his head in puzzlement, smiled and exclaimed, 'As long as we get our Green Cards, you can call me what you want.'

They went back to work, two souls with a renewed purpose and a hope that things would somehow get better in the Promised Land.

10

KAMALA ARRIVED FROM India and visited the office. David's mood turned sullen after he greeted her. His body language grew increasingly antagonistic. 'Vulture,' he thought, 'she looks like someone who lives on dead, rotting flesh.' She had changed. It seemed that the burden that was Achyuta was now a distant memory. Her black eyes glistened with a new luminosity as she called a meeting. Beginning with humility, she acknowledged that her husband had been difficult to deal with, and that she intended to change what had happened in the disagreeable past. She stated that she would be 'in charge overall', but David would make all the professional decisions. She was here to help, and together they would make the business flourish. She told them that starting next week, their salaries would be doubled. She said that she would handle 'the books' as she had done all along – from home because Achyuta did not want anyone to know that she was his accountant.

Deepak asked, 'What about the sponsorship for our Green Cards?'

'I promise you,' she said, 'I will work on that, okay? As soon as we all settle down, I will get my attorney to file your papers, okay?'

David seriously doubted that, but what choice did he have? He had to hope that she was not lying.

She looked at David, sensed his thought,: 'We have to trust each other, Cabral, otherwise things can get difficult. The important thing is that the newspaper makes money. So, let's get to work, okay? Things will settle down soon, okay?'

David thought, 'First she was a simple housewife. Now she is an accountant who has an attorney. There is something. She is planning something. I will have to play her game for now to see where this goes.'

Kamala asked to speak with David privately. They went out to the fire escape, where he stood as far he could from her body odour.

'I want to thank you for all that you have done, okay? See, I don't blame you for anything, okay? See, Cabral, if you did give him those extra pills . . .'

David cut her off savagely: 'I did not give him anything. When Deepak discovered him slumped in the bathroom, I called 911. That is the truth.'

Kamala looked at him and David could tell that she thought that he was lying. 'Let us forget all this, okay?' she said, looking down at the alley. 'Cabral, we must concentrate on the newspaper.'

David could not let her think that she had a hook in him that she could manipulate in the future. 'I need you to listen to something,' he said, teeth clenched. 'Stay here, I will be back.'

He walked back to the office, pulled out the mini tape recorder and walked back to the fire escape.

'What is this?' Kamala asked, slightly alarmed.

David pressed play. Her eyes widened in horror. Her voice played back, sounding tinny and eerie as it crackled through the mini speaker. Her body tensed, her eyes narrowed and her lipless mouth hardened in a steel line.

She heard her voice, stared at the mini recorder as if it had suddenly come alive.

And then David's voice came through.

'You are asking me to murder your husband. Why don't you just say it?'

'I don't like that word, okay? Achyuta has not much time left anyway, what is his use?'

'I don't want to do this. I do not want to murder your husband, or be an accessory to the murder of Achyuta, OK? If you want to do it, that is your business, your problem, your husband. I don't want to know anything about this from now on. You don't want his blood on your hands so you are asking me to do it. Fire me. I don't care. I am not a wild animal for hire.'

He switched the machine off, looked at her thunder, and said, 'I am just protecting myself, that's all, just in case you get any ideas . . . you know. Once again, I tell you, I was not responsible for Achyuta's death. He was probably already dead when I made that 911 call. I don't know, but I was not responsible for his overdose. I have five copies of this recording, just in case this one disappears, know what I mean?' He paused, then added sarcastically: 'Okay? Kamala.'

The opaque darkness in Kamala's eyes scared him, but David knew he had sucker-punched her. The rules of the game had changed. She might call the shots, but he owned the bat and ball. He had the option to walk away.

Kamala forced a laugh. 'I never thought you would resort to something like this. You surprise me. Don't worry, Cabral, I need you, okay? Cabral, we both stand to lose if this gets out. What do you say, we both forget all this and work, just work, okay? Achyuta overdosed. He was responsible, okay?'

David had thought about a work-related issue that he wanted to discuss with Kamala. He paused and looked straight into her dark eyes. 'I have a girlfriend, whom I love very much. So, whatever you think is happening between us has to stop.'

Kamala patted him on the shoulder. 'I respect that, Cabral. No worry. We have enough on our hands as it is. No worry, okay? Who is she? Hope she is a nice girl. Is she Indian?'

David ignored the questions. 'Okay,' he said. 'Let's get back to work.'

Kamala nodded calmly, but her eyes flashed lightning, and in her silence David heard a thunderclap and flinched inwardly. She still had one more poison quill.

'Cabral,' she said slowly, 'if you knew I was planning to murder my husband, why did you not tell the police?' She smiled.

David looked at her, hating her ugliness, hating her as a human being.

'We are both here together. I do not want problems and you do not want problems. Let us forget what happened, okay?'

David grunted. Their cumulative guilt made them accessories to a death both had desired. The NYPD would have loved a case like this.

He concentrated on the newspaper. This was his catharsis. It helped him get away from Kamala's threatening insinuations. He began by restructuring the contents of the paper in his spare time. He worked on a dummy. It took him five months. He showed it to Kamala, explained the nuances and significant details. He e-mailed journalist friends in Bombay, and pleaded and cajoled them to contribute free articles. He assured them that once the paper began to do well, they would get paid. It worked. He began writing serious analytical pieces, on politics, life of Indians living abroad and devoted a full business page to the pitfalls and advantages for Americans who wanted to do business in

India. He sat with Deepak, week after week, redesigning the paper, the logo and the typefaces. Even Kamala was impressed.

A film journalist from Bombay provided him with snippets of who was doing what to whom and how many times. David began to build a library of photographs that they could use for free. He ran a byline and the photographers were happy. Six months after Achyuta had passed away, *India InTune* launched its first new revamped edition.

Kamala looked at a copy and smiled. 'Cabral, this is fantastic. Seriously, I had my little doubts about whether you could do all this, but here we are, we are okay.'

David smiled and felt a huge personal satisfaction as he waited for the advertisers to pass judgement. He called Brian. Spoke to his father. Told them that he would be home soon, assured them that his Green Card was on its way.

He talked about the paper with Hatsumi. She loved his ideas, did not understand the politics and laughed at the Hindi movie gossip. The advertising support had been great. More advertising assured them that the paper was on the right track. David made bigger plans. He had contacted a distributer in Canada. Maybe they could move into new territory. Things were beginning to happen. Kamala gave them a big Christmas bonus. Kamala said that in January the procedure for their Green Cards would begin. She had talked to the attorney. Next week, she would give them the paperwork. Deepak was overjoyed.

David thought: 'My God, this is really going to happen.' Finally, New York city was going to be his home. He had arrived.

David thought back to a conversation he had had with

Marty. He had run into Marty and Hank in Central Park. Hank was pushing the Target cart, Marty strolled along, watching the pigeons.

David had walked up to them, and said hello. 'Oh, it's you, David, my friend,' Marty had said pleasantly. They sat on a park bench and Marty began fishing in the Target cart, a twinkle in his eye. David could smell the rank odour emanating from it. He wondered when they had last washed their clothes or themselves. Marty found the brown paper bag. He passed it to David and then to Hank. Marty took the bottle from Hank, sucked the whiskey, belched, and asked: 'Are you happy?'

'I don't know,' David said, 'maybe sometimes ... maybe ...'

Marty laughed his Santa Claus ho, ho, ho and pounded his fists on his thighs. Then he grew quiet, looked at David with a glint in his eye and said, 'I was friends with Robert Oppenheimer, remember him? I visited him when he was diagnosed with throat cancer in late 1965. I was still teaching at Princeton and unhappy with the routine. I never was a good teacher anyway. Three days before he died, we talked of the bog I was sinking in, we discussed my cage, my frustrations. I remember he quoted some lines from the Upanishads. This in particular I remember: "There is a path of joy and there is the path of pleasure. Pondering on them, the wise individual chooses the path of joy; the fool takes the path of pleasure. Don't be a fool." Robert went into a coma on 5 February 1967, and died at his home in Princeton on 18 February. The next day, I left Princeton, leaving all my belongings behind. I decided to walk the path of joy. David, my friend, you will have to make that decision, to be happy, all by yourself. It does not matter where you are or what you are doing, if you are not happy, there will always be a dull charcoal line that will define the edges of your life, like the chalk lines the police draw around the dead. That's all there is to it, really. Oh, and try to give up smoking.'

Having said that, Marty lit a cigarette, swallowed a mouthful of whiskey and laughed. It was time for David to leave. He stood up and walked away. There were no goodbyes.

At the office, David now worked with a renewed enthusiasm. He was going to make a difference. He was going to turn this newspaper into a respected successful journal.

And then, a day before the year passed on, Kamala introduced them to her boyfriend. Her body odour had been replaced with a pungent-smelling perfume. Her boyfriend was a slick south Indian. His name was Anthony Thomas. He was born in Kerala.

'People call me AT,' he said, smiling.

His handshake was strong, his eyes insincere. He was an investment banker who lived and worked in Manhattan, did alright, he said with fake humility. Yes, yes, he drove a BMW and lived in an apartment overlooking Central Park. They were welcome there anytime. Kamala's friends were his friends. He said he had a few good ideas for the newspaper and would talk to David about them in the New Year.

David was instantly apprehensive. Things were going to go south.

He celebrated New Year's Eve with Hatsumi. They drank and danced the night away at a house party in Scarsdale. When the ball in Times Square told them that it was now the

Bloodline Bandra

New Year, they kissed and hoped that the New Year would be better than the last. Finally, at 3 a.m., they staggered home and slept as the New Year's first sunrise illuminated the east coast. It was a holiday. They spent it at her home and talked of their aspirations and hopes, and wondered what surprises were in store for them.

David left early in the evening and took the train back to Grand Central. Tomorrow was a workday. They were working on refining the masthead of the newspaper when AT and Kamala walked in, smiling, wishing them all a Happy New Year.

'Let's have a small meeting,' Kamala said. 'AT has a few ideas. He has taken the day off so that he can help us, okay?'

AT smiled, looking mildly embarrassed, patted his grey suit and said, 'I think we can all make this paper bigger than it really is. Cabral, you and Deepak have done an excellent job, I must say. I have seen old copies of the newspaper and compared it with the new *India InTune*. Excellent job, Cabral, excellent.'

David thanked him. Deepak squirmed. He was not used to people congratulating him for any kind of excellence.

AT continued, 'As an investment banker, I nurture business relationships, develop, organize, administer and monitor capital ventures. We can triple the monetary strength of our advertising revenue with the right marketing approach if it has a sound financial basis for our clients. What I am trying to say . . . and, Cabral, you have done an excellent job, no doubt about that . . . what I am trying to say is that we can give our advertisers more "bang for their buck". Supply them with demographics, advise them on restructuring their ad content. See, most of our advertisers do not have the money to go to big advertising agencies, so their ads are not adequate. We will supply them information free of charge, and this will triple the feedback that they will receive for their products. That means more advertising for us, more money. Everybody wins.'

And then AT delivered the punchline: 'I will be taking over the advertising. No offence, Cabral, but it will be better that way. Now you will have more time for editorial content, which is your forte, yes! It's common sense, no? Together we will make this newspaper great, make some real money. Now, financial transactions involve a lot of paperwork.' He looked at Kamala. 'We have been discussing this. Cabral, you now draw an okay paycheck. We will need the small space that you live in, no hurry, take your time.'

David began to protest, but saw the futility of making a rational argument. He nodded his consent.

'We need you here, Cabral,' AT said, softening the blow. 'Please do not assume that I am firing you. What I want to say, Cabral, is that with your editorial expertise and my financial knowledge, we will do very well.'

David thought of the sculptor Arturo Di Modica, who installed the bronze charging bull without permission in New York City. There seemed to be something shifty here. AT was confronting him with the sculptor's bombastic arrogant attitude after he had installed his bovine: 'So, what are you going to do about it now, eh?' The sculptor had labelled what he did 'Guerrilla Art'.

Di Modica had driven his 7,054.8-pound baby to Lower Manhattan on 15 December 1989. He then surreptitiously installed it beneath a colossal Christmas tree in front of the New York Stock Exchange. He said it was his Christmas gift to the people of New York. The police impounded the bull, while the artist passed around his publicity materials to the hundreds of people gathered to watch the spectacle. It was a classic marketing strategy, full of bull, but it worked. And then New Yorkers began to scream and agitate. They wanted their bull back. The press moaned. Politicians made bovine noises, not wanting to say yes to all that bull, and simultaneously wanting to appease the ferocious culture warriors. Finally, the bull was installed at Bowling Green Park. Now the whole world knew about Arturo Di Modica and his eleven-foot bull. He ran out of publicity materials. He had to print more, many, many more. Tourists were known to rub the bull's testicles for financial luck. David wondered what it was he needed to caress to turn his fortunes around. And he wondered what moral the story held for him anyway.

Deepak had a solution to David's housing dilemma. David could move into Deepak's one room at his Harlem tenement. The landlord could use the extra money. 'I know it's Harlem,' Deepak apologized, 'but it is better than nothing. New York is an expensive town and I think we both need to save as much money as we can. Who knows what can happen tomorrow?'

David agreed, packed the few things he had and moved in with Deepak.

The poverty in Harlem stunned him. He met people who were illiterate and street smart, literate and dangerous, junkies and career loafers, welfare queens and paupers, the working poor and rich pushers. The squalor shocked him because here was an open sore, just outside Manhattan, the glittering house on the hill. This was America. He had no idea that the

United States had places like this. Harlem's notoriety for danger and poverty was a universal talking point. But to be there, smell the dissatisfaction, sniff the atmosphere and sense the underlying paranoia and danger of the streets stunned him. Sure there were slums in India; bigger wounds than this, but Jesus, this was America!

Deepak said that people on his street left him alone because they now knew that he was poorer than they were, and he had grown to like some of them. He had absolutely no idea what most of them did for a living and was scared to ask. His landlord was a retired musician who had played saxophone with 'a hot' jazz band at the Apollo in his younger days. Now he lived off his savings, social security and the rent he collected from the four apartments he owned in the tenement. He called Deepak D-Dog and told him stories about Harlem's glorious past. David liked the sound of D-Dog.

One evening, David was walking from 125th Station to the tenement. A six-foot, slender black man approached him, and asked ever so politely: 'Do you have the time, sir?'

David nodded, told him it was 6.30 p.m.

The man thanked him, turned to leave, then stopped. 'My name is Duke Ellington,' he said, smiling, 'no relation to the great piano man who wrote for the orchestra.' He offered a hand for David to shake and said, 'Nice watch.'

David nodded.

'I would like to have it, that's if you don't mind, sir.'

David stood there confused. Duke put his hands into his back pocket, fished out something and held it behind his back. David heard a switchblade snap behind Duke's back, or had he imagined it? Duke was still smiling, polite, rocking

Bloodline Bandra

on the balls of his feet. David looked at the jeering grin and froze. He was being mugged. People were moving around them. Mothers with children, men going home after a day's work. The usual loiterers were hanging around, smoking, joking, jiving each other. It looked like David and Duke were amicably chatting, so nobody looked their way.

Duke asked if David liked jazz. David mumbled something about Charlie Parker.

Duke laughed. 'That Cat was the be-bop king, man, no question. But he mainlined heroin and was just thirty-four years old when he died. Just thirty-four, sad, isn't it? Imagine what the Cat could have done. You know he used to ride the New York subway all night long sometimes. Just tripping man, far out, strung out. Someone once asked him why he did that, you know what the Bird said, man? Ha ha ha ... The Bird said he was looking for the lost chord. Go figure.'

David wanted to get away. Duke told him he was hungry, asked to see David's wallet. David had seven dollars. He handed it over to Duke. David told him that he was too poor to afford a credit card.

Duke sympathized and said, 'We poor people need to stick by each other, man, you know. Well, nice meeting you, sir,' Duke said, finally. 'Keep in touch. I would love to stay and chat, sir, but I have some urgent business that needs tending to.'

Saying that, he put his hand into his pocket, restored the small switchblade that he had been cupping behind his back, turned and disappeared into the evening bustle. David just stood there, amazed and frightened, his open mouth dry. He had heard of muggings. They were usually violent, scary experiences for the one being robbed. This had been a smooth operation; nonetheless, it had scared the Jesus out of David. It was not even a stereotypical mugging. David actually laughed when he narrated the story to Deepak. It was funny in a tragicomic sort of way. He decided that the next time somebody asked him anything on a street in Harlem, he was going to turn around and walk the other way, fast.

AT took over the running of the newspaper. His clients began advertising in *India InTune*. As a bonus, he ordered David to interview them and run public relation pieces. *India InTune* slowly began changing. All the work and effort that David had put in was slowly eroded. AT was always polite, always smiling, saying: 'It is for the newspaper. We are doing alright.' Both David and Deepak complied. They could see their Green Card aspirations take flight and go out of the window on the wings of a carrion fly. When D-Dog dared ask Kamala about the paperwork for the application, Kamala morphed into Achyuta and snarled at him: 'Is that all you think about? What about work? Why don't you think about work for a change, okay?' David had to interview the wife of an advertising client on her Indian doll collection. When he protested that the subject matter was far too trivial, AT smiled, Kamala smiled.

'My dear boy,' AT said mildly, 'her husband is giving us an advertising campaign that will bring in 50,000 dollars over a one-year period. Now, do you want us to lose that money? Come on, we need the money and let's face it, *India InTune* is not exactly the *New York Times* now, is it? And what does it matter to you anyway. Just do it and everything will be okay.'

Kamala nodded in agreement. In five months, the paper had become an advertorial jumble. David worked like a slave. His eyes averted, head down, back bent, never questioning, agreeing with everything. Something was going to snap soon.

The influenza attack came in the middle of the night. A potent viral assault. Nasal congestion woke him. Half an hour later, he was twisting with pain in his joints and throat, as fever washed over him like running lava. D-Dog helped with ice packs to his forehead but the shivering continued until dawn. Tylenol pills calmed the rage, but his body felt limp and wasted; his mouth was on fire as fever blisters swelled in soft, jellied agony. D-Dog realized that David could not be left alone, he might get worse and he could not go to a doctor because he had no medical insurance.

He found Hatsumi's number and called her in the morning. David was asleep. When he awoke, he heard movement in the kitchen.

'Hey D-Dog,' David called in a small voice, 'why did you not go to work?'

'Because I am making you some chicken soup,' Hatsumi answered.

'What is she doing here?' he thought. He was ashamed of the poverty of his existence. She walked into the shabby minuscule bedroom that he shared with D-Dog and saw the naked embarrassment in his fevered eyes.

She held his hand and said, 'D-Dog called me without telling you. He did the right thing. David, you and me, we go beyond these cracks and walls, we go beyond this neighbourhood, I want you to know that.'

He clung to her hand, and he wept. She had brought Japanese herbal medicines and fruit and a bag full of different cough medicines, fever relievers and soups. She had taken time off work and driven to Harlem. 'I don't deserve this kindness,' David thought. 'What good have I done, for a woman like this to be part of my life?' She mixed the Japanese herbal medicine in soup, and spoonfed David like a child. Finally, the fever broke and sweat poured off his body. She helped him shower, changed the sheets on the bed and lay him down. Her voice seemed far away. She was telling him a story of a twenty-two-year-old English photojournalist, Dan Eldon, whose biography, *The Journey Is the Destination*, she was reading.

'You and me, David, we may never get there, wherever there is; but these stops on the way, each of them are destinations. We are there already, and there are many more stations, better destinations.'

Then, like a train leaving a deserted platform in the midnight hour, the sound of her voice grew distant as it entered a tunnel and merged with the darkness. David drifted off to sleep. When he awoke, he felt better. She was in the kitchen. He could hear her.

'I am awake,' he called out weakly.

'Okay,' answered D-Dog.

Was he delirious? Had she really been here?

'Where is she?'

'She went home,' D-Dog called out. 'I am making us chicken soup.'

David looked at the Japanese herbal medicines to reassure himself that her visit had not been manufactured by his high temperature.

D-Dog walked out, eating a plum. 'How are you feeling? You look better than you did in the morning. Sorry, I had to call her. I did not want you to be alone.'

David nodded.

'I like your girlfriend,' D-Dog said, smiling. 'She is very nice, she brought a lot of nice things to eat.'

David laughed, it made him cough violently. 'Yes, D-Dog, I like her too. Now, can I have some soup please?'

11

KAMALA WAS NOW her late husband incarnate. She snarled at petty mistakes, criticized David's writing and told him that he was being paid too much.

'Now that you handle just editorial, I don't see the necessity of paying you all that money, okay? I can get somebody cheaper any day. Next week, your pay goes down.'

It had not been a good day, and the night was about to get worse.

Hatsumi called, five minutes to midnight. There had been an earthquake in Japan. Yokohama was devastated. Hatsumi's father was missing, presumed dead. David rushed to Grand Central Station, boarded the train for Scarsdale. He ran to her home. She was weeping. She told him that she was going to call him earlier because she had some good news. Juilliard had finally accepted her, she was ecstatic, and then five minutes later the call came. A relative called to say her mother had collapsed, their home had been destroyed, their town was no more, and she had to go back, look for her missing father.

She broke down. 'I may never come back, David,' she sobbed. 'I may never come back.'

David sat there, stunned. He held her shaking body, but there was little he could do to comfort her. She needed to go home. To find her father. To be with her mother. The bank would take care of her belongings, store them and ship them to her when things settled down. With typical Japanese efficiency, the bank booked her ticket within the next hour. Hatsumi was flying away. David told her that he would leave New York behind and journey with her to Japan.

She shook her head. 'Not now, David,' she said, sobbing, 'please, not now.'

A bank employee was driving her to JFK airport. David kissed her, held her, looked at her crying face one last time and walked out of the door. He walked to the Scarsdale station, weeping. He wandered, he stumbled . . . he looked up, he was lost.

David found himself on Carman Road. The Immaculate Heart of Mary Church stood before him and David fell to the ground like a stone, his body shaking, his voice cracking with sorrow.

'Why? Why?' he screamed. 'I cannot climb another mountain. Take my life. I don't have the guts to kill myself. What have I done to deserve this? What have I done?' He lay there in the dirt, clutching his knees, begging for an answer. 'Why have you done this to me? Why?'

People passed him by, some stared at his trembling body lying in the mud. Nobody helped. They thought he was another insane New Yorker, hallucinating. He could be dangerous. David knelt before the church, his pupils were dilated, there were white froth-bubbles on his lips. His body rocked with epileptic spasms. He lost control of his bladder. He spread his arms and cursed God, the mother of God and the heavens, giving them an excuse to terminate his misery.

Nothing happened.

Silence, pure and soundless, dripped on his tears.

The Immaculate Heart of Mary was closed.

He shut his eyes and tried to pray, in sadness and helplessness, a confused cause looking for reasons to justify the nothingness. Glorification of the Almighty turned to pleading, then begging. Intractable terror exploded as the soggy straw, at which he was clutching, wilted and dissolved. And then, there was that sinking, as his heart shifted into overdrive, and sank slowly into the belly of blackness.

Is this drowning a divine retaliation for his past transgressions?

Mea Culpa.
Mea Culpa.
Mea Maxima Culpa.

For the next six months, David slogged at work. He had muted his suffering and refused to complain or feel sorrow at his predicament. A letter arrived at the office. It was from Yokohama. David let it sit unopened. There was nothing he could gain from reading her letter, it would only underline his loss. He and Deepak talked incessantly about their futures. His existence in New York City had come to resemble a crazed hamster riding the rodent wheel. On Sundays, David had begun strolling aimlessly in the city.

It was Sunday, much like all the other Sundays of the last few months. He thought of the line 'life, liberty and the pursuit of happiness' in the *Declaration of American Independence*, and smiled with bitterness. He walked along Fifth Avenue, hands in his pockets, spine bent. He was at Central Park on the corner of Fifth Avenue and 59th street. David walked into the park, past the jutting black rocks to the left and the shirtless men, with their eyes closed as they soaked in the heat on the lawn, to the right. Bikinied women lay on their stomachs on beach towels, their bra straps undone, sprawled in the sunshine. To the left was a children's park with swings and slides, he paused to look at a street artist working on a summer landscape. It was a perspiring, wet-armpit, mid-August afternoon. David stopped to listen to a banjo player picking a blue grass tune, somewhere around the corner; a blues harp wailed a crawling Southern lament. Something made him look down. He was standing on a storm drain. And there, etched on the circular metal, he read 'Made in India'. David bent and caressed the alphabets on the warm metal. Later, sitting on a park bench, he realized with a little embarrassment, what he had done and why. The moment had come.

Back at his apartment, as they tried to drown their sorrows with Jim Beam, David told D-Dog that he had decided to go back to India.

A week later, he was all set. 'There is nothing, nothing left for me here. My best friend, a big part of my heart, has gone to Japan forever. I will never see her again. New York has nothing for me and I have nothing for New York. Working for *India InTune* is a torture every day, and Kamala will never sponsor my Green Card. It is all over, D-Dog. It is really all over. If you ever come back to India, come to my home. You will always be welcome, anytime, always. You are a good man. I will never forget your kindness.'

Deepak smiled and hugged his friend. 'Cabral, Cabral, I am going to miss you very much. God willing, we will meet someday in better times. God willing and luck by chance, I will come to your Pali Village.'

He looked at Deepak. 'Saturday, I fly back home. I have booked my ticket. Don't tell anyone. They don't need to know.'

Saturday morning he said goodbye to his friend D-Dog, who had to leave for the *India InTune* office.

'I will tell them I don't know where you are. I will tell them that you left my apartment to stay with friends.'

David shrugged, he didn't care anymore.

He spent the day packing. He called Martin and Veronica, told them that he was leaving for India and would explain it all in a letter. David had to see Marty and Hank before he left. He walked through the city in anticipation, hoping to see that Target cart, hoping to hear that familiar laughter. He quizzed the homeless, the Central Park buskers and the bums. He walked through Hell's Kitchen between 34th and 59th streets. He came close. Someone had seen them yesterday, maybe they would return. Through the Bowery and Jackson Heights, through the east and west village and Washington Square Park, he looked for them. He waited in Times Square amid the neon nuclear invasion of huge alluring advertisements that towered like sparkling monsters of fierce light. It was three in the afternoon. The tourists were heading back to their packaged tours. It was time to leave for the airport. David whispered one last silent farewell to Marty and Hank.

When the sun set over New York City, he left America, and let the jet stream dust the shadows of the American dream from the tortured soles of his feet. As the jumbo lumbered across the sky, David's existence ran a quicksilver mile across his mind. Bitter bile rose thorough his gullet. He had failed. He consoled the angst, telling it that his American sojourn had been just another journey, a learning experience and now he was free. Faces flashed. Kamala, Anna, Manu Laxman, Achyuta, AT, Deepak, his father Bertrand, his mother Olive, Salt Peter, Brian, Marty, Hank, Duke Ellington, Hatsumi . . . He wondered what she was doing. He thought about her pain at forsaking the Juilliard dream. He wished that they would meet again, somewhere.

Bloodline Bandra

A young man sitting next to David introduced himself as Manohar Shetty. 'You can call me Manny. In Noo-York, that's my handle. I'm in the computer software racket.'

His pseudo Americanisms irked David. He said he was going home to Pune to see his future bride. His parents had arranged a 'good homely girl'. He was then going to take her to America. Something snapped inside David.

'Is she fair and lovely?' he asked in a jagged, shark-bite voice.

Manny's jaw dropped in shock.

'Is the dowry sufficient? Does she have a college degree? Did your parents check to see if she is a virgin?'

Manny recoiled. He was just 'trying to make conversation', and there was no reason for 'uncalled hostility'. Manny, now visibly furious, continued: 'I don't know where you're coming from, man.'

David retorted with a sneer, 'Ah-ray, I am coming from the bleddy Pali Village, men. I am a bleddy Bandra bugger . . . MAN.'

'What is your problem?'

David ignored him, looked out of the window at the blackness outside. He wanted to be left alone. Manny pressed the buzzer that summoned a stewardess. He requested for a seat change. David sighed, he had not meant to be rude and thought about apologizing, then thought, 'The hell with it all.' He laid his head back and closed his eyes.

12

PALI VILLAGE WAS in darkness. It was Sunday, 8 September. The first day of the feast of Mount Mary and the Bandra Fair. He had told no one that he was coming back. The taxicab pulled up in front of David's house. He looked at the old building and the cracked balcony, and tears came to his eyes.

'Home,' he said. He knocked. His father opened the door, peering at him in the dim porch light.

'Papa, it's me. I have come home.'

His father was stunned and cried. He kept touching David to assure himself that this was real, that his son had finally come back. He wiped his streaming tears, and stroked David's forehead with still-moist hands. David hugged his trembling father and told him that everything was going to be alright.

An hour later, after a long bath, a rickshaw dropped him off at Yacht Restaurant. He used to come to this restaurant when he cut classes as a disgruntled student at St Andrew's High School. Here, a group of 'class-cutters' would smoke cigarettes, drink tea, ridicule the ignorance of their teachers and lie about their sexual exploits. St Andrew's Church stood beside the restaurant, glorious in its Portuguese decor. He walked to the cemetery, which lay in a U-shape around the church. The gates were locked. He climbed over the low walls, walked left past the grotto, to where his mother lay buried. The tears came before he reached the six feet of soil she was under. He fell beside her grave and sobbed, telling her again, and again, and again that he was here now, that he was sorry he could not come when she was sick, that he wanted to be there when she died. He begged for forgiveness, pleaded for her to hear him. He lit candles on the white-marble gravestone, promising that he would come back. He told her he was home and that he would take care of Papa.

The night watchman arrived; he wanted to know how David had got in. He told him to leave at once. He could lose his job. David slipped him a ten-rupee note, told him that he had just come from America, he was just visiting his mother's grave, and that he would leave soon. The night watchman nodded, tucked the bill into his front pocket, asked David to hurry and walked away. David knelt and said a prayer for his mother and begged God to take care of her soul. He placed his hand on the cold marble and whispered, 'I promise, I will never leave you again.'

That night he knocked on Brian's door.

'Oh my God, oh my God,' Brian exclaimed, 'I never thought dat I would see you again, men. Yes, yes, I heard, your papa told me. When did you bleddy come, men? I came looking for you but you were not home, you bugger. Why didn't you bleddy write, men, saying you were coming? Are you on bleddy holiday or wot? When are you going back? Come, come, come . . . oh my God.'

They got drunk as David painted his American odyssey. Brian sat there, listening in disbelief to the humiliation that his friend had gone through.

'Wot happens to these bleddy Indian buggers when they go abroad?' he asked.

David spread his hands and shrugged. 'I don't know, Brian. I really don't know.' Then David grew silent. He turned to Brian and said, 'I am sorry for telling all those lies in my letters, of how happy I was in New York and all that, I hope you understand, I don't know what else to say.'

Brain patted him on the shoulder, smiled and said, 'Have a drink, it is over, good to have you back. Wot happened to your girlfriend, dat Japanese girl?'

The next day, news spread through the village that David was back and a steady stream of visitors came and went. When the villagers discovered that David did not plan to return to the United States, they were flabbergasted and disappointed. But he expected the barbed queries: 'You don't like America or wot? Now wot you going to do, men? Catch one and shake two?' He was not surprised by the sarcasm and suspicion either. 'Why for you bleddy left a good job to come back here again, men? Bugger, tell da whole truth, men; people just don't leave a big job in America just like dat and come running back. Wot bleddy happened? Why for you not going back? You got sacked or wot?'

'I did not like New York City,' he told them. 'I prefer it here.'

Tommy-Eat-Shit-A-Lot snarled, 'Oh, you like it here, with all dis bleddy shit and pigs! You like dis better than New Yock? Ah-ray, you gone bleddy fully mad or wot, men?'

Jadi Steamboat's fat folds around the neck jiggled as she shook her head and exclaimed, 'Hut, men, we thought dat you would bring home a nice fair American girl, and now you come back like a bleddy, useless, bekar bugger, with your tail between your legs. So many bleddy Indians live in New Yock, and dey is all happy. Shee baba, I don't understand. Now better for you to stay here, and bleddy slog like dogs, like all of us.'

A few of the villagers were conciliatory. One evening,

Acknowledgements

Dominic Big Stomach accosted him on the junction as David made his way home after buying bread from the bakery. 'Ah-ray, David,' he said, 'good to see you, men. I want to bleddy tell you something, will only take short time, keep it just between you and me, okay?'

David nodded.

'I am having problem with someone in da village, I cannot take his name. See, men, we are eating from da same plate. But da bugger is eating 75 per cent and I am eating 25. And den, when it is coming time for paying, he is telling dat we have to pay pip-tee, pip-tee. Ah-ray, bleddy bugger thinks I am stupid or wot? And when I am saying why for pip-tee, pip-tee, bugger is getting angry and making big noise. My God, I cannot believe my eyes, men. But I am keeping quiet, you know, I know his wife. She is bleddy, very nice thing, men. Po thing, how she has stayed for so long with da idiot bugger, I don't know, men. Now tell me, baba, why should I pay pip-tee per cent when he is eating 75 per cent, huh?'

David looked at Dominic Big Stomach, perplexed and amused. Was he speaking literally or metaphorically?

So he answered, 'Yeah, men, the bugger's mouth is getting bigger and fatter every day, men. Wot to do? Soon da bugger will want to eat da full plate, men, and he will still say pip-tee, pip-tee, when it is coming time for paying. I cannot fully understand. Best thing is, you should not bleddy go out to eat with him, den no tension.'

Dominic Big Stomach nodded vigorously, the loose ample flesh of his mid-section heaved. He clasped David around his shoulder and said, 'See, I knew dat you would bleddy know da answer. All those stupid books you read sometimes helps.'

David smiled at the friendly insult. He needed to recalibrate and exist within the confines of a new setting. The milling of people, the incessant honking of automobiles, the garbage heaps being sniffed by bony, stray dogs hoping for a rotten morsel, the illegal street vendor stalls on both sides of the streets that encroached on the narrow roads all offended his recently acquired New York sensibilities. He had to get used to the thick, queasy noise and pollution, the eunuchs, beggars and lepers.

He was walking through the crowded, narrow Pali market road, and winced as he had to step over garbage and the smell of fish rotting in the burning sun. Through the jostling crowds, a stream of traffic tried to muscle its way through. Rickshaw drivers cursed the people; the people abused them back. Car drivers in expensive BMWs and Mercedes-Benzes hurled insults at everybody when traffic stalled and the people simply manoeuvred through, ignoring the storm. David looked around, no one was really offended by the insults or the chaos. It was a familiar fury. David felt his foot sink into something soft. It was a rotting, half-papaya that his heel had squished to pulp. David shook his head in disbelief and smiled. This was home. It was not new to him, and yet, it was now different. After New York, everything had a twist of the new, in a familiar sort of way.

That night, he bought a bottle of Old Monk and walked out of Pali Village. He stood at the junction, looked at the white cement cross to the right, and said hello to the usual bunch of loafers. To the right, up the road, drunks were stumbling out of the Janata drink hole. He turned left, sauntered down the road, past good old Dr Care's dispensary, now closed, and arrived at Hill Road. He turned right, past

St Stanislaus High School. Passing Mac Ronnel's, he remembered that his father sometimes used to buy him chicken sandwiches from this landmark restaurant. Through the locked gates of the church, he tried to locate his mother's grave and bid her goodnight. He walked to Bandstand and the old Portuguese fort. It was almost midnight.

David sat on the low walls of the fort and began drinking straight from the bottle, looking out at the blackness. Half an hour later, he thought he heard a cello playing. He stood up on the wall, looked down, the rocks merged into the night. It all seemed like a painting in soft focus, and seventy-nine feet down, David could hear salt water crashing somewhere. His body moved ever so slightly, maybe it was the wind, maybe the rum. He licked his lips, New York on his mind. He looked out at the sea that he could not see, there was no horizon. He was back, and now what? He was standing next to nothing but the stones of the Castella de Aguada built in 1640; its yesterdays were long gone and all that was left was a crumbling tomorrow. His decisions had led him back to the starting point.

His neck seemed to lose its traction and his head slumped forward. And he thought of being cut adrift . . . *Dhobi ka kutta na ghar ka na ghat ka*. David smiled. Then he thought of Martin Chevalier. Marty was the washerman's dog, which belonged neither to a home nor the washing place on the riverbank. Marty would have loved this proverb. D-Dog's smiling face came through, David laughed, and the memory was good. New York flashed again, a rotating kaleidoscope, small, bloody, glass shards coagulating into symmetrical patterns of pain and hopelessness. He stood there, slightly incoherent, swaying. The time was now. He looked at Old

Monk, raised the bottle to his lips and swallowed a burning toast to Martin Chevalier. Then he got off the wall and began the long stumble home. David felt a decision had been made. He would extinguish the backburner that was New York and bury the fragments of a love that was never going to be consummated.

Pali Village now began to feel like the old routine. When someone asked him what he was doing standing at the Pali junction, he answered, 'Nothing, men, just standing, passing da bleddy time.'

Here, they could not deport him. He could quit his job and not feel like an illegal alien. He was not afraid anymore. A minuscule incident brought it all back home. He was buying some butter and bread from the bakery. He pulled out his wallet, opened it and saw that he did not have enough money. David told the bakery owner that he did not have enough money and would come back for these things. The man said, 'Ah-ray, wot are you worrying about small things, men. Take da bread and butter. Come tomorrow or next week and pay me. Don't be making tension for nothing.'

David smiled.

His friend, Small Tree Big Fruit, saw David at the bakery and offered to pay. 'Good to have you back, men. You have to come and meet my husband. He is quite a useless bugger. Wot to do, men, my fate is like dat only. Come home, I will make American chopsuey for you. See, you take elbow macaroni, mince meat, onions, put a little salt . . .'

David held up his hand, started to protest, 'I don't have . . .'

Then Small Tree Big Fruit said, 'David, my husband is thinking of applying for a bleddy job in America, some

Bloodline Bandra

Indian company in California needs accountants. Can you give him a few tips or something about America?'

David smiled. 'Yes, I will come over tomorrow. Yes, I have a few tips for him.'

Epilogue

DAVID FOUND WORK as a journalist with *Spear India*, a political magazine. He was happy. This was real journalism. He worked long, immersive hours every day. It was a cathartic tool that helped ease some of the pain of the past and the memory of Hatsumi. He seemed to have lost all interest in women and ignored village talk of finding him a 'nice, fair, homely East Indian girl'. Three years passed. But he thought of Hatsumi every day, wondered what had happened to her life. Had she forgotten him? Did she think of him, still, sometimes? Did she find her father? Was she back in New York, studying at Juilliard? Had she met someone? Did she have a Japanese lover? Where was she? He touched her locket around his neck, wondered if she was still wearing his bracelet. Tears were replaced by answers he did not want to hear and eventually resignation set in. Hatsumi Nakamura was a girl from his past, a pleasant memory that had no relevance to his life today. Still, he often heard her voice singing, the wind would whisper her name and a gentle breeze would blow it out to the open sea.

Amputating the past is not easy. Fibrous scar tissue remains. There were spaces in time when the cogs turned and New York minutes began ticking in his brain. His head ached with the futility of it all.

He was soon promoted as the bureau chief of *Spear India*'s Bombay branch. He travelled often within India, covering events that were socially relevant and journalistically exciting. An outbreak of Maoist violence took him to Nepal. He considered himself fortunate that the editor had given him this assignment. David managed to interview rebel leaders – it took four weeks, but David came back with a great exclusive story. He filed the feature from the office at Nariman Point, caught a cab to Churchgate station and rode the train back to Bandra. It was late, 11.30 at night. Brian was at his home. His father was laughing at nothing. 'Bleddy bugger's drunk again,' thought David. Brian was looking at him in a peculiar manner; there was an idiotic smile on his face.

'Wot?' said David, raising his voice. 'For wot you bleddy laughing like dat? Like a bleddy donkey, men. You gone bleddy mad or wot?'

From the kitchen, they heard a loud metallic clang of a pot being dropped. Hearing the sound, David quizzically looked to the kitchen. Standing upright, near the kitchen door, was a leather cello case. David stared at it, speechless. From the kitchen, he heard a lilting familiar voice doing an unforgivable imitation of Bandra bugger-talk: 'Ai-ey, mens, dinner eees the become. You coming to bleddy eat or wot, men?'

David clutched the small locket around his neck.

He threw his head back, laughed, clapped his hands and walked into the warm kitchen, and the rest of his life.

Acknowledgements

TO ALL THOSE nameless East Indian men and women in Bombay who let me record them speaking, thank you. To the American Professor of Linguistics, who listened to the tapes and reminded me of the phonetic wonder of East Indian English; I am grateful that you led me through the stylistic patterns and convinced me that this was worth documenting. Part I of *Bloodline Bandra* happened because they helped me decipher the sound behind the lilting words of the East Indians.

I must thank my agent, Priya Doraswamy, for her indefatigable energy and zany sense of humour. When we were set to meet in Hoboken, New Jersey, for the first time, I told her that she would recognize me by my large moustache; I asked her to describe some small characteristic by which I would be able to identify her. She laughed and said, 'I have a large moustache too.' Priya held me together through that long torturous process of editing. I would also like to thank my editor in Upstate New York, Shobha Viswanathan, and Ajitha G.S. at HarperCollins India, for their deft handling of the editorial scalpel.

Bloodline Bandra would not have seen the black of print if my friend in Bombay, Shobhaa De, had not read the first raw draft. The story touched her and she graciously handed it to Priya in Jaipur. Thank you, Shobhaa, you rock, tattoo and all.

Part II of this book would not have been written if it were not for the people listed below; without their help, I would have died.

Homeless in New York City, skin-burning winter deep

freeze, sleeping near a garbage can, Kenneth and Vanessa Desouza found me and took me to their minuscule basement home in Queens. They were very poor then, struggling to survive with many problems of their own, but they offered me shelter, warmth, food and hope. How does a stranger thank people who have absolutely no ulterior motive when they offer unconditional help? With what valid emotional currency do you try and repay this immeasurable kindness? Saying 'Thank You' seems glib, trite and inadequate.

Dinesh Balgi was my fellow 'Legal Slave', shackled to an abusive, alcoholic, porn-addicted, paranoid publisher of a despicable Indian rag in New York City. Dinesh helped me survive. We were galley slaves in the underbelly of the same damned ship. We talked about dying in this land we had journeyed to, all promise and hope had gone by then. I remember meeting Dinesh one night, wandering in Times Square in midtown Manhattan; wild-eyed, slurred speech, rambling incoherently. I can recall the gigantic Broadway billboards flashing *Les Misérables* as he walked away. I looked up; the prophets seemed to be writing our fate in neon signs. I cried for him and for me; we were not going to survive. I lost him after that night. Our lives were dragged in different directions. Dinesh eventually escaped the labyrinth of despair and hopelessness. One day ten years ago, he managed to connect with me. Dinesh is well today, safe and content, far from the American Dream. His remembrances will always stand as a sad testimony to the time when we were exploited and enslaved by our own people. We met in India a few years ago, it was beautiful. We hugged and laughed, overjoyed that we had survived and connected, and inevitably we recalled 'the days of absolute darkness'. We drank black rum and talked of the future. This was something precious. We were both aware of how this privilege of envisioning a future had been savagely ground to hopelessness and stolen from us in the past.

One evening after Dinesh disappeared, travelling to White Plains on the Metro-North Railroad, via the Harlem Line, I thought I had seen a familiar face on the train. I walked up to him; it was Brian Mascarenhas from Saint Paul's Road in Bandra. We had known each other in Bombay. The chance of two Bandra boys meeting on a train travelling to Upstate New York was a strange and mystical coincidence. This happened in a city where neighbours do not know or see each other for years. This happened in a city of millions, infamous for its legendary urban isolation. Alarmed by my physical appearance and shocked by my state of mind, he took me and my family to Florida, let us stay at his home and set me up as a vendor at the 192 Flea Market in Kissimmee, Florida. It was a dead-end job for a dead-end man, but it helped me stay alive. He is gone now; but wherever he is, I hope that he is walking on the Sea of Galilee with that man from Nazareth, the one who changed water into wine, the one that transformed Brian's existence. I was not there when Brian left. I would like to tell him here, 'Vaya Con Dios, Brian; for you and me, there are no goodbyes. You will always be here with me, here in my soul.'

Interview with Godfrey Joseph Pereira

Tell me, how did 'Bloodline Bandra' start?

G.J.P: The literature student in me had always wanted to document the way Roman Catholics in India spoke the English language. Phonetically, it is a ear-tingler, with harmonic and rhythmic cadences that dance, and the flow is amusing and entertaining. As a child I had heard this talk, and then like the ancient Pali language, it disappeared, almost. I wanted to document those glorious dialogues, pickle that cocksure swagger and capture its rustic essence so that it would be preserved in words bound by paper. I mean, where in this world, will you hear something like this: 'Sandra, what you cooking, men, everybody knows you bleddy can't boil rice to save your face?' And Sandra answers, 'Yes, men, I'm making ball curry and cock soup. Bugger, when you bleddy go home, pull your pants down and see what is missing. You coming to eat or wot, men? Want to bring your bleddy wife to my supper?' The sarcasm, the humour, the abuse, the double entendre, the innuendo . . . it's absolutely bloody brilliant, and it is all delivered in a sing-song musical way without sounding crass, obscene or offensive. The way they talked was a linguistic wonderland. I had to try and put this down on paper. I have to add this, ball curry is a famous East Indian beef dish; you will have to figure out what cock soup is. I am an East Indian. I had to do this. I sometimes think it's my psychological payback for leaving and running off to America.

The novel moves from Bandra and travels to New York City. How did that happen?

G.J.P: Once upon a time, encouraged by a nervous breakdown, ceasing to exist seemed like an appropriate release to a tumultuous sad period in New York City. Through those times, I had scribbled notes of misery, trying to understand what was happening to me. I was chained by what I now term 'legal slavery' by my own Indian people in New York City. What is 'legal slavery'? In the United States, the H-1B work visa forbids you to work for anybody else. You are chained to the employer who 'sponsors' you, and often, these employers throw you a minimum wage meatless dry bone, treat you like an animal, humiliate, threaten and abuse you, demand you work overtime and on holidays with no pay, and in some cases, physically torture you – all this in the Land of the Free! You cannot quit the job because sponsors are near impossible to find and leaving would make you an 'illegal alien'. Of course, I could have cut those shackles and escaped to my home in Pali Village, Bandra, Bombay, but at that time, the logistics of doing this seemed insurmountable. I had no money, I was homeless and scared, and going back would mean defeat and humiliation. I was a legal slave for a long time.

Is that the time that you started writing *Bloodline Bandra*?

G.J.P: No, that came later. I was in the process of finishing my first novel, *What the Mountain Said*. Defeated and mutilated from the psychological beatings I had endured in New York City, I journeyed to Florida, dragging my unhappy marriage and manuscript. Later, visiting an old friend, Hartman de Souza, in Goa, India, I started talking about my New York City years and the horror stories I had heard from other Indians, and he said, '*That* is the novel you *must* write.' I ignored him for many reasons. The remembrances would bring devastating sorrow, and the liquor bottle would be once again a venomous comforter. I had lain semi-conscious in that sewer a long, long time ago. That place frightened me. I was familiar with the odour of dying. It stank of sour hangovers, bitter vomit and self-loathing.

What happened to *What the Mountain Said*?

G.J.P: It's still up there on the mountain. My agent is reading it, trying to figure out the madness. But I have begun a third novel, titled *Letters to Esther*. It is set in The Village in New York City. It started out with me writing letters to my sister Maria, who tragically died when she was three-years old, and then the story morphed into something different. I don't know where it's going to go.

You seem to have walked down some long winding roads . . .

G.J.P: You have no idea, and it got worse. Years later, I left Florida one September morning and crawled to Hoboken, New Jersey; divorced, frightened and free. I was drifting again and writing. That's the time I started writing *Bloodline Bandra*. One afternoon in Hoboken, waiting for the 34th Street Path train to New York City, I walked to the bench I was sitting on, the bench from where I had tried to jump under an oncoming train. Devastating pictures of my days as a legal slave began flashing.

What happened next?

G.J.P: When I got back home that night, David Cabral floated out of Manhattan and began telling me his story. He brought back vicious unpleasant times. The bottle appeared, profusely sweating, appealing, beckoning . . . these were the hand-trembling consequences of visiting that stinking gutter again. Now I was working on two novels, fuelled by liquid energy and cigarettes. The Bandra Bugger talk book, and the New York story of human bondage. I was flummoxed, it started to get confusing. I copped out and stopped writing for a year.

Is David Cabral a real person? Is he you?

G.J.P: No, he's a fictitious character, but he is real inside my head. To me, he is flesh, blood, skin and bone. Parts of my life are incorporated into the psyche of David Cabral. The approximately ten-million bonded labourers in India and the myriad Indians abroad whose voices have been castrated by other Indians are the heart and soul of David Cabral. Part II of *Bloodline Bandra* is the searing scream of anguish as a dream lies dying. It is the sound of silent destitution, humiliation and hopelessness that human bondage brings. David Cabral's DNA is an amalgamation of the powerless.

By this time you had stopped writing. How did that make you feel?

G.J.P: Terrible, just awful. This was not writers' block or anything like that. I was just confused. I did not know how to pull it off. I mean, here I was, trapped between two novels and I wanted to write just one. The question was; how do I solder the two into one seamless piece? At that time, I did not seem to have the literary capability to do that. The more I tried, the more I began wandering. I just stopped. I visited Goa again. When I told my friend that I did not want to write anymore, he jokingly said, 'Why don't you just kill yourself?' I told him I had tried; 'does not work for me'. We both laughed. Still, as a journalist, I wanted to tell people what had happened to David Cabral. Speaking to friends in Canada, England, South Africa, New Zealand and Australia, a common horrifying Indian trend began emerging. It amazed and saddened me. Now I knew I had to document this. Hartman sat me down in Goa and talked to me for hours. I listened to his wisdom, anger and fury, aided by a lot of alcohol.

What did he say?

G.J.P: I can't verbalize what he said, there are international laws that forbid it. Ha! Lots of four-letter multicoloured three-dimensional words and clenched-fist gestures. But he explained why I had to do this, even if it meant placing my sanity on a knife's edge. Kris Kristofferson wrote a song titled '*Pilgrim*': 'He's a poet, an' he's a picker, he's a prophet, He's a pilgrim and a preacher, and a problem when he's stoned.' You should listen to that song. That's Hartman for you. When I tried to explain why I could not, did not want to write, he sat there in silence and listened. He sipped his whiskey, lit a cigarette, blew smoke in my face and barked, 'Don't use big words. Shut up and start writing.' Ha! If you ever need a shrink, contact Hartman.

What happened next?

G.J.P: It got worse, for me. Hartman is a great writer. He had read my manuscripts. He said to me, 'Don't write. Paint pictures. If you can't manage to do that, do not write.' I left Goa mired in doubt and confusion. I have a problem drawing even stick figures, and now this . . .

Why and when did you decide to start writing again?

G.J.P: I could not hold it back anymore. If it meant that the recollections would bring despair, so be it; and remember, I had to try and weld the two novels into one. It was a daunting literary challenge that was beginning to torture me. Back in New Jersey five years ago, one quiet night I began writing again. I started painting pictures, and the two novels began fusing, savagely twisting into each other in a strange lysergic-acid word-dance.

Why is it so important to you to tell this story?

G.J.P: First, for the first time in the 500 years of East Indian history, the way the East Indians really talked, and the salt of their everyday lives has been documented in a novel; and of course, part II of *Bloodline Bandra* just had to be told. What happened to me is shameful and humiliating. Dreamers of a better life in the West are still trapped and exploited by their own people. My tragedy is not unique or even extraordinary, but the totality of this exploitation, this human bondage, is a global crime that demanded a hearing.